STIFF ARM STEAL

A MIAMI JONES CASE

AJ Stewart

Jacaranda Drive Publishing

Los Angeles, California

www.jacarandadrive.com

Cover artwork by Streetlight Graphics

ISBN-10: 0-9859455-7-5

ISBN-13: 978-0-9859455-7-2

Books by AJ Stewart

To my reader, my coach and my muse, Heather.

And Mum and Dad, for pointing my boat in the right direction but letting me sail it myself.

Sometimes dreams are fulfilled later rather than sooner. It beats the hell out of never. Thanks to everyone who believed along the way, and those who doubted but had the good grace to keep their mouths shut.

CHAPTER ONE

I sat in the outside bar at Longboard Kelly's looking at the worst drink ever invented. The fall breeze was playing with the back of my shirt, the blue one with white prints of palm trees on it. Despite the season the humidity was up and I could feel the sweat soaking into the fabric. Ron sat next to me with a smile and a Miller Lite. He was enjoying my pain. I was pretty sure that tonic water and a lime wedge constituted cruel and unusual punishment. I made a note to check the law on that.

The guy walked in the rear of the courtyard bar from the parking lot. He didn't belong. At least not here. It wasn't that Longboard's was discriminatory. All sorts celebrated, waited out time and drowned their sorrows here. Some, like Ron and me, were outdoor bar types. Our backsides were practically imprinted into the wooden stools. Others preferred the darkness of the indoor bar. We looked straight into it from where we sat, but nothing short of a hurricane drove us to sit in there. Others still preferred the tables in the courtyard, under the sun-bleached umbrellas. But this guy belonged in a yacht club. His blazer was blue and his khakis had a sharp press from his ankles to his balls. His hair was short on top and shorter on the sides, and his glasses looked like something Don Henley would have sung about in his day. The guy walked over to the bar. It was a strong walk, the walk of an athlete who never got injured—at least not badly. A walk of confidence. Except for his soft skin and unblemished hands, it could have been the walk of an enlisted man. The guy took off his shades and leaned on the bar.

"You Miami Jones?" he said, looking across me at my drinking buddy and business associate.

"Who's asking?" said Ron.

I sipped my drink. It tasted like battery acid with lime squeezed in it. I was as big a fan of lime as the next guy, but why anyone would waste it in tonic water was beyond me.

"I represent BJ Baker," said the guy.

Ron curled his lips as if this impressed him greatly.

The guy glanced at me. He was clearly unimpressed with a wardrobe inspired by Jimmy Buffett. He looked back to Ron.

"Is there somewhere we can talk privately?" he asked.

Ron smiled. "You got a name, kid?"

"Murphy."

"Well, Murphy, take a load off and let's get you a drink." Ron turned to Muriel behind the bar. She had a face like tanned leather, strong arms and breasts that exploded beneath her tank top. "Another for me, and one for the kid."

"Murphy," I said.

Murphy sat and Muriel banged down two icy glasses of beer. I used my straw to play water polo with the lime wedge in my tonic.

"Cheers," said Ron, lifting his glass in salute. Murphy did likewise, but with less enthusiasm. "My name's Ron. Ron Bennett."

Murphy stopped mid-sip and frowned. "So who's Miami Jones?"

I smiled at him like Tom Selleck back when he was Magnum. Not that I look anything like Tom Selleck. I'm blond and don't have a mustache. But I wasn't worried if Murphy thought I looked like Magnum. It wasn't about Murphy. It was about me, and getting my mind off this abomination of a drink in front of me.

"You? You're Miami Jones?"

I winked. "In the flesh."

Murphy sipped his drink while he considered this news. No doubt the locale had not impressed him. A watering hole with no water view was no place at all in this guy's mind. But he was under instruction, so he was here. He wasn't impressed by Ron, whose shirt was plain, no palm trees, not even a magnolia. But Ron had looked like the best option at the bar, and Murphy was under instruction. Now he looked me up and down, stopping for a moment at the board shorts, and considered if his instructions could be wrong. His eyes wandered back to my face, then to Ron and then to Muriel's ass as she stacked the glass washer under the indoor bar.

He sipped his beer again. "You're *the* Miami Jones?" I was impressed with the *the*.

"I hope there isn't another wretch with that particular albatross around his neck," I said.

He sipped again. Then he put his beer down on its mat, like he'd made a decision. "Mr. Baker requests your presence immediately."

I played with my lime and looked at Ron. "Immediately," I said. Ron nodded and made his impressed lip curl again. I turned to Murphy. "He's just started a new beer."

"Mr. Baker isn't requesting him."

"He's my associate. We're kind of a package deal."

"Then he can leave the beer."

Ron coughed.

"You've just started yours," I said.

"I don't mind. Mr. Baker is waiting."

"Well, he can wait."

Murphy spun on his stool and tipped his beer over, pouring it onto the ground. It ran between the dry paving stones. "Mr. Baker doesn't wait."

I looked at him. Then I looked at my drink. It was just daring me to leave. Ron picked up on it and pulled his beer in one shot.

"Well, let's not keep him waiting," said Ron.

"You're driving, sport," I said to Murphy, casting a final goodbye at the sorry-looking lime wedge in my glass.

CHAPTER TWO

BJ Baker's sprawling home sat in gardens overlooking the Intracoastal in Palm Beach. It was someone's idea of a Tuscan villa, if Tuscany were full of prefab, hurricane-proof concrete. Murphy drove a black Suburban at the speed limit. He even used indicators. Ron and I sat in the back, watching the cranes and pelicans glide across the water. The driveway was as long as a par 5 and as well manicured. Murphy stopped in front of a service entrance on the side of the home. He got out and stepped up to the house. He didn't open our doors. The service entrance led into a kitchen the size of a minor league ballpark. There were two marble islands and a forest of stainless steel. Murphy led us through the kitchen into a long corridor. A dining room fit to seat a battalion was on the right, a staircase on the left. We strode across the marble foyer at the base of the stairs and into a large room. It was all mahogany panels and bookcases. There was a massive desk at one end, a solid piece that looked like it might have come off the USS Constitution. BJ Baker sat behind the desk. He was on a cell phone that looked tiny in his gigantic mitt. There was a Cuban in his other hand. He sucked at it and the end glowed red.

Murphy stopped at the doorway. I assumed we were supposed to stop behind him. I stepped past into the room.

Murphy frowned. "Excuse me," he said through clenched teeth.

"You're excused." I ran my finger along the binding of one of the sets of leather tomes on the bookshelf. Gilt writing told me they were the Great Books of the World. The introduction was three books long. Then there was Aristotle and Plato. There must have been sixty volumes. The spines were as flawless as a model's cheeks. I heard the swoosh of a chair on felt pads being pushed back on the hardwood floor.

Murphy stepped forward. "Sir, this is Mr. Jones, and his associate, Mr. . . . ah. . ." He looked at Ron.

"Ron." He smiled.

BJ Baker stepped from behind his desk. He was a big unit. I wondered how he looked so good for someone his age. He'd played college ball before I was born. But he was tan and trim. He wore a full pate of gray hair and his gray-blue eyes were like traps. He had a chin of granite, which matched the chest that pushed at the seams of his Greg Norman signature golf shirt. His chinos were creased in the lap. I was taller than most, but Baker could have inspected the top of my head for fleas. He didn't. He held out his huge hand. I offered mine and he grabbed it like he was pulling a coconut from a tree. Then his other hand closed around my wrist and he gave me the double pump.

"Thanks for coming on such short notice." He had great teeth. Straight, white and all accounted for. Not the mouth you expect to see on a retired pro footballer. Some dental guy was driving around in a fancy car on the proceeds of that mouth.

"It's what we do," I said.

"Well, I'll get to the point," he said.

I was glad. I was getting tired of all the small talk.

"I asked around," he said, stepped back to his desk. "You came recommended."

"We aim to please."

"I didn't say highly recommended." He gazed at me like he'd nailed me with that one.

"We like to leave our audience wanting more."

Baker scrunched his brow. "Is your attitude going to be a problem?"

"Are you asking me on a date?"

"What?"

"Cause if you are, then yeah, it's a problem. I don't do that kind of thing. But if you've got some detective type work needs doing, then I can help. Attitude or no."

He looked at me like I was a defensive lineman, summing me up, deciding whether he should step around or just go right through me. "I'm told you played football," he said.

"College. University of Miami. But you already know that."

"You think I followed your career?"

"I think you did more than ask around before you sent your manservant to get me."

"You were second team."

"Backup QB. That was me. I took a few snaps here and there."

"Never started."

"Nope."

Baker fiddled with a pencil on his desk. "Why?"

"Two reasons. One, the coach didn't like me much."

"Hard to believe. What was the second reason?"

"The other guy was better."

He nodded. "At least you're honest."

I said nothing.

"So you've heard of the Heisman."

"The go-go dancers at the Pink Flamingo have heard of the Heisman."

"What don't the go-go dancers know?"

"You won it back in the sixties. Your senior year at USC."

"And?" he asked.

"You were a first round draft pick. Detroit. Spent a few unhappy years in Motown and got yourself traded to Pittsburgh."

"Where. . .?"

"Where you won the Super Bowl in '75. But you didn't call me here to give you a mental hand job. You've got a whole staff who can do that."

The frown returned. "I want to make sure you know who you're dealing with. I am a successful man. I make no pardon for that and I don't need a practice team quarterback to remind me of it."

"So we're almost on the same page then."

"Almost?"

"I still don't know why the hell I'm here."

Baker looked at Ron and then back at me.

"Come with me."

CHAPTER THREE

BJ Baker led us down the corridor on the opposite side of the staircase we had come past on arrival. He took long strides but was light on his feet. Through the corridor I saw a large living area that spread out through French doors to a patio and landscaped pool. A waterfall ran down a wall of fake rocks. Baker opened a door and led us to the side. He flicked a light on despite the bright sunshine flooding in through the floor-to-ceiling windows.

I looked around the room. Lots of guys have a room that they use as their sanctuary. They might call it the office, or the den, or the man cave. Perhaps the study. But mostly it was the same room for all functions. A desk for paying bills, a favorite chair and a flat screen for watching the game. A bookshelf with some favorite reads or the trophies of youth. Some sports medals, a ball caught in the bleachers at Camden Yards.

BJ Baker's man cave served one role. It was a shrine to BJ Baker. We had left his office and with it his desk, and the books. This room was all about a golden career. A Detroit jersey hung on one wall, a Pittsburgh jersey on another. Next to the Steelers jersey was one from the University of Southern California. All bore the name Baker and were framed behind museum-quality glass. There were photographs of Baker the player in full flight. A *Sports Illustrated* cover with him breaking the tackle of a hapless Bills defender. There was a front page of the *Pittsburgh Post-Gazette* with the headline *Super Steelers Win, 16-6.* Then there were more photographs, framed and matted. BJ Baker with Chuck Noll, with the governors of a handful of states, with Jack Nicklaus and Greg Norman. BJ In his Fox Network commentary blazer. With President Bush version 2.

The floor-to-ceiling windows made up another wall, through which was a private lanai that wound its way around to the pool. Baker placed his hand on the back of a black leather recliner that looked like a sleeping bear. He wasn't smiling, but his eyes told me this room gave him a serious hard-on. I couldn't blame him for that.

"So?" he said.

Ron nodded to himself. "Impressive."

"Notice anything?"

"You get your photo taken a lot," I said.

"Anything else?"

"You mean apart from that empty trophy case?" I nodded at the glass case designed to hold a single trophy. LED lights in the top of the cabinet shone down onto an empty space.

"You're everything they say, gumshoe," said Baker.

"Someone stole your Heisman trophy."

"My Bassett hound could have figured that out. I asked you about the Heisman earlier. So that's not even a lucky guess."

I wasn't digging being asked to drop everything to come and salute the chief while he belittled me. If I had something better than a tonic and lime to return to, I would have told him to go play Lord of the Manor with the pet iguana. "Someone knew what they wanted and where to get it," I said. "Nothing else was taken. There's nothing else of value."

"Nothing else of value?" said Baker. He pushed himself off the recliner and stood erect, making himself tall. I figured he imagined it made him more imposing, and I was sure he was often right.

"Nothing of value to the burglar. He didn't go into any other rooms. He didn't take any cash or look for a safe full of jewelry. The Heisman was the only thing of value to him."

Ron stepped over to the empty case and peered inside. "If he was a football nut, what about BJ's Super Bowl ring?"

"What about that, hotshot?" BJ asked, clasping his hands together.

I had to smile.

"You and I both know the answer to that. This guy didn't want your ring because he wasn't just after memorabilia. There's a garage sale's worth of memorabilia in here that hasn't been touched. So he was after the Heisman specifically. Besides which, if he wanted your Super Bowl ring, he'd have to pry it off your cold, dead body, since you always wear it. It's on your left ring finger, which is odd, but I get it."

Baker unclasped his hands. On the ring finger of his left hand sat the ring. It was a huge thing, but in the gaudy world of sports rings it was remarkably restrained. A single diamond surrounded by the words Pittsburgh Steelers, World Champions. On the left side the number 19. On the right, 74.

Baker looked at me. "How do you mean odd?"

"Most men, married men at least, wear a ring like that on the right hand because they wear their wedding band on the left. A ring like that makes a wedding band look like the lawn out front of the Taj Mahal."

"The Taj Mahal?"

"It's a nice lawn. But who sees it, because it's in front of the Taj Mahal, for crying out loud. But you don't care. Lucky for you, you've got big hands. You wear your wedding band behind it, on the left, because you shake hands with your right. Then you do that stupid double-handed shake and put your left hand over the top, all friendly like. But you're making sure the guy you're shaking gets an eyeful of that ring."

Baker fiddled with the ring. "You think you're smart, gumshoe?"

"Yep. And there's more. The robbery happened yesterday evening, during or after a function your wife organized here. The guy who did it had been planning it for four days, so he was adaptable."

"How on earth could you know that?"

"It happened last night because that gave you enough time to get the cops involved, for you to then get pissed at their lack of progress, and for you to ask around and find me."

He put his fists on his hips. "Who says I'm pissed at the cops?"

I wandered toward Ron and the empty case. "You don't figure any of the guests for it. They're all such upstanding citizens. So you think it had to be the help. But not your help."

I glanced at Murphy. He was stone-faced. "Outside help. Caterers, cleaners, et cetera. You stop in here to take a load off after the event, see the old Heisman's disappeared. You get the cops in. Hell, the chief was probably here for your function. They canvas the help, get nowhere. You've got some sway in this town, so someone pulls an all-nighter. Background checks, surveillance video. Full-court press. You wake up this morning and the chief tells you they've got a donut. Nada. So you get all itchy and have to mount your own search. You spend the morning asking around. Not for just any private dick. One who understands the sensibilities of your situation. Someone tells you I played college football, maybe they mention I played pro baseball. But they also mention I don't suffer fools lightly. So you hesitate. Waste an hour on it. Then you figure you're getting nowhere fast, and you can handle anything I can dish up, so mid-afternoon your manservant is dispatched to find me. Most people who know me know where I drink. I bet after my office, Longboard's was the second place he checked." I waited and took a breath and looked at Baker. "That about it?"

Baker grinned out the side of his mouth. "I didn't hesitate because of your attitude. I can handle you. I hesitated because of the baseball. It's a boy's game. And who the hell spends their best years playing second-rate minor league ball?"

He waited for a reaction but didn't get one. He'd never understand the answer even if he knew.

"But the rest was on the money." He looked at Murphy and nodded, and Murphy slipped from the room. "How'd you know there was no cash or jewels taken?"

I turned from the trophy case to face him. "You don't keep that sort of stuff in here. It's in a safe, in your office. If there was anything missing from the safe, you would have shown us when we were in there."

Baker nodded. "What makes you think the guy had four days to plan? That was just baloney, right?"

"Four days ago I read a piece in the Palm Beach Post about the upcoming charity event you were hosting. It was held last night." I walked across the room to the French doors. "These doors were open. The photographer was there on the lanai, you and your wife were here, just inside the room. A nicely framed shot, with your Pittsburgh and USC jerseys as backdrop."

"Yes, okay. That's right. So what?"

"So just to your left in the shot, slightly out of focus but unmistakable to any college football fan, was your Heisman trophy." Baker turned his head back and forth between me and the empty cabinet. Murphy stepped back into the room and handed Baker a thick envelope.

"You think they saw the picture and decided to steal it?"

"It's a working theory. You ever done a press photo in here before?"

"No."

"Staff come in here?"

"Only our maid, Carmela. But she's been with us for years."

"Then it's a working theory."

Baker held up the envelope. "Then work it hard. I want my trophy back."

He dropped the envelope into Ron's palm with a thud. Ron smiled.

"And I want daily updates."

"Look, BJ, I have to tell you, the police will do everything they can. And they'll do it for free."

"I know that. I want you to do what they can't." He looked at the envelope in Ron's hand. "There's more there if you make progress."

I shrugged. I'd done my moral duty. He wanted me to sniff around for a week for a wad of fresh bills, so that's what I'd do.

I looked at Murphy. "Give us a ride back?"

"I have a dinner to get to," said Baker. "Murphy will order you a cab."

CHAPTER FOUR

Ron and I ditched the cab at the office to deposit the cash in our safe. Ron slipped out a couple of bills traveling money and we jumped in the Mustang. The colored party lights were on in the courtyard when we got back to Longboard Kelly's. The beer-brand umbrellas had been folded up, but left in the middle of each table, like giant flowers that had closed with the falling of the sun. The tables were nearly full. The autumnal heat had abated from its summer furnace down to just plain hot, and a light breeze made for a pleasant evening. Ron and I took our seats at the bar. Muriel had come off shift and Mick had come on. Mick owned the joint. He was built like a pipe bomb and had a fresco of tattoos up each arm. He wore a white tank top that said Longboard Kelly's on the back with a picture of a Hawaiian longboard. I didn't think Mick surfed. I wasn't even sure he could swim. He'd owned Longboard Kelly's as long as anyone could remember. How he came to be in possession of the bar was anyone's guess. He nodded and poured a Yuengling. Ron never drank full-strength beer during the day. But once the sun dropped over the yardarm, all bets were off. Mick dropped a highball of tonic and lime in front of me. It was a conspiracy.

"Got any vodka?" I asked.

"Yep," said Mick, walking away to serve a customer inside.

"Cheers," said Ron.

"If you think," I moaned.

I sipped at the tonic. My impression of it hadn't improved. Ron slugged half a pint and wiped foam from his mouth. Ron was the same vintage as BJ Baker but had a few more miles on the clock. His hair was more silver than gray, and he had a glow that was more rum than pushups. He had a few faded scars on his face, neck and hands, the result of skin cancer removals. Despite all that, he still had a way with the ladies that I never quite got my head around.

"So what do you think?" he said.

"I don't agree with our Mr. Baker that all his guests are such swell people that they wouldn't steal his trophy. Probably some pissing contests among them. Someone might just steal it for kicks, like they would have done to a college mascot, thirty or forty years ago. So give Lizzy the number for his guy Murphy and get a guest list, and one of all staff, internal and those hired for the event. Ask her to do the usual checks. We won't turn up anything the Palm Beach PD won't, but we should earn our cookies anyway. I'll chat with Sally tomorrow, see if he has any thoughts on the matter."

I played with my lime wedge as Ron slipped off his stool and fired up his cell phone. He walked away from the music coming from inside the bar, toward the rear of the courtyard, where a longboard with a bite out of it hung on the bamboo facade that was nailed to the fence. Ron held the phone to his ear and smiled as he sauntered by three women who looked like they'd just walked off the eighteenth at PGA National. I swiveled my barstool around to survey the crowd. They were easy and happy to be out of the air-conditioned prison that is South Florida in the summer. I glanced at the paved path that led to the parking lot and saw her walking in. It is not possible, in my learned opinion, to make a uniform look any sexier than she did. I didn't have a fetish for such things, but I was developing one. Her green trousers were crisp and curved in all the right places. Her shirt was pressed and starched and tucked in tight and her badge gleamed off her left breast. She was tall and lean and athletic. Her belt was snug around her taut waist and her sidearm swayed with her hips as she walked. Her hair was short enough to be low maintenance, but long enough to be as feminine as hell. The combination of the hips, the uniform and the gun had every eye on her. She walked straight to the bar. Not oblivious, but not caring either way.

She stopped at the bar and smiled at me. Her golden nameplate said Castle. "Your butt print in that stool yet?"

"Not at all, Deputy. I've been out and about today."

"You don't say. And such a fine day to sit and drink and ponder the world."

"Depends on the drink."

She dropped her eyes to my tonic water and then turned to the bar. "Mickey?"

Mick put his hands up. "I swear, on pain of an IRS audit. Nothing but tonic water."

She raised one eyebrow and gave a quiet "mmm." Then she smiled at me. "I'll have what he's having."

Mick squirted some tonic into a highball and tossed in a lime wedge. She picked up the drink and sipped it. Condensation rolled down the glass. I watched her drink. She had thin lips and big brown eyes I could waste whole afternoons in.

"Cheers," she smiled.

I sipped my tonic. "You're trying to kill me."

"On the contrary, I'm trying to keep you alive." She leaned toward me and I caught a hint of jasmine and vanilla. She put her palm on the side of my waist. I could feel the heat of her hand through my shirt. Then she pinched the small muffin top she found there. She gave my skin a good squeeze.

"That's gonna leave a mark," I said.

"All part of the service."

"It's police brutality, that's what it is."

"I'm not the police."

"A mere technicality."

"A bet's a bet," she said, sliding onto a stool. I saw her eyes glance over my shoulder. I turned and saw Ron sitting down with the golf ladies, his calls made, the night young.

"You on tonight?" I asked.

"Yep. Graveyard and a half. Got to get in early."

"What's the beef?"

She sipped her drink. "Some big hotshot in Palm Beach had a party, and someone pinched a prize trinket." She put her glass down and pointed a slender finger at me. "Hey, you probably know him. He's some football guy."

"BJ Baker."

"Yeah," she smiled. "How'd you know?"

"Guess where I spent my afternoon?"

"Seriously?"

Ron appeared at my shoulder. "Evening, Danielle. Don't you look dashing."

"Hi, Ron. Yeah, dashing was what I was going for."

Ron signaled Mick. "Three white wines and another for me."

Mick pulled a cleanskin bottle of wine from his fridge below the bar. Wine of unknown varietal and region was as fancy as Mick got.

Ron put his hand on my shoulder. "Left a message for Lizzy. We'll get into it first thing." He picked up his drinks. "Evening, Deputy," he said, turning back to his new friends.

"So why are you involved with Baker?" I said, watching Ron settle at the table with the golf ladies. "I thought the PD would be on it."

"They are, and we're all being awfully careful not to step on each other's toes. But Baker put a good bit of cash into the sheriff's election campaign, and he's called in a marker."

"So he's got two law enforcement agencies and a P.I. on the case." I shook my head and downed my tonic and lime. It was so sour it made my eyes water.

"Just to get back an old college trophy," she said.

I spluttered tonic back into my glass. "While I agree it's a little excessive, it is a Heisman."

Danielle narrowed her eyes. "What does that mean, exactly?"

"It's only the most prestigious award in college sports."

"So it's like an MVP award."

"Exactly. It goes to the best player in college football."

"Who chooses the winner?" She sipped her drink.

"There are selected judges in media and press across the country. The nation is divided into regions and then they tally all the votes."

"And they get a cup or something."

"Not a cup." I took out my phone and found an image of the Heisman trophy.

Danielle looked at the picture and frowned. "What is he doing?"

"The trophy is an image of a football player carrying the ball in one arm and laying what's called a stiff-arm. He's fending away a tackle."

"So why would anyone steal it? Could you sell it?"

"That's a question I hope to answer tomorrow, but I would have thought it'd be tough. But there might be black market collectors who just want something they can't buy."

"So what's he like? Baker?"

"He's a successful man who's gotten used to being successful. So now he expects it. I think he's more miffed that someone got one up on him than the actual trophy itself."

She pushed her drank away. "Did you play nice?"

"Nice enough to get a retainer."

"I'm so happy for you." She grinned and slipped off her stool. "I gotta get going."

"Give me a ride?"

"Of course. What do you think your property taxes are for?"

I wandered over to Ron and tossed him the keys to the Mustang. He winked and I turned and followed the khaki trousers out to the parking lot.

CHAPTER FIVE

Sally's Pawn and Check Cashing sat on Okeechobee Boulevard, on the wrong side of the turnpike. It was in your typical low-rent strip mall. A package place, a nail salon, a Chinese restaurant that also did American cuisine. I parked my motorcycle in front of Sally's. It was already hot, away from the coastal breezes, and I was regretting giving Ron my car. The bike was fine, but it meant I had to wear jeans that stuck to my skin, and a helmet that made me sweat and look like a greaser when I took it off. Ron suggested I leave it off. But I've seen too many guys who came off bikes. Few of them come back, and those that do rarely come back all the way. Nothing cool about being dead.

I hung the black helmet on the bars and slipped on my Patriots cap. Sally's store had bars on the windows as a permanent fixture. A check-cashing booth sat at the front and a young black girl I didn't know sat behind the Plexiglas. I nodded as I walked by. She didn't smile. I didn't blame her. It didn't look like a particularly rosy place to waste away your day. A low glass cabinet ran along one side of the store, holding everything from diamonds to Smith and Wessons. The rest of the store had cheap shelving with other items for sale. Old CDs, DVDs, small electronics, musical instruments. There must have been more starving musicians in West Palm than I gave the place credit for.

It looked like a small change operation, which is exactly how Sally wanted it to look. He stepped through the rear door and shuffled along behind the glass cabinets.

"You wear that friggin' hat in my store? What, you trying to kill me?"

"How's your Jets going?"

"Aach," he said, throwing his hands into the air. "Don't get me started. You think if they're gonna lose every week, they could take some guys out at least. I mean they're representing Jersey, for Chrissakes."

"You should try a Dolphins' game some time."

"Aach. Dolphins. I can't follow a team dressed in orange and teal." He looked at my cap again. "But there's no excuse for that."

"Hey, I grew up in New England."

"Aach. You grew up in Connecticut."

"Last time I checked, that was New England."

"You're killing me. Fairfield County's just part of New York."

"I grew up in New Haven."

"Southern Massachusetts, that's what I say. I mean, what the hell is Connecticut for, anyway? Only good thing about it is that it puts the Red Sox an extra two hours away from Yankee Stadium."

"Connecticut's the insurance capital of the world."

He threw his hands up again. "Zurich's the insurance capital of the world. Connecticut's a waste of a star on a flag."

I shrugged.

"Let me ask you this," he said. "You ever go back?"

"Why the hell would I go back?"

"Insurance?" Sally smiled his nicotine grin.

"I got an insurance broker in my building right here."

"Exactly my point. Exactly my point." He shook his head and laughed. "So what do you need, kid?"

"Got a question for you. A Heisman trophy."

"Aha."

"What's it worth, on the market?"

Sally scrunched his face like he was passing a stone. "Depends on when, depends on whose. But no less than a hundred grand, and easily more than two hundred for a popular player. Why? You got one?"

"No. A client had one stolen."

"Who?"

"BJ Baker."

"Aach. Steelers. He's a blowhard. Where'd he go to school?"

"University of Southern Cal."

Sally nodded. "Yeah, be worth something to somebody. But hard to move."

"That was my next question."

"Tough. High-profile piece. Well known. Hard to move through usual channels."

"You know someone who could do it?"

"I know everyone who could do it. But I ain't heard nothing."

We stood in silence for a moment. I could see the cogs working in Sally's head.

"If it were me, I wouldn't move it. I'd hire the guy direct. Get him to steal it for me. Pay him direct. No need to put it on the market."

"Makes sense."

"Sort of. But here's the thing. You can never show it. To anyone. The kind of guy wants a Heisman, he wants things money can't buy. He's a sports fan for sure. But he wants the things others can't have. A guy like this, he wants you to know he's got stuff you can't have. He wants to show it off. But a Heisman? They're unique. There's not many of them and they almost never come up for sale. But they're so well known, by sports fans at least, that you'd never be able to keep it secret. Word would get out."

"So why do it?"

"If it were me, one of two reasons. One, to hurt BJ Baker. I mean, who goes through life being called BJ? It's like the guy wants to be called a homo."

I lifted my eyebrows at that, but let it go. "What's the second reason?"

"The Heisman means something else to me. I want it, but I won't show it off because I don't care about that. I care about it for other reasons. It represents something else to me."

"What something else?"

Sally looked me in the eye. "The hell should I know?"

I smiled and shook his hand. His skin was papery and loose. "Thanks, Sally. Say, we should catch a ballgame sometime. I still know the GM up at St. Lucie. Get some box seats."

"Aach. You, I'd pay money to see. Not these babies today. You were the real deal, kid."

"Organization didn't seem to agree."

"The hell do organizations know? You had the stuff."

I opened the door and the little bell rang. The girl in the booth looked at me with weary eyes.

"Appreciate it, Sal. Appreciate it."

CHAPTER SIX

It was a conspiracy. I sat in my office, jeans discarded for a pair of Quicksilver board shorts. I was tossing around the case with Ron. Lizzy, my office assistant, walked in, all pouty lips and jet-black hair. She put a steaming glass of something on my desk.

"Should I ask?"

"Green tea," she said. "Full of antioxidants."

"Full of what?" I said.

Ron laughed.

"Antioxidants. If I can't save your soul, maybe I can just save your life."

"Did Danielle put you up to this?"

She looked at me, impassive. "Let's just say—for reasons neither of us understand—we both seem vested in saving your life."

"I'm not dying! It was just a bet, for chrissakes."

Ron laughed again. "What was the bet this time?" he said.

I shook my head. "Sit-ups. She bet me I'd fatigue first."

"And obviously you did."

"I got forty-four. I used to do over hundred when I played ball."

"Such a long time ago," said Lizzy.

"Not that long ago."

"How many did she do?" said Ron, suppressing a chuckle.

"She stopped at eighty. Invoked the mercy rule, she said."

Ron laughed. "That's one fit lady."

"She did the last twenty as crossover crunches, just to make a point."

"And that point is, you have been enjoying life just a little too much lately," said Lizzy.

"Jesus doesn't want me to enjoy life?"

"Jesus wants you healthy."

"Great," I groaned.

"Until he's ready for you."

"Awesome."

The phone on my desk rang and Lizzy leaned across and picked it up. "LCI," she said.

"Get me Miami Jones, now!" I could hear BJ Baker bellowing down the line.

I leaned forward to take the handset, but Lizzy wasn't finished with Baker.

"Sir, I am afraid Mr. Jones is presently indisposed. Can he call you back when you have located your manners?" said Lizzy, calm and steely, like an irritated librarian.

"Excuse me!"

"Of course, sir. Forgiveness is what I do."

"Listen lady, if you don't get Jones now, I'll have your job!"

"Sir, I think we both know that you couldn't handle my job."

"I don't mean that. I mean I'll have you fired!"

"And whisk me away from this middle-class urban squalor? Well, bless you, sir. Thank you."

"Now listen here!"

"No, you listen. If I can find a notepad, I will write a message that you called. If I can find a thumb tack, I will pin the message to Mr. Jones's corkboard. If Mr. Jones comes in, I will point him in the direction of the corkboard. And if you call here again and use that tone, I will see to it that the archangels rain fire and brimstone down on your soul. Good day, sir." She dropped the phone back in the cradle and walked out of my office, closing the door quietly behind her.

I looked at Ron.

"BJ," he said.

I nodded.

"Didn't sound happy."

I shook my head, and looked at the steaming tea in the glass before me. It smelled faintly of cat urine. I tasted it. Not as acrid as cat urine. It was more like putrid irrigation flow. It was definitely a conspiracy.

The phone beeped like a hospital heart monitor and Lizzy's voice broke through the static. "Detective Ronzoni to see you."

I didn't answer, because Ronzoni wasn't going to wait. He came through my door and closed it behind him. He was average height, a few inches short of me, and trim in the face and limbs. His flat chest dropped to a bulb of a belly that didn't match the rest of him, like he was a healthy guy who had spent too much time sitting on his butt. A cop's dilemma. He wore a brown polyester suit with an open shirt and loosened tie, to help ventilate. Ronzoni didn't sweat. Literally. It was some gland thing. He had to drink a lot of water to regulate his body temperature. That was the word on the street.

"Detective Macaroni, can I offer you some water?"

He clenched his jaw. "It's Ronzoni, and yes, I'll have some water."

Ron opened the bar fridge and tossed him a bottle. He cracked the top and sucked some down.

"What kind of name is Miami, anyway?" he said.

It wasn't fair. He was a decent cop, honest enough. He wasn't the sharpest tool in the shed, but he was as determined as a bulldog. It wasn't his fault glib repartee wasn't his thing.

"It's a city. Couple hours south of here. You should check out South Beach." I watched the words filter through his mind like slurry in a gold mining pan.

"Very funny. I thought you played in California."

"Couple years at Modesto."

"So why aren't you called Modesto Jones?" He smiled like he'd delivered a zinger.

"Because that would be stupid."

Ronzoni frowned for a moment, like he was processing that. "Well, whatever Jones. I came here to tell you to keep your face out of my case."

"What case would that be?"

"You know very well what case. BJ Baker. You and your"—he looked at Ron—"your team, have been calling Mr. Baker's friends and suggesting they are suspects."

"Everyone who was there is a suspect."

"No genius, not everyone is a suspect. I say who is and isn't a suspect."

"You or the chief?"

"Me and the chief. We are a team." He sipped his water.

"Go team."

"Just leave Mr. Baker's friends alone. You've upset some important people."

"Should I send a card?"

"What? No, just butt out."

"Mr. Baker has retained me."

"I wouldn't be so sure about that, hotshot."

I flicked my feet up onto the desk. My boat shoes were crusty with dried salt. Ronzoni looked at my shoes and my shorts. He ran his hand down his tie, stroking it.

"This is a PBPD matter, so don't go sticking your nose where it's not welcome."

"What's the sheriff say?" I asked.

"This has nothing to do with the sheriff. Burglary happened inside the city limits."

"Okay."

"Just give me an excuse, Jones."

"Thanks for dropping by."

I watched him process that for sarcasm and finding none, he nodded and held up the bottle in thanks and left.

When he was gone, Ron turned to me. "You want we should call BJ Baker's friends again?"

"So tempting. But let's hold off for now."

Ron stood and smoothed the wrinkles in his trousers. "I think it's drink o'clock. Coming?"

I shook my head. "I can't stomach another tonic water."

"How long is the bet?" He smiled. He was enjoying my torture.

"A week. One week of no alcohol. Three long days to go."

"What'll you do? Work on the case?"

I took my feet off the desk and sat up. "Not sure where to go with the case. Need to think on it. But if I have to be so damned healthy, I might as well go for a run."

Ron shook his head. "I'll leave you to that." He walked to the door.

"By the way," I said. "How'd you go with the golf ladies last night?"

He gave me a huge grin. "You know what they say about girls who play golf. They love to play around with balls."

"You didn't really just say that."

He laughed and closed my office door. I could still hear him laughing as he wandered down the stairs and out of the building.

CHAPTER SEVEN

I ran on the sand, along City Beach, past the Marriott and the Hilton. I got to where the island thins out to a finger at the north end, then turned and ran back. My calf muscles burned before my lungs did. Once my feet left sand and hit pavement, I ambled in the early evening sunshine. I headed along the canal streets that fed out to the Intracoastal. Walked past nice homes with big driveways, and pools inside bug-proof cages that looked like massive bird aviaries. Headed straight for the ugly house at the end.

It was a seventies rancher that, unlike its neighbors, hadn't been redeveloped or knocked down to start again. There was no pool, but I was a two-minute run from the beach so I really didn't see the point. I had picked up the place at a foreclosure auction, as the property market in South Florida had tanked. I wasn't really Singer Island material and neither was my house. We were both comfortable with that. By the time I got home I was breathing normally but sweating like a fat man eating vindaloo. I dropped my clothes in the hamper and stood under the cold water until my temperature dropped below that of a raging fever. I put on some workout shorts and wandered into the kitchen. I opened a Diet Sprite and found a can of black beans in the pantry and put them on the orange Formica counter. The kitchen was retro, and had been in the eighties. I looked through to an open living space that was a lot of wood paneling and not much furniture. I didn't care for the clutter and never had parties. That was what Longboard Kelly's was for. I'd read something at college that had always stuck with me. *It is preoccupation with possessions, more than anything else, that prevents us from living freely and nobly.* Henry David Thoreau. Or maybe Bertrand Russell. Either way, it spoke to me. Hell, I wasn't a monk. I'd just bought a Mustang, for crying out loud. But I didn't own a television, so I figured that made it about even.

I got out some lemon and garlic and some cuttings of cilantro and whipped up a quick black bean dip. I was done before I realized I had nothing to dip in it. I was pondering eating it with a spoon when there was a knock at the front door. I'd left the door open to let the cross breeze flow through, so I just yelled, "Come in."

It was Deputy Castle. If she made a sheriff's uniform look good, she made Levi's and a white t-shirt absolutely hum. Her hair was damp from a shower and her face was moist from the heat. She dropped a suit bag over the back of the stool at the counter and a paper grocery sack on the Formica. She looked down at the Sprite and bean dip and smiled.

"You are being a good boy."

"A bet's a bet."

"Well, I spoke to the governor. He's giving you time off for good behavior." She opened the grocery sack and took out a container of olives and a bag of fresh Pita bread.

"Better than a spoon," I said.

Danielle frowned quizzically. Then she pulled out a cold bottle of sauvignon blanc.

"You are an angel. Anything you want, just name it."

She arched an eyebrow. "I'll take a rain check on what I want until later tonight. For now, glasses and a corkscrew."

We sat on the patio and watched boats drift by. The sun sank low behind Riviera Beach in the west. The wine was dry and fruity and the second glass made me forget about tonic and lime. We nibbled olives and didn't speak again until the sun sent deep orange spears into the atmosphere. Danielle let out a loud sigh.

"World on your shoulders?"

She gently shook her head. "Thinking about BJ Baker."

"Gorgeous sunset, sparkling company and delicious wine, and you're thinking about BJ?"

She arched the eyebrow, and then dropped it. "I've spent the better part of the last two days looking for that man's memento. The police are doing the same." She sipped her wine. "I just think it's wrong that one man can demand so many resources for something so unimportant."

"It's important to him."

"But in the scheme of things. If you lost something important to you, you wouldn't get to mobilize the full law enforcement capabilities of the county."

"If I lost something important, I'd go find it myself."

"But not everyone can do that. And some people won't get the attention they deserve because we're strung out chasing trophies."

I stood and poured a little more wine. I moved behind Danielle's chair and rubbed her shoulders. They looked smooth and tan, but felt like a bag full of marbles. I massaged some of the knots out. Danielle reflexed against my hands, as if it hurt.

"It's the way of things," I said. "People are self-motivated. You're working the case because your boss tells you to. The sheriff is telling you to because it's in his interests to help a major campaign donor." Danielle grunted as I pressed a knot the size of a chestnut. "The police chief doesn't get elected but he gets hired and fired by the mayor, and I'll bet BJ Baker put some cash into his campaign, too."

"So everyone's looking after each other and the little people miss out."

I smiled. "That's why I'm here."

I stopped working with my thumbs and started with my fingertips, soft and slow. Danielle moaned. When I was done I smoothed out her shoulders with my palms. My hands were cramping. I managed to pick up my wine and look at the lights across the water. The breeze was still warm.

"Thanks," she said, rolling her shoulders. "That was great."

"You needed it. You should try some gentle swimming. Helps with the tension."

"Maybe I should just get a weekly massage."

"You should. I do."

She turned to me and frowned. "From who?"

I smiled. "No one you know."

"I have the full resources of the Palm Beach County Sheriff's Office to find out."

"Not this week you don't."

"And I have a sheriff-issue sidearm and the training to use it very effectively."

"From a physical therapist. When you play pro sports you get more rubdowns than most people have showers. I learned there were benefits, both physical and mental. So when I quit the game, I kept getting worked on."

"What physical benefits?"

I smiled again and sipped my wine. "Where is your mind right now? I'm talking about working out the knots like I just rubbed out of you."

"This person better be a he."

"No."

"Then three hundred pounds and called Helga."

"Nope. Michelle, and closer to one twenty."

"She sounds horrific."

"Blond, and a yoga instructor in her spare time."

"Remind me why she isn't sitting on this patio with you right now?"

"Because she isn't you."

Danielle looked across the water and sipped her wine. "Good answer."

"And she's gay."

"Better still."

We watched a Beneteau cruiser motor past with its running lights on. Danielle stood and placed her wine glass down to wave at the passing yacht with a flick of her hand. She turned to me and extended the hand, like she was asking a wallflower to dance.

"This is me showing you what I can do with my hands." She raised her eyebrow again. "And various other parts of my body."

I put my wine down like it was a tonic and lime, and took her hand.

CHAPTER EIGHT

The secret to a good smoothie is dates. I've tried every ingredient in combination, and the common factor in anything that turned out palatable despite a nasty list of ingredients was dates. Like massage, I learned this playing minor league ball. People don't realize it, but the minor leagues are cut-throat. If you can get there, the *bigs* are a high tea with Dom Perignon mimosas on the side compared to the minors. In The Show, lots of guys still have that deer in the headlights look, or have been there so long and done so much that they can be forgiven even a whole season-long dry spell.

But in the minor leagues, guys are either young and desperate to get to The Show, old and desperate to not get cut, or old and dropped from the bigs and desperate to get back. No one plans on making minor league ball their career, so you look for every advantage you can get. Some I didn't do, like sabotaging another guy's equipment or spiking his All-Bran with laxative. Others I did, like steroids, for a few months before I realized that pitching was more timing than muscle and the 'roids started to monkey with my hand-eye coordination. But a big part of the minors was just staying on the park. Keeping healthy and managing injuries. You take a day off, the guy who takes your slot might pitch a no-hitter, or blast one out of the park in the ninth, and you'll find yourself selling Craftsman tools before your head can stop spinning.

Some guys will try most anything to stay healthy. One that made sense to me was eating more fruits and veggies to keep my immune system strong. But I wasn't about to start eating a plate of mustard greens every night. Then I was introduced to smoothies. A high-powered blender and a pound or two of vegetables and fruit and I got all the immune fighting power I could drink. And even the most disgusting mix of kale, flaxseed and fish oil could be made palatable by a handful of dates. Which was what I had in my hand when Danielle padded out into the kitchen wearing a faded Modesto Nuts t-shirt. She looked at the graphic on the shirt, a peanut holding a bat, and shook her head.

"I'm really not sure what you're trying to tell me," she said. I dropped the dates on top of some cut oranges, pineapple, flax seed and kale.

"The bounty of my youth. They were called the A's when I played there, but they changed their name and affiliation the year I got traded. A friend in the front office sent me that. The Modesto Nuts. It's a winner, don't you think?"

She smiled. "It's everything a baseball team should be."

I hit the button and the Vitamix screamed to life and the whole house shook. There was no conversing over a Vitamix. When it was done, I poured two glasses and tossed in straws. I handed one to Danielle.

"How's your shoulders?" I asked.

She rolled her arms over. "Not bad. How's your. . . " She finished the thought by sucking some smoothie.

I didn't get to answer before her cell phone rang. She picked it up and listened. I washed out the blender. Danielle said a couple *ahas* and nodded. Then she rang off and looked at me like she was ending a scene in a daytime soap opera.

"What?" I asked.

"You are not going to believe this."

"What?"

"Someone just stole another Heisman trophy."

CHAPTER NINE

The Bellingham residence was situated in the Tropicana Palms Mobile Home Park, in an enclave of similar parks that sprouted up north of the airport between I-95 and the turnpike. The homes were all single-wides in pastel blues, peaches or white. The lawns were green and only a week overdue for a cut. There were no sidewalks but the roads were smooth asphalt. Danielle stopped the cruiser behind an old but well cared-for Dodge Ram.

We walked up the side of the mobile home. It was a misnomer. The home was about as mobile as a school bus with no wheels. It was a basic rectangle, thin end out to the street, the long edge at seventy degrees to the road. The door was a little over halfway down the long edge. There were no foundation plantings. There were no plantings of any kind.

Danielle knocked and a short woman with a utilitarian haircut answered. Her hair was blond but not naturally so. She was a little plump, and pink-cheeked, like a cherub. She saw the uniform and ushered Danielle in. The inside was basic, but neat and clean. A well-loved brown sofa sat opposite a television that itself sat in a cabinet surrounded by shelves of family portraits. A man in a blue tank top and jeans sat on the sofa. He was resting a soda can on his gut. A floor fan blew directly on him. He looked at Danielle, and then took a second look.

"Bout time," he said.

Danielle spoke to the woman. "Mrs. Bellingham, is it?"

The woman nodded.

"You called about a burglary?"

The man on the sofa snorted and spilled some Mountain Dew on his belly.

"Yes," she said. "A man broke in." She was looking at her shoes and picking at her fingernails.

"What time was this?"

The woman looked at the clock on the wall, and then back at her feet. "About two hours ago?"

"Tell me what happened."

"Yeah, Jenny, tell us all what happened," said the slob on the sofa.

"Sir, who are you?" said Danielle. She unconsciously put her hand on her waist, an inch above her sidearm.

"Who am I? I am the lord of this domain." He smiled at his wit.

"Your name, sir?"

"Bellingham."

"What is your first name?"

Bellingham nodded at me. "Who's this guy?"

"This is Mr. Jones. And your name is?"

"He's not a cop."

"No, Mr. Jones is assisting us with our inquiries."

He snorted. "The hell does that mean?"

His attention was diverted by a segment on SportsCenter. He looked at the screen and sucked on the can. I stayed leaning against the back of the door. I was tempted to give the guy a clip around the ears, but this wasn't my show.

Danielle turned back to Mrs. Bellingham. "Ma'am, do you want to tell me what happened?"

"Well, I got home from work."

"Which is?"

Mrs. Bellingham looked at Danielle. I couldn't tell if she was on the verge of tears or was one of those people who always looked like they'd just lost their favorite puppy.

"I'm an ER nurse. At St. Mary's."

Danielle nodded. "So you got home."

"I came in through the front door and there was a man. There." She pointed to the pine shelving around the television.

"What happened?"

"He was standing there, rubbing my daddy's trophy."

"How do you mean, rubbing it?"

"It's a man playing football, with one of those old fashioned helmets on. He was sort of rubbing the helmet with the palm of his hand." She made a fist with her left hand and rubbed it with her right.

"Then what happened?"

"I think I startled him. He looked up at me and we both froze. I didn't know what to do."

"Understandable," said Danielle. "So you saw him. You could identify him?"

"Yes. No." She shook her head. "I mean, he was wearing sunglasses, big ones. Like Newt wears at work."

She turned to the sofa. The man looked up.

"Newt," said Danielle.

"That's what they call me."

"You wear glasses for work?"

"Protective eyewear."

"What do you do?" asked Danielle. She even slipped him a little smile.

He responded. "I'm a construction foreman. Sometimes we wear protective eyewear on site." He bent over and pulled a pair of glasses out of a canvas tool bag that lay at his feet. The glasses were black and had large dark lenses, like a giant fly, or an Irish rock star.

Danielle nodded. "Like that?" she said to Mrs. Bellingham.

"Uh huh. And a cowboy hat and mustache. Fake one."

"How do you know it was fake?"

"No one would shave at the angle this thing sat. 'Sides, I work with people up close every day. Shave a lot of folks before OR. This wasn't human hair. More like polyester."

Danielle wrote that down. "Then what happened?"

"What happened is, she blew it," said Newt, rising from his sofa. "Like always. Blew it, blew it, blew it." He took a step toward his wife, and she recoiled back into the small counter separating the kitchen from the living space.

"Sir, I need to ask you to sit down," said Danielle.

"Newt, he had a knife!" said Mrs. Bellingham.

"A knife, ha! Why don't you ask her how come we're stuck in this crapper of a trailer park?"

"Sir."

"And how come she's always sneaking around? Ask her that."

"Sir, I won't ask you again. Sit down."

I bumped off the door, ready to evict Newt Bellingham from his own home. But he stopped mid-rant and grabbed a pack of Marlboros off the picture shelves.

"Ask what you want. I'm going for a smoke."

He stepped to the door but I was in the way. Standing, you could see he had once been fitter, maybe a high school athlete back when. His forearms were strong, but his midriff showed the hours spent in front of the idiot box.

I looked at Danielle who shook her head. I stepped aside. He threw open the door and stepped down onto the grass. I nodded to Danielle and stepped out, closing the door behind me.

The morning had lost its early dew and the grass was dry. Bellingham was sitting on a cheap plastic chair that was part of a set. A matching table had a sun-bleached umbrella through it. The umbrella wore the Miller High Life logo. Bellingham lit a cigarette and watched me walk along the side of the mobile home. I looked around the park. It was neat enough. No trash or cars on blocks. All the same, it was the kind of place a news crew would flock to after a hurricane. I stood by the table, the sun over my shoulder. Bellingham had to look straight into it to look at me.

"What's your story?" he said. He didn't appear to be smoking the cigarette. He held it in his fingers and let it burn.

"I'm a private detective."

"Like Columbo?"

"No, not like Columbo."

He tapped some ash onto the ground. "So what are you doing here?"

"I'm working on a case that might have something in common with yours."

"How's that?"

"You had a trophy stolen."

"You say so." He squinted and turned his head. The cigarette burned.

"You didn't have a trophy?"

Bellingham coughed a laugh. "Yeah, we had a trophy."

"What was it?"

He shook his head and curled his lip like he'd eaten a sour grape. "A Heisman."

"Real?"

"Oh, it was real."

"How'd you get a Heisman trophy?"

"Who says I didn't win it?"

"I do. You're too young that I wouldn't recognize you if you'd won it. Besides, to win a Heisman you have to play college football, and you look like you sweat opening a pickle jar."

"Funny guy."

"So how'd you get it?"

Bellingham glanced at the side of the trailer. Then he put his hand up to his forehead to shield the sun. "My wife's father won it.

Years ago. Never saw him play. But the old man passed it to us when he died."

"Which was when?"

"Few months back."

"You get on with the old man?"

"He was a crotchety bastard."

"So he wasn't keen on his daughter marrying down."

"Hey."

"You put in a good word to get the Heisman?"

He shook his head. "Never even knew he had it. Until he kicked the bucket."

"Anything else go missing?"

He shook his head.

"You think whoever broke in was looking for the Heisman?"

He shrugged and dropped the cigarette butt to the ground and crushed it with his foot. "If there was a break-in."

"You think your wife made it up? Why would she do that?"

"To piss me off."

"Fair reason."

"You're a comedian."

I looked around the park again. The mobile homes looked like shipping containers. Couldn't be too many places to hide a Heisman.

"You working?" I said.

"Yeah. Left just after six. Came back when she called."

"Your wife was getting home?"

"She works nights, on and off." He picked out another cigarette. "So you're looking for BJ Baker's Heisman? I saw it on TV."

I nodded.

"Maybe you find his, you find mine."

"Or your wife's."

He shrugged. "You got a card?"

I pulled my wallet out and took out a card. It was bent to the shape of my right butt cheek. I handed it to him and he looked at it.

"Miami Jones?" He looked at me. "That's your name? Geez, what's your brother's name? Kansas?" He grinned again at his own hilarity.

"Guy called Newt making fun of other people's names. Now that is funny."

CHAPTER TEN

"Could he be the same guy?" Danielle said as we got into her patrol car.

"Two Heismans in a matter of days. Got to consider a link."

Danielle turned the key and the deep engine rumbled.

"You think he might be escalating?" I said as Danielle pulled the car out of the trailer park.

"Hard to say. Mrs. Bellingham said the guy had a knife."

"Did she tell you what sort of knife?" I said.

"Kitchen. She thought it was one of those Japanese-style ones. Santoku."

"Question is, did he have it last time?"

"What do you think?"

"Gut says no. Last theft was during an event, so too public to carry a knife."

"Unless he was supposed to carry one," Danielle said.

"Like a caterer?"

"Just a thought."

"You guys come up with anything on the staff yet?"

"The PD are doing more of that, but not that I've heard. How about you guys? You checking?"

"Yeah," I smiled. "Ronzoni wasn't too happy about it. But we haven't come up with anything much, either."

"What about the husband? He say anything?"

"Newt? Nice guy. He thinks his wife is making the whole thing up."

Danielle pulled onto Australian Drive to scoot around Clear Lake. "Why? Attention?"

"Maybe. Attention might be something she craves. I don't think spooning in bed is too high on old Newt's nighttime routine."

"Could he be right, though? Could she have heard about BJ Baker's trophy going missing and saw a chance to get some attention?"

"I can't rule it out. People do funny things to get some attention. Even the bad kind."

Danielle pulled the patrol car into the lot beside my building. The solid concrete nameplate advertised the tenants. An insurance agent. Three sets of attorneys. A computer software company. A couple of companies whose names gave no clue as to what they did, and were run by people I'd never met in the elevator. Then the nameplate for Lenny Cox Investigations. It was a new building with double-glazed windows and environmentally friendly HVAC. Not the usual ratty space detectives inhabited in the books I'd read as a kid. Danielle didn't switch off the engine but I didn't get out. The air conditioning was cool.

She turned in her seat to look at me. "What is it?" she said.

I let out some air. "Just something nagging. On the one side, how did the burglar, if it is the same guy, know about the Bellinghams' trophy? They haven't had it for long, and they weren't making a big song and dance about it. Maybe he showed it to a few buddies. But how does that get back to our guy?"

"Maybe Jenny Bellingham is making it up."

"Well, that's the other half of it that doesn't sit right. Her description of events."

"How so? She walks in on the perp, they freeze, he pulls a knife, tells her to get on the floor and if she looks up for ten minutes he'll cut her. She does what she's told and he flees."

"Sure it all fits," I said. "Whether it's real or she's faking it, that's a plausible story. But I'm talking about when she described him. When she first walked in. She said the guy was holding the Heisman and rubbing its head. She even showed us with her hands."

"Right."

"So Mrs. Bellingham doesn't strike me as the creative type. She's a nurse, working nights, tired from her shift. She wore boring, practical shoes and had a haircut the military would have been proud of. So I buy the idea of making the burglary up, but the head rubbing? That's one detail too far. She didn't make that up. She saw that."

Danielle nodded, and then turned as her radio crackled. The dispatch came over with a callout. "Duty calls." She smiled and I seriously missed a beat.

"I'll keep on it."

As I got out of the car she said she'd drop by if she could.

"If not, I'll be home later. In case you get swamped," I said.

"Or in case I spend my day chasing tails for BJ Baker."

"Go save the world." I slammed the door and she drove around the parking lot in a loop and came out by me. She waved as she drove out onto the street.

CHAPTER ELEVEN

Ron was at the water cooler when I came in the door. He wore a lightweight linen suit, blue shirt and a red striped tie.

"Nice costume, bro," I said.

"You only wish you could look this dapper."

"If you only knew how true that is." I turned to Lizzy who was retrieving something from the printer behind her desk.

"Miss Lizzy, how are you?" She ignored me and packed a sheath of papers into a presentation folder. She handed the folder to Ron.

"You're good to go," she said.

"Gorgeous, thanks." He winked at her, which earned him a small smile. It would have earned me a slap.

"Good news?" I said.

"Indeed," said Ron. "The Melito insurance fraud case. What I have here is going to make the insurance company very happy. They won't have to pay him a dime. So some of those dimes will come to us."

"Making a livelihood. Way to go Ron. How'd you get him?"

"The spinal injuries he suffered in his fall may be catastrophic, but they aren't enough to prevent him from smoking a very long and true ball down the eighteenth fairway on the Links course at Bear Lakes."

"For him it truly will be a good walk ruined."

"Indeed. And how about you. You're rather tardy today."

"Got a callout with Deputy Castle."

"I'll bet you did."

"Guess why."

Ron shrugged.

"Somebody stole another Heisman trophy."

"You don't say."

"I do."

"A serial snatcher?"

"Possible. I've just got to figure out where it takes us with the Baker case."

"Here," said Lizzy. She handed me a pile of Post-it notes. "Your Mr. Baker has called four more times. His assistant has called eight times. I think they've got me on speed dial."

"How were his manners?"

"The assistant was brought up right. As for Mr. Baker, he knows he won't get far with me using his gruff voice, but he certainly won't be getting his manners merit badge anytime soon."

I looked at the handful of notes. "I guess I'd better give him a call."

"I've got a meeting to get to," said Ron. "You know, if it is a serial snatcher, that might help."

"How so?"

"We just need to know where he's likely to strike again. And it isn't lightning. He has a specific target."

"Other Heismans."

"You just need to find any other Heismans in Florida."

I shook my head. "I wouldn't know where to start."

"But you know someone who does." He raised his eyebrows.

"No. No way."

"You know she'll know. If anyone has their ear to the ground on this, it'll be Beccy."

"I'm sure there's another way."

Ron opened the door and smiled. "There isn't a better way." He was grinning like the proverbial cat as he stepped out and closed the door. Performance exits were becoming a thing with him. I looked at the notes from BJ Baker. The idea of reporting to him that I had gotten nowhere didn't fill me with joy. And the road forward was a thorny one. I looked at Lizzy. She shook her head like a schoolteacher giving a pupil an emphatic no. I stuffed the notes in my pocket and headed out to Longboard Kelly's to ruminate on my options.

CHAPTER TWELVE

Two beers and a turkey sandwich did nothing for me or the case. Thinking about Ron in a suit, out earning our pay packet while I sat ruminating over a beer drove me from the bar. I walked into the office, grabbed a cup of water from the cooler and asked Lizzy to get BJ Baker for me. I sat behind my desk and kicked my shoes off. My phone beeped and I picked it up and Lizzy told me she had Mr. Baker on the line.

"BJ," I said. There was nothing but the sound of the ocean coming down the line. That was the thing about rich people. They never answered their own phones. They had people. My people called their people and the last people on the line was the winner. The phone made a thunking noise.

"Jones," came the boorish voice from the handset.

"BJ, how's tricks?"

"Where the hell you been?"

"Out looking for your little trophy."

"It's not a *little*. . . I've been calling you."

"I know. This is me returning your call."

"You need a new secretary."

"I don't think Jesus would agree," I told him.

"What? Look, don't you own a cell phone?"

"I do."

"Why the hell don't I have that number?"

"Because I don't want you to call me on it."

There was a grunt of dissatisfaction. "You need to remember who is paying your bills."

"How could I forget? What do you want?"

"What?"

"What. Do. You. Want. You've been calling me, remember."

"Yes, I have. I want you to stop harassing my clients and friends."

"Who?"

"You've been calling guests at my party and accusing them of being suspects. I made it clear when I hired you. None of my guests are suspects."

"Actually, I decide who is or isn't a suspect."

"You do no such thing! I am paying you, so I'll tell you how to handle things."

"No, you won't. You hired me to investigate the theft of your trophy, and if possible to find it. You did not buy the rights to belittle or bully my staff, to direct this investigation or, as stated, decide who is or is not a suspect."

"Excuse me?"

"I will excuse you. But this is the final time. If you don't like the way I work, then you are free to terminate my services and put your stolen Heisman in the hands of the Palm Beach Police Department, the Palm Beach County Sheriff's Office, the United States Marshals, the Federal Bureau of Investigation, the Florida National Guard, the United States Armed Forces, the Navy Seals, the Army Rangers, the Joint Chiefs and any other body you have managed to co-opt into this search."

There was silence on the phone.

"BJ?" Nothing. "Oh, BJ? Shall I consider myself terminated?"

"No."

"What's that?"

"No. You are not terminated. You don't get off that easy. I hire someone, they do the job right or they never work in this town again. I don't care who finds my Heisman. You, the cops, the sheriff. I don't care." His voice went deep and cold. "But you. I don't want you to bring back just my trophy. I want you to bring me the guy who took it. The cops won't do that. You will. I want him first. Before the cops. I just want to spend half an hour with him."

"What are you going to do? Get him to polish the trophy? I think he might have done that already."

"Just find him, smart guy. Find him and bring him to me. Don't, and I hope you've got a branch office in Guam. Because you'll never work around here again." He hung up and left me listening to the ocean again.

I put the phone in its cradle and flipped my bare feet up onto the desk. BJ Baker couldn't ruin my business. Not completely. He didn't have that kind of sway. I figured I'd still get the odd missing cat case from the snowbirds in Palm Beach Gardens. Or I could find BJ's Heisman. And Ron was right. To find one, I'd have to find them all. And to do that, I'd have to call my one source who would know. Beccy. Then my cell phone rang.

"Hey, boss," said Ron. He sounded like he was walking.

"How goes it?"

"Guess who just deposited a big fat check in our bank?" I could hear the smile in his voice.

"You're a prince among men."

"Celebration libations at Longboard's."

"I'm there."

I dropped the phone in my pocket and slipped back into my shoes. I walked to the outer office and told Lizzy I had a meeting with Ron.

"Don't drink too much," she said.

I stepped out the door, thinking about Beccy Williams and wondering how warm the winters were in Guam.

CHAPTER THIRTEEN

I must have forgotten to tell Ron about BJ Baker's mandate, because the next day he kept calling everyone on the lists from the charity event. Both guests and staff. As fate would have it, he got his first hit on the staff list. We drove out to what my father would have called a halfway house. Hell, I would have called it that too, but in my father's day he would have gotten away with it. It was, in real estate vernacular, a multifamily residence. We parked on the street in front of the large two-story house. There were two front doors that gave the impression that the house had been converted into a duplex at some time in its history.

Unlike the other houses on the street, this one had no decrepit cyclone wire fence and the lawn was neatly mowed. I took a good look around. It wasn't the sort of area you left a shiny new Mustang sitting around for long if you expected the wheels to still be attached when you got back. We walked up the concrete path toward the gray painted porch. We each chose a door. Both opened into the same small foyer, barely big enough to swing a domestic animal. There were closed doors off a corridor and stairs heading up to the second floor. The only difference was on my side. One of the doors was open. I heard someone call out.

"Help you?"

I stepped in and Ron followed. The floors creaked underfoot. There was no sneaking around in this place. Perhaps that was intentional. I poked my head in the open door. The room was the size of a small bedroom. But it held two messy desks and a large man with bags under his eyes and a Marine-style buzz cut. He wore a white tank top and both shoulders were covered in ink. He had a boxer's nose. He smiled. He had a boxer's teeth, too.

"Help you?" he said, again.

"You the super?" I asked.

"Facility Manager. That's the official title, I believe."

"Miami Jones," I said, extending my hand.

He took it. He had big mitts. "Lex."

"We're looking for some information on Dennis Rivers."

"He in trouble?"

"No," I said. "Employment verification." I handed him my card. He took it and looked it over.

"You guys don't got a phone?"

"I prefer to do things face to face."

Lex nodded like he didn't care either way.

"What do you do here, Lex?"

"We run a re-entry program."

"A halfway house?" asked Ron.

Lex smiled again. "Transition from Prison to Community Initiative. That's the official title, I believe."

"How does that work?" I asked.

"We assist offender re-entry into the community. We get them training, help them find work, give them a place to bunk for a while."

"Does Rivers live here?"

"Nah."

"Did he?"

"Nah."

"So how do you know him?" I asked.

"Dennis trained in culinary skills while inside. Worked in the kitchen. When he got out he did a work placement with us in our kitchen."

"Does he still work here?"

"No. He got a job."

"And he lived elsewhere?"

"Family, I think."

I nodded. "What was he in for?"

"Committing a crime."

Now it was my turn to smile. "Do you know what crime?"

"Yeah."

"But you're not going to share."

He grinned and shook his head.

"Was he a good worker? Good in the kitchen?"

"It ain't the Ritz, you know. But yeah, he was good. Did what he was told."

"And how did he get the job at. . .?" I looked at Ron.

"Black Tie Catering," he said. I nodded and looked at Lex.

"He applied for it." He shrugged. "He worked here, kept his nose clean. Did the job program, learned how to put an application together and he applied."

"Anything else you can tell us?" I asked.

Lex shook his head. "What kind of job is he going for now?" he said.

"He's trying to keep one."

I thanked Lex for his time.

"Look, no one who comes through here is a saint," said Lex. "But Rivers isn't a bad kid."

I walked back to the car, looking around the street. I wondered how bad jail must be that this place was the more attractive option.

"It's a step on the road to somewhere else," said Ron, reading my mind.

I nodded.

"What do you think? Could he just be a good kid?" asked Ron as he slipped into the car.

"He was *good* enough to end up jail. So I suspect my baseline for such things is a little different from Lex's." I turned the key and revved the Mustang. "We need to find out for ourselves. We need to chat with Dennis. I don't suppose the caterers will give us his home address?"

"Not necessary. I happen to know that Black Tie is doing the food at a function at the yacht club tomorrow."

I smiled. "Tally ho."

CHAPTER FOURTEEN

Sitting at the bar in the courtyard at Longboard Kelly's reminded me of a Billy Joel song. Only it wasn't five o'clock and it wasn't Saturday. Saturdays were for tourists and office clerks. It was midweek when the true regulars shuffled in. Ron and I sat on our stools, the old fan attached to the palapa shade shifting the warm breeze onto us. Ron had a Corona, I had a Dos Equis. It wasn't Cinco de Mayo, but what the hell.

We were small talking with Muriel. She looked like she'd spent the day on a tanning bed. Danielle walked in from the parking lot. She was in a sleeveless red button-up shirt and denim cutoffs. Her hair was wet from her post-shift shower. She came and stood between Ron and me and ordered a vodka tonic. Muriel handed her the drink but didn't ask for any money. I thought she might give freebies to law enforcement, but then realized it would land on my tab. There wasn't a spare seat at the bar, so I stood up. Danielle nodded toward a table at the rear of the courtyard, near the water feature. It was a big gold-colored urn, with water bubbling across the top and spilling down the sides. Danielle took the seat closest to the bubbling water.

"Another day alive," she said, holding up her glass.

Ron and I clinked our drinks.

"Amen to that," said Ron.

Danielle sipped her drink and leaned back. "You get anywhere in the Heisman hunt?"

Ron glanced at me, and then busied himself taking a long, slow drink from his glass.

"Baker's on the warpath but wants to keep us on the case," I said.

"He wants the guy, doesn't he?"

"He does."

"You're not going to give him the guy, are you?"

"No, ma'am. If I can find his prize trophy, I'll consider my duty discharged."

"Glad to hear it. No other news?"

"Not much. Found an ex-con on the payroll of the caterers."

"And?"

"Spoke to a guy from the re-entry program. More or less vouched for the kid."

"Who's the kid?"

"Name of Rivers. Dennis."

"Speak to him?"

"Tomorrow. You know if the PD has had a chat yet?"

"I don't, but I can find out. I expect if you know, they'll know."

"That's a vote of confidence."

She smiled. "You know what I mean. Getting at that kind of info is easier for us."

"I know."

Danielle rolled her shoulders and grimaced. "It's driving around in the cruiser. Murder on the shoulders."

"I can get you in with my masseuse."

"I might just take you up on that."

We sipped our drinks.

"So how was your day, dear?" I asked.

She rolled her eyes. "Took a call for a missing person. Frantic woman out near Wellington. Her husband's disappeared and we've barely got the time to take the call, let alone find him."

"Busy, huh?"

"The Heisman hunt. And for what? This poor woman can't sleep at night, but because it doesn't look like foul play we can't put the proper resources into it."

"The guy up and leave?"

"Who knows?" she said. "Possible. His car's gone, an overnight bag. So maybe. But most of his clothes and stuff are still there. She thinks he's harmed himself."

"People leave. We don't always know our loved ones as well as we think we do."

"I get it. But I'd still like to be able to tell her if he's alive. Even if he did take off. She just looked so sad. Not like she'd been crying. More like she'd been sad for years."

I sipped the last of my beer. "You can't help everyone."

"I know. But like you said the other night, when the little guys get left behind, that's what you're here for."

I smiled my Tom Cruise toothy grin. "You got it."

"I'm glad you agree," she said, finishing off her drink. "Because I gave her your number. Said you'd be able to help her out."

I looked at Ron, who removed his mouth from his glass to say, "Just finished the Molito case. We're good for a new one."

"Not sure she's going to be able to pay much," said Danielle.

"How much is not much?" I said, standing and collecting our empty glasses.

"Possibly nothing."

I looked at Ron.

"Bit of *pro bono* might be good for the soul," he said. He handed me his glass. I frowned at Danielle.

"You keep getting me work like that, I might have to make you a partner."

"Promises, promises," she said as I headed for the bar.

CHAPTER FIFTEEN

I ran across the hard sand, my feet leaving a second set of prints. The morning sun burned across the right side of my face. I sacrificed a little speed for position, which was a couple of strides behind Danielle. She wore a sports bra and Lycra running shorts. Her legs looked like they'd been stolen off a gazelle. I knew her abs looked like steel, but the view from behind was equally impressive. And motivating. If she had taken off in a rocket I would have developed the gift of flight. She turned from hard, wet sand back up toward the park. I lifted my knees as I pushed across the softer beach. We both stopped running when we hit pavement and walked back along the streets. We didn't speak. When she turned and caught me looking at her backside, she just smiled. We got back to my house and had one hell of a shower.

I was wearing a towel and tossing some fruit in the blender when her phone rang. We frowned at each other. It was her day off. She answered the call on the patio, wrapped in a sarong, the origins of which escaped me. She strode back in to grab a pen and paper and write something down. She hung up and looked at the note, and then began punching in a new set of numbers.

She looked at me as she let the phone ring. "Jenny Bellingham called the office asking for me. Dispatch said they could send a car out, but she said she needed to talk to me."

She turned and walked back out to the patio. I hit the blender and poured two smoothies. They came out green despite the absence of any green ingredients. But they tasted just fine.

Danielle came back in and grabbed hers. "She doesn't sound good. Wants to tell me more about the burglary."

"Hubby at work?"

She nodded. "You mind?"

I smiled. "What else would you do on your day off?"

We drove to the mobile home park, listening to the radio. The weather report said we should expect some rain. I couldn't see it. I parked the Mustang in front of the Bellingham home, behind an old Honda Civic I hadn't noticed last time. I followed Danielle up the side of the home for no other reason than I wanted her to be the one who knocked on the door. Jenny Bellingham answered. From the darkness of the mobile home I could see a massive shiner. She looked like she'd walked into a Mike Tyson right hook. Her left eye was puffy and red. It was going darker as we stood there. It was recent.

She looked at Danielle, puzzled. It often happens. We train ourselves to see things without paying attention. What Jenny Bellingham saw the first time we visited was Danielle's uniform. Now she saw none.

"Mrs. Bellingham? Deputy Castle. You called me?"

"Oh, yes," she said, a flash of recognition running across her face. She turned her shoulder and opened the door. Danielle stepped through. I stopped at the threshold. Mrs. Bellingham looked at me, tense.

"Ma'am, would you like me to wait outside?"

She looked at me, and then Danielle. "No, come in." She didn't sound convinced.

The mobile home still looked neat, but it was dark. The blinds were dropped and this time it was the inside that reminded me of a shipping container. It was warm and dark. Maybe that was how nightshift people liked it. Darkening the whole house to sleep in one room seemed like overkill to me. Maybe she had other reasons. The two women sat on the sofa. I stayed in my position against the door.

"What happened?" said Danielle, looking at the bruise on her face.

Mrs. Bellingham touched it reflexively, and then recoiled. "Oh, that. I fell."

"Ma'am, that doesn't look like a fall."

She looked at Danielle, angry and confused. At whom, that was the question. "It's nothing, really. I fell."

"Why did you call me, Jenny?"

"I don't know. You left your card. I didn't know who to call." She looked at Danielle's attire and shook her head. "I'm sorry. It's your day off."

"That's okay. Just tell me what you wanted to speak to me about."

Mrs. Bellingham glanced at me again. "You know about the Heisman, right?"

"Yes, ma'am," I said. "I played a little college football myself. Not as good as your dad, though."

"You saw him?"

I shook my head. "No. Never had the pleasure. I heard he had an arm, though. Biggest Hail Mary in the game."

She almost smiled. "He loved that game. He played NFL, you know."

"Cleveland."

She nodded. This time she did smile. It was only temporary. I could see now she had a split lip. "I was born there. We left when I was three. He was good, my dad. But not good enough."

I knew the feeling. "It's a hard thing to leave behind. But there are other challenges, other things to strive for."

"That's what my dad used to say." She looked at her fingers, and then at me again. "He used to keep the Heisman on a shelf in his den. It was never really on display. Like it wasn't the center of anything, just another part of his life."

"Some winners define the Heisman, and some are defined by it."

She nodded and remembered not to smile. "I was the one who used to watch the games with him. Thanksgiving, especially. My sister would help my mother make turkey and cranberry sauce and I'd sit with Dad and watch football." She paused, and then glanced at Danielle. "It's why he wanted me to have it. When he passed away." We waited in silence for a moment before Danielle spoke.

"Did someone really steal the trophy?" she said.

Mrs. Bellingham glared at her. "You think I made it up?"

"I don't know what happened, Jenny."

"It happened just like I said. No one believes me."

"I believe you," said Danielle. "What I don't understand is how anyone knew you had it, in order to steal it."

"My husband." She shook her head. "I probably should have pretended to have it stolen, then hidden it from him."

"What did your husband do?"

"He tried to sell it."

Danielle and Mrs. Bellingham both looked at me, and then back at each other.

"Sell it, how?"

"On the Internet. He listed it on the Internet," Mrs. Bellingham said.

"But you weren't okay with that."

"No. It was my daddy's."

"But Newt didn't agree."

"No."

We waited in silence again, each of us thinking.

"Ma'am, do you have a computer?" I said.

She nodded. "In the spare bedroom. Newt does his fantasy football on it."

"May I?"

She nodded again.

I walked down a corridor that ran down one side of the home. The corridor had rooms off it, like on a sleeper car on a train. The first room was a bathroom. The second room was the spare room. I figured the master bedroom was the room at the end. I flicked the light on in the spare room. It was full of the junk of life. An old two-seater sofa, maybe a pullout for when Newt's buddies came over and drank too many to stand up and get to their trucks. There was a stack of moving boxes, filled with detritus. A couple of As Seen on TV exercise devices. A desk covered in envelopes and paper. Bills and junk mail. A computer monitor sat in front of a tattered red office chair. There was a desktop system on the floor underneath. I got down on the carpet to look at the back. I was getting up when Danielle entered the room.

"Something?"

"Hard to tell," I said, brushing off my hands. "The carpet could do with a vacuum." I stood up. "If he listed the Heisman online, then he might have had communication with the burglar by email. It might tell us something."

"You think we should take the computer?"

"No. That might set old Newt off. I found a USB port on the back, so if we get an external hard drive we can copy everything over."

"There's a big box store just on the other side of I-95."

"I'll go if you wait here."

"No," she said. "I'll go. I need you to talk to her. She won't open up to me about the bruising. I need you to come from another angle. Help her understand that we can help her. Whatever her situation."

"Lawful or not so?"

Danielle looked hard at me.

"She needs to know all her options."

CHAPTER SIXTEEN

Jenny Bellingham offered me coffee. I watched her pour boiling water on the instant granules and she passed me the mug. It had a bass on one side. The other side said *I'd rather be fishing*.

"Sugar or NutraSweet?"

I shook my head. "How long have you lived here in the park?"

"About five years." She poured water in another mug and filled it to the brim with milk.

"How long have you been married?"

"Seven."

"No kids?"

She closed her eyes and sipped her coffee. There were daffodils on her mug. "Newt isn't interested. Says they'll suck the money out of you. You got kids?"

"No. Not married, either."

"Why?"

"Lots of reasons. Never met the right woman, or if I did I let work get in the way."

"What do you do exactly?"

I took a card out and slid it across the kitchen counter. "I help people solve problems."

"What sort of problems?"

"All sorts. I help find people, or discover if people are doing something wrong. I help people escape bad situations. Sometimes some corporate work."

She picked up the card. "LCI?"

"Lenny Cox Investigations. He was the original owner."

"And now?"

"Now it's my place."

She put the card down. "I can't afford a private investigator, Mr. Jones."

"You don't need to. Someone else is paying me. But in finding their thing, I might find yours."

She nodded slowly, and then sipped her coffee. It stung her lip and she grimaced.

"Keep the card anyway. Like I say, I help people out of situations. You ever need help, you call me."

"What can you do? The police can't do anything."

"The sheriff can do more than you think. And I can do even more."

"How?"

"I have a little flexibility in my approach. I've helped women like you before."

"Women like me?" She said it defiantly, like she wasn't ready to admit she was being abused.

"Women who are sometimes a little clumsy and fall down," I said.

I finished my coffee as I heard the Mustang pull up outside. Danielle came in and we connected the hard drive to the USB port on the rear of the tower. I got the transfer going and we went back to the living room. It was still dark inside. We drank more coffee and Mrs. Bellingham told us about her father. Some of his stories. About her sister in Tequesta. After my second coffee I went and checked the transfer. It was done. Pretty quick. No videos. Very few pictures, I guessed. I unplugged the drive and put it back in its box and carried it out.

Danielle got up and put her hand on Mrs. Bellingham's shoulder. "We'll check this out and see what we find. I'll let you know."

"Thank you."

Danielle stepped down onto the path and strode toward the Mustang. I got to the threshold and Mrs. Bellingham put her hand on my elbow. I turned and looked at her. The bruise on her left eye had gone black and blue. It was a hell of a nasty fall.

She smiled with her cheeks, not her lips. "My daddy would have liked you."

I nodded. "I would have liked him." I paused for a moment, and then said, "You need anything, you call. Okay? Anything."

She nodded and I stepped down into the glare as she closed the door behind me.

CHAPTER SEVENTEEN

The yacht club overlooked the glittering water of the Intracoastal. The sun bounced off the ripples between sprouts of cloud. The radio was still talking about a storm, but it was nowhere to be found. Motor yachts, each worth more than my house, lined up along the docks that spidered out from the promenade on Flagler Drive. We found two vans belonging to Black Tie Catering on the promenade, at the end of the dock that led down to the clubhouse. We followed a girl in a plain white blouse, black skirt and black stockings. She carried a stainless steel tray containing some kind of hors d'oeuvres down to the water. A large motor launch was tied up against the shore. The girl stepped aboard the boat via a small aluminum gangway that rattled as she tiptoed across.

Ron and I stood on the promenade in the sunshine. I had my shades on, and I'd even put on trousers. One should look the part. We watched the hubbub on the boat. It was a pontoon boat with a wide flat deck, like a miniature ice rink without the ice. Chairs and tables had been set up in cocktail fashion. A bar and buffet were set up near the back. Or was it the front? Next to the cockpit, or the wheelhouse, or whatever the little shed with the steering wheel in it was called on such a barge.

Someone walked past us. It was a guy in the same black and white uniform that the girl was wearing. He carried another steel tray onto the boat. I watched him step around the tables. He moved well. He had dark brown hair that was neat, if a touch long. He was tall, but not large. Big enough to take care of himself, but small enough to not attract unwanted attention. I watched him help move a *bain-marie* on a stand into the corner of the deck. Then he ambled out across the gangway. He walked toward Ron and me and squinted up into the bright sky. His shirt was open at the neck. I assumed he had one of those clip-on black bow ties in his pocket.

"Dennis," I said as he got to me.

He looked down from the sky and blinked. "What?"

"Dennis Rivers?"

"Yeah. Who are you?"

"You got a minute to talk?"

He looked me up and down. I thought I looked pretty snappy. "About what?" His body coiled some.

"We're investigating a theft from the Baker residence."

"C'mon, man," he groaned. "The cops already hassled me. That was nothing to do with me." He walked toward the van.

"You did work at the event. The night of the burglary."

"Beat it, man."

I looked at Ron. "I guess we'll just have to take it up with the catering company."

Rivers spun around. "C'mon man. They'll can me."

"Couple minutes, Dennis."

"I'm workin' here, man."

"So give us a card. If they ask, we're interested in getting some catering done."

He hesitated, and looked at the boat. Then back to the van.

"Two minutes," he said, walking down the promenade, away from the boat.

"You guys aren't cops," he said.

"We work for Mr. Baker."

"So why you ragging on me?"

"You were at the event, yes?"

"We all were. You asking everyone else these questions?"

"Possibly."

"C'mon, man. You hassling me 'cause I got a record."

"That doesn't help you."

"So you just gonna lay it on the ex-con? Easy done, right?"

"Like you said, we're not the police. We're just trying to get Mr. Baker's property back."

"Well, I don't got it."

"What were you in for?" said Ron. His voice was soft and caring. He sounded like a grandpa.

"GTA. Stole a few cars. I don't do that no more."

"You learned how to cook inside?" said Ron.

"Yeah. We had to learn a skill."

"You like it? Cooking?"

"Yeah, it's not bad."

"But this isn't cooking," Ron said, pointing back to the boat.

"Nah, man. It's just waiter stuff. But it's a job."

"So what can you tell us about the event at Mr. Baker's?" I said.

"Look, I don't know nothing, man. It was just another gig. I didn't even know the man's stuff was pinched until the cops came knocking on my door."

"Did you see the Heisman?"

"Nah, man. That's what I'm telling you."

"What about two days ago, early morning? Can you verify your whereabouts?"

"Why?"

"Can you?"

"You mean like an alibi?"

"Yes, Dennis, an alibi."

"Why?"

"There was another burglary."

He shook his head violently. "Man, I knew it. You trying to nail me."

"Just tell us where you were, Dennis, and the problem can go away."

"Why, man? It's not like you're gonna believe me. Guy like you in your fancy clothes never believe a guy like me."

So I did look pretty snappy. I knew it. But I also knew the kid had a point. I wasn't going to buy anything Rivers said at face value.

"Look, man. I gotta get back to work. Just leave me the hell alone."

"Dennis, did you tell Black Tie Catering you were an ex-con?"

His face changed, to something I suspect he didn't have before he went to prison. He looked completely devoid of emotion. Not angry, but capable of anger.

He held up my business card. "I know where to find you."

He turned and strode back to the van. We watched him grab a plastic crate of glassware and carry it to the boat. He didn't look back at us.

"Don't ever get that guy to do catering for you," said Ron.

"That's a bit harsh. He might be an okay chef, even if he is a crook."

"I don't know about his cooking. But based on the look he just gave you, I can guarantee he'll spit in your food."

CHAPTER EIGHTEEN

The rain came down for twenty-four hours straight. It was unseasonably late and unusually long. It hit the roof on our building like we were at the bottom of Niagara Falls. I was sitting in a visitor's chair in the front office, watching Lizzy type slowly. Or play solitaire, I couldn't tell. I was considering breaking into my scotch stash in my office when there was a knock at the door. A mousy woman in a long raincoat poked her head in.

"I'm sorry," she said. She was hard to hear over the rain. "The office downstairs sent me up here. Do you know where I can find a Mr. Miami Jones?" If she wore makeup, it had washed away. Her hair was only a touch damp. She must have been holding an umbrella behind the door.

"I am he. How can I help?"

She looked at me, unsure. I was wearing chinos and a shirt with station wagons and surfboards on it. I had boat shoes on. I was presentable enough. Then she looked back at the nameplate on the door.

"LCI," I said. "That's the name of the company. I'm the owner."

"Oh," she said. She was holding onto the door. "Would it not be easier to have your name on the door?"

"Yes, ma'am, it would. If I wanted everyone to know this was my office. That's not always the case." I stood up and put my hand out. "Miami Jones. And you are?"

She took my hand. Hers was soft and small, more bone than skin. She couldn't have been much past forty, but she presented like she had given up a long time ago.

"My name is Arlene Ferguson. I was given your name by Sheriff's Deputy Castle."

"Yes, Mrs. Ferguson. She mentioned it. Won't you come through?"

Mrs. Ferguson stepped into the office. She held a long black umbrella with a polished wood handle.

"Let's sit in my office." I put my hand on the back of her shoulder. I felt like I was dealing with my grandmother. "Would you like coffee?"

"Do you have tea?"

I looked at Lizzy for help and she nodded. I ushered Mrs. Ferguson into my office and sat her on the sofa that spent most of its life as Ron's daybed. She wore a dress with red flowers on it. Big petals. Hibiscus or something like that. She adjusted her hem below her knees and clasped her delicate hands in her lap. I turned around the visitor's chair that was facing my desk and sat. Lizzy came in with a tray. She placed two mugs of tea on the table between us. I didn't know where the tea had come from. She smiled at Mrs. Ferguson. They couldn't have been more different. Lizzy wore enough makeup to stock an opera company. They were about the same height, five five-ish, but no one in their right mind would call Lizzy mousy. She stood to leave.

"Grab a chair," I said. Lizzy put the tray on my desk and turned the other visitor's chair around. Mrs. Ferguson held her tea like she was cold. It might have been raining cats and dogs, but it was still seventy-two degrees out.

"Deputy Castle tells me your husband is missing."

"Yes," she said into the tea.

"When did he disappear?"

"A couple of days ago. He was gone all night, which isn't like him. The next day I called the sheriff."

"And you haven't heard from him."

"No," she whispered. The rain kept tapping against the window.

I made no move to pick up my tea. "What do you think might have happened to him, Mrs. Ferguson?"

"I have no idea. I don't understand."

"What does your husband do?"

"Do?"

"For a living?"

She nodded. "He sells cars."

"At a dealership?"

"I guess you could call it that."

"What sort of cars?"

"Cars are cars."

I nodded. I didn't care about the cars. I just wanted to get her talking. Conversations need momentum.

"Has he always done that? Sold cars?"

"Pretty much. He got a job with a Ford dealer when we lived in Belle Glade. That was out of college. When our son started high school we moved to West Palm. Sandy got a job at the lot."

"Sandy, that's your husband."

She nodded and sipped her tea. Lizzy was watching her, studying her face.

"Tell me about your husband, Mrs. Ferguson."

"The thing you need to know, Mr. Jones, is my husband is a good man. He's just sad, is all. We met in college and he was so full of life. He was charming and athletic and just so full of life. After we graduated and our son was born, well. . . he lost his spark. He had a family to support and bills to pay and I don't think selling cars was his dream job. Not sure it's anybody's dream job."

She sipped her tea. I didn't speak.

"But he always found the money for us to get by, and for our son to go to college."

"I'm sorry to ask this, but did he ever hurt you, Mrs. Ferguson?"

Her eyes flashed. "Good God, no. No, never. He isn't an angry man, Mr. Jones. Just sad. It happened so slowly I never really noticed. Our lives became gray. We did all the things people do. We vacationed on the Gulf, went to school recitals, had backyard barbecues with the neighbors. But the whole time, the world was turning gray. We existed, but we didn't live. Sandy lost his verve. That boy, so full of life? I don't even know who that was anymore."

I looked at her face, and wondered if she realized the absence of any makeup made her look gray. "Is it possible that Mr. Ferguson might have harmed himself?"

"Why on earth would you say that?"

"Mrs. Ferguson, I'm no psychologist, but your husband sounds depressed."

"Well, that's what I'm saying. He was sad. That doesn't mean he would hurt himself. Goodness me."

"I'm not suggesting he was sad. I'm suggesting he might have been suffering from depression. Sometimes people suffering from clinical depression can feel so isolated as to harm themselves." I was thinking that Mr. Ferguson might have taken his own life, but I couldn't find the words to say it to her.

"No, Mr. Jones. No. Sandy would not harm himself. He has a family."

I changed tack. "Is there anywhere your husband might have gone? A favorite place? Some old college buddy?"

She shook her head. "No. He never kept in touch with anyone. All he did was sit in his den and do goodness knows what."

"Okay, Mrs. Ferguson. We'll see if we can track down some information on your husband. But I have to warn you. What we find may not be good news."

"What do you mean?"

"Sometimes the people we find don't want to be found. Sometimes they'll run away for reasons we can barely fathom. Sometimes we can't find them. And sometimes they've done harm to themselves. Or worse." I looked into her eyes to make sure she got my meaning.

She blinked slowly. "Don't think me cruel, Mr. Jones. But I don't care. I'm beyond caring. I'm tired, and I'm old, and I'm gray inside, too. And I'm only forty-five. I just need to know, Mr. Jones. If he's run away, or he's found another woman. Or he's dead. I don't care. I love my husband, Mr. Jones. But I just don't care anymore. And that makes me even sadder."

I took a deep breath. "Okay, Mrs. Ferguson."

I stood up and Lizzy followed my lead. Mrs. Ferguson collected herself and stood with us.

"You'll go with Miss Staniforth here. She's an expert at these matters. She'll work with you to go through bank records, credit cards, everything we can use to track your husband and get you some news."

"I don't know anything about that. My husband took care of all that stuff."

"That's okay. Miss Staniforth will help you get what you need."

"You don't understand. I don't have any money. Sandy gave me housekeeping, but he took care of the banking. I have no way to pay you."

"Don't you mind that. The money doesn't matter."

"I can't even pay for groceries."

I ushered her to the door. "We'll sort that out, too. You just go with Miss Staniforth now. She'll help you. And I'm here if you need me."

"You take a seat at my desk," said Lizzy. "I'll be right with you."

We watched Mrs. Ferguson sit down. Lizzy turned in the doorway of my office and frowned at me. She shook her head. "Just when I'm about to give up on you, Miami Jones, you go and do something Christian on me."

She smiled and closed the door behind her and left me listening to the patter of the rain.

CHAPTER NINETEEN

The rain was letting up by the time I drove over to Gun Club Road. I parked in the lot of the Criminal Justice Complex and went in the front. The reception desk was staffed by a civilian named Ted. He was a good egg and I'd thrown him a few tickets for Mets spring training. He nodded when he saw me.

"You armed?"

"No."

He buzzed me through.

"Thanks, Ted."

He handed me a visitor's tag. "You have a good one, Miami."

I wandered through the corridors and found Danielle at her desk, eating an apple and looking at a computer screen.

"Hey, you," she said.

"Any news on the hard drive?"

She picked up a pile of papers off her desk. "The tech boys got a bit there. Some nudie shots, which they enjoyed."

"Jenny Bellingham?"

"God, no. Off the web. Nothing illegal, though. And these." She handed me the papers. They were printouts of emails. Exchanges between Newt Bellingham and what appeared to be prospective buyers of the Heisman trophy.

"So he was trying to sell it."

"Back page."

I flipped through to the last page. It was a print out of a web page. An ad on a classifieds site, offering an original Heisman trophy for sale.

"This is still online?"

"No. Looks like Newt pulled it. But our guys retrieved a cached copy."

I flipped back to the emails. "So how do we find out if one of these buyers is our guy?"

"Each email is sent from an email service provider. Three of these are from the cable company. Two of them are free online email accounts."

"Gotta be a free account. He wouldn't be stupid enough to use his home cable account."

"Can't rule out stupid. He is a man."

"Touché. So what do we do? Email them?"

"Each email provider keeps a log of when, where and who sent an email."

"What about free accounts? They can be accessed anywhere, right?"

"They can. But for security, the email provider logs an IP address that tells us which computer location sent the email."

"So how do we get that info?"

"The providers need a warrant to access that info. I've got an eyewitness to the crime, the victim's authorization to access the drive and five emails that specifically mention the stolen item. Wasn't too hard to get a warrant."

"So when will you hear?"

"Usually within forty-eight hours, give or take. They can do it within an hour if we push hard."

I smiled. "So you're pushing hard."

"No."

I stopped smiling. "Why not?"

"These guys do have work to do. We push on every case, then soon the pushing stops working and the forty-eight hours becomes the minimum. We save pushing for important cases like missing kids. This ain't that."

"I agree. Not sure your boss or BJ Baker will, though."

"Actually, my boss did agree. He knows how it works. And he knows one day we'll need this done yesterday. He said BJ Baker will just have to wait for a change."

"Perhaps I've misjudged the sheriff."

"Perhaps."

I looked around the floor. It didn't look like a New York police drama off television. It looked like a brokerage firm with uniforms. "What's on your agenda?" I asked.

She shook her head. "I got a ton to get through."

"Well, I'll let you get to it then. See you around, Deputy." I winked.

"You too."

I returned my pass to Ted and walked outside. The rain had stopped. The sun had broken through the clouds and was already heating up the wet pavement. I felt like I was being sautéed.

I got to my car and started her up and turned on the air. I sat for a moment. My evening had opened up. I could go for a run, grab a cold beer and make it an early night. Or I could do what BJ Baker was paying me for and go find his Heisman before the cops. And to find his, as Ron had put it, I'd have to find them all.

CHAPTER TWENTY

"I was surprised to get your call," said Beccy Williams. She put a martini on the table next to me. I was in a wicker lounge chair that was built like a first-class seat on an airliner. She didn't sit. Instead, she leaned against the balcony railing and sipped her martini. She was wearing a red silky dress that in my father's day would have been called an undergarment. The neckline dropped deep across her chest and the bottom ended only inches below her navel.

I sipped my martini. It was dirty with three olives. "Like I said, I need your help."

"You always needed my help, sugar." She wiped some condensation off the glass onto her finger, and then stroked her finger across the length of her collarbone. A blind man could see she wasn't wearing a bra.

"How's work?"

"You came all this way to ask about my career?" She smiled and small dimples appeared on one side of her mouth. Her blond hair dropped across the side of her face.

The sun was setting behind us and Hollywood Beach was drifting into darkness. The breeze had blown the clouds away and the humidity was comfortable on the coast. Despite that, I felt steamy.

"Just making small talk," I said.

She took another sip. "Well, since you asked, I have been approached by ESPN."

"That's great. What for?"

"Initially, mainly sideline stuff. I plan to anchor, eventually."

"I saw you on Fox. Doing the sidelines at the Dolphins. You looked good."

She looked at me with eyes the color of the Caribbean Sea. I knew for a fact the color was all real. Truth was, she didn't look good on television. She looked sensational. In real life she looked like she could do with a feed. I could see bones above her breasts and her arms spoke of an eating disorder, which she didn't have. Unless you considered a liquid diet a disorder. They say television adds ten pounds. On Beccy, it added it in all the right places.

"Will you go to New York?"

"The audition meeting is in Bristol, Connecticut."

I nodded. "Their main campus."

"Why don't you come with me?" She smiled. "You could show me your old haunts."

"They're called haunts for a reason."

We sat in silence for a while. I couldn't think of anything to say. I figured Beccy would fill the void.

"You look good," she said.

"Thanks."

"Working out?"

"Not much. Running mainly."

"You were always a good runner. For a pitcher."

"Maybe too good."

"Yeah, you could have done with a little more beef on your bones." She giggled. "You remember that line drive that Tucker hit at St. Lucie? Charlotte down three-four. Tying run on third and Tucker drives a humdinger back at you."

"I remember."

She shook her head and smiled. "And you catch it with your pitching hand."

"I couldn't pick up a ball for a week."

"It didn't seem to affect your performance later that night if I recall."

I shrugged. "You ever miss those days, working for the papers?"

"Not for a second."

She finished her drink and sauntered to the bar to mix another. I was only halfway through so she topped mine off. She sat on the wicker chair opposite and stretched across so her feet lay between my legs.

"You got a great memory," I said.

"I remember every inning I saw you pitch." She wiggled her toes as she drank.

"If you get the gig will you move to New York?"

"When I get the gig. And yes, probably. So this might be your last chance to say goodbye."

"Then I have a question."

"Shoot."

"How many Heisman trophies are there in Florida?"

"Ooh, football trivia as foreplay."

I shrugged.

She pinched her eyes. "Seriously?"

"It's important."

She took a long sip from her drink. "How many winners from Florida?"

"No. Trophies. From anywhere. Currently in Florida."

"What do I look like, the Census Bureau?"

"You don't know?"

"This is the retirement capital of the world. The Heisman has been awarded since 1935. You do the math."

"Okay," I said, edging back in my chair. "So let's say your buddies at ESPN wanted to do a feature on Heisman winners. How would they track them down? Who would they ask?"

"They'd ask me."

"So what would you do?"

She sipped her drink as she thought. I saw muscles in her slender thighs contract. She stared at me.

"There's a lot I could do. But the first would be to contact the Heisman Trust. They present the award now. They probably have some kind of alumni mailing list."

I nodded. "Good idea."

"Of course it's a good idea. Now tell me that isn't the reason you drove all the way down here."

"It's not that far. But yeah, that was pretty much it."

She shook her head and teased her hair. Then she stood up, stepped over to me and sat on my lap, straddling me. She dipped her finger into her martini again and traced her finger around my lips. She put her drink aside and leaned into me. Kissed me hard. She tasted salty and dry. Memories came flooding back. This part was always oh-so-good. But the rest was like trains in the night. Headed in opposite directions. Now she was going to New York City. She wanted to say goodbye. We were consenting adults. I tried to convince myself there was no reason not to. I failed.

I must have broken speed records getting back to West Palm.

CHAPTER TWENTY—ONE

Tropicana Palms Mobile Home Park was starting to feel like a second home. It wasn't growing on me. I sat in the Mustang, being as covert as one ever is in a bright red sports car. The streets around the park were full of kids and teenagers with nothing better to do than stand around doing nothing. The Mustang attracted some attention but not as much as I thought it might. There were more late-model cars in the park after work than I assumed there would be. Heavy on the trucks: F-150s, Silverados, Rams. A few sportier models. Nissans and Mazdas. Some people put more effort into their cars than their homes. Perhaps that was simply because they could.

I sat kitty-corner from the Bellinghams' home. The sun was low. Newt Bellingham had arrived home in his Ram and parked right behind the old Civic. He got out of the cab slowly. He looked like a man who had worked a long day. He ambled up the path and kicked his boots on the doorstep. Little puffs of cement dust swirled around. Then he went inside. There was no movement for a couple of hours. Some kids left the streets and went inside. They were replaced by other kids. It looked like they worked in shifts. I waited patiently. There was no point getting worked up, wanting something to happen. It was like a rain delay at the ballpark: the rain stops when the rain stops. Getting worked up meant you were in knots when the game actually started. Better to be relaxed and ready.

I watched the door to the Bellingham home finally open. Jenny Bellingham stepped down. She was dressed in a pink nurse's uniform and she wore soft white shoes. She walked to the Civic and used a key to unlock the door. In the night light I couldn't see the shiner, but I guessed it to be mauve and yellow. She got in the car, checked her mirrors, put her seatbelt on and started the engine. She did a K-turn across the street and drove away from me. I waited fifteen minutes, and then I got out and locked the Mustang. When I got to the door I banged hard with my fist. The home swayed a little with the impact. I shuddered to think what would happen in a hurricane. I heard movement and heavy footsteps inside. The door flung open.

"What!"

"Mr. Bellingham."

"The hell do you want?"

"A chat. About the Heisman."

"I'm in the middle of SportsCenter."

"It'll be on again in half an hour."

I stepped into the mobile home, and he had to choose to take bodily contact or move out of the way. He moved. I walked into the room and waited for him to close the door. He was in a blue tank top and brown shorts. He had a can of Bud Light in his hand. He took a moment to gather his forces, and then he marched on.

"You found my Heisman yet?"

"You mean, your wife's Heisman?"

"What's hers is mine."

"It's her father's, actually."

"Well, he ain't here no more," he said, flopping down on the sofa. Two guys were on screen, yelling at each other about who was the best basketball player ever. One said Jordan. The other had obviously never seen Michael Jordan play. I picked up the remote and turned the television off.

"Hey, I'm watching that."

"Not anymore. Tell me about the Heisman."

"What about it?" He had to crane his neck to look up at me. "Some guy took it. You're s'posed to find it, but you're here busting my chops 'cause you're hopeless and you got nothing."

"So you don't think your wife took it?"

"No."

"How do you know?"

He gave me a tight grin. "Because I asked her."

I took a deep breath. It was a thing. I always took a deep breath before a pitch. It calmed me. And I needed calming. I really wanted to put Newt Bellingham's head through his flat-screen television.

"Who took it?" I said.

He frowned. "How the hell should I know?"

"Maybe someone you tried to sell it to?"

He looked dumbfounded for a moment, and then I saw a flash of anger. "She told you, didn't she? The bitch."

"If you are referring to Mrs. Bellingham, that's not a very nice way to talk about your wife."

"I call it as I see it. And she's a disloyal bitch."

I took a step toward the sofa and stood off at an angle so he had no way to reach me with his feet. No point getting kicked in the nuts if I happened to annoy him.

"You put the damned thing up for sale on the Internet. You're dumb enough to think we wouldn't find it?"

"I took it down."

"Yep, seems you are that dumb."

"Hey, you can't talk to me like that." He tried to sit forward in the sofa but failed.

"Why the hell not? You're an idiot. I saw how much you priced it for. How'd you come up with that magic number?"

"Guy at the pawn shop offered me a thousand bucks. I know he's a crook, ripping me off. So I figure I list it myself. It's got to be worth at least double what he says. So I put it up for a deuce and a half. Leave a little negotiating room. That's how deals are done."

"You're a regular Donald Trump."

"Why? What's it worth?"

"Couldn't be more than eight hundred bucks." I watched him process this information. The genius could put a trophy up for sale on a classifieds site but couldn't use a search engine to find the price.

"You get takers?" I said.

"Some nibbles."

"You arrange to meet or give out your address?"

He looked more sheepish than a spring lamb. "No."

"Who?"

Nothing.

"Who did you give the address to? Do I have to shake it out of you?"

"I dunno the guy's name. He used one of them free emails."

"What email address?"

"RealPro. That was it. RealPro. The thing got stolen before our meet. Didn't matter none. I forgot to email him it was gone. But he didn't show, anyway."

CHAPTER TWENTY—TWO

I sat in my office with the window open and the breeze blowing in. My shoes were under the desk somewhere. I'd spent the night wishing I'd thought of the Heisman Trust thing myself. Saved myself the trip and an evening of night sweats. But I knew what I knew now, so I moved on. I found a phone number online and dialed New York.

"Good morning, Heisman Trust." The woman on the phone sounded pleasant and professional.

I gave her my name and credentials and mentioned that I was working for Heisman alumni BJ Baker. I didn't think she knew BJ Baker from Colonel Sanders, but the Heisman alumni thing helped. She told me she would see who could help me. I waited a long thirty seconds and another voice came on the line.

"Hello, Mr. Jones?" It was the kind of voice you expect to hear if you call a trust in New York City. Clipped and nasally and smart-sounding. An NPR listener. Hell, probably an NPR donor. It didn't sound like a voice that was the slightest bit interested in football. In my head a football voice came from Austin or Oxford.

"Yes," I replied.

"I understand you wish to speak to someone in Alumni Relations?"

"Yes."

"May I ask the purpose of your inquiry?"

"As your colleague may have informed you, I represent Mr. BJ Baker, a Heisman alum, in the matter regarding the theft of his Heisman trophy."

"Yes, ghastly business. How is it we can help?"

"I'd like to know who else in Florida might have a Heisman trophy. You know, past winners who have moved here, or are from here. So I can warn them."

"Warn them? Yes, I see." He went quiet for a moment. "The person you really need to speak to is our alumni and community relations manager."

"That's pretty much why I asked to speak to someone in Alumni Relations."

"Yes, well the thing is, he's currently out of the office. Visiting schools, you see."

"And there's no one else who can help me?"

"No, he's really the person with the information you require." Another pause, then, "What I can do is this: I will leave your name and number and the nature of your inquiry and ask him to call you directly."

"Let's hope he does that before another one of your trophies get stolen."

"Indeed. Thank you for your call."

I dropped the phone in the cradle and leaned back in my chair. I bet myself dollars to donuts that Beccy Williams would have gotten the information. But when it came to getting what we wanted, I was a bloodhound. Beccy was a wolverine.

CHAPTER TWENTY—THREE

Ron lay back on the sofa in my office, nursing a glass of Woodford Reserve. I sat with my feet on my desk, sipping my scotch.

"You know, our accountant doesn't think getting paid in scotch is such a great strategy," I said, tasting the leathery spice on my palette.

"He's wrong. I once fixed an IRS problem with a case of scotch."

I smiled. It was probably a tall tale, but with Ron it just might be true. The door snapped open and Lizzy popped her head in.

"I'm out of here," she said.

I nodded. "Okay. Any luck with Mrs. Ferguson's missing husband?"

"Nothing firm. She's getting me some stuff. I'll keep you posted."

"Great. Have a good evening."

She pulled her head back and closed the door. I looked back at Ron and swished the liquid around in my glass. Then my phone buzzed.

"State Attorney Edwards is here to see you," said Lizzy.

I smiled at Ron. "Tell him I'm here, but I don't want to see him."

The door to my office opened and a man in an immaculate Italian suit stepped through. He was tall, almost too tall to fit through the door. His thick black hair was combed back. He had high cheekbones but divots where he should have had cheeks, and he was marathon-runner thin. He looked like a well-dressed light pole.

"Jones," he said.

"Come in, Eric, please. Great to see you."

He looked around the room as if it were the first time he was in it and he was assessing escape routes. His eyes got to Ron on the sofa.

"Ron." He smiled. His was an elected position, and he was always in campaign mode.

"How's things on the Fifteenth Judicial Circuit?" I said.

"We're fighting the good fight."

"Well, good for you."

"I hear you're working on BJ Baker's burglary?"

"I am. So what brings you here?"

He helped himself to one of the visitor's chairs. He smoothed his tie with his hand after he sat.

"I just wanted to relay some information that came to my attention."

"Being?"

"Sal Mondavi."

I didn't speak.

"You know Sal Mondavi?"

"Remind me," I said.

"You were seen entering and leaving his premises on Okeechobee Boulevard last week."

"You watching me, Eric?"

"Not you."

"Is Sally charged with something?"

He ran his hand down his tie again. It looked as smooth as an ice rink after the Zamboni had done its rounds. "So you do know him."

"We both know I do. What's your point?"

"I don't think Sal Mondavi is the kind of person you should be associating with right now."

"Thanks, Dad."

"I'm serious."

"That's always been your problem, Eric. I was just visiting a pawnshop. That illegal now?"

"You took nothing into the pawn shop and brought nothing out."

"That you guys could see. Maybe it was something small."

"Like what?"

"Like a diamond ring."

State Attorney Edwards was a cool customer. He wasn't easily put off balance. But it was a hell of a lot of fun trying. I saw his jaw clench at the mention of the ring. But nothing more.

"Getting yourself implicated in underworld dealings won't just hurt you, Jones. You need to think about that."

"So you're not really worried about me?"

"I couldn't care less what happens to you, Jones. You and I both know that." He smiled at me, but it wasn't the politician's smile. "But being linked to you could hurt Danielle's career."

"And you're worried about Danielle."

"Yes, I am."

"Where was that worry when you were married to her?"

"You're not as clever as you think, Jones."

"And all that concern you had for her when you slept with your secretary?"

He stood up. I had to hand it to him. I'd put in the low blows and he hadn't lost his cool. He got up slowly and smoothed his tie one more time. At least it saved having to iron it.

"I should just let you go down, Jones. You're no good for her." He turned and strode to the door.

I let him get halfway out.

"That makes two of us."

CHAPTER TWENTY—FOUR

Sometimes stakeouts are extended, tedious affairs, where you sit in an uncomfortable car for longer than the seat was designed to hold you, trying to keep your attention up, or at least stay awake, while watching nothing happen for hours on end. Other times you find yourself sitting at a bar watching leggy women in lingerie wander around an overly cooled function room.

Ron had been doing most of the sitting in cars. I decided to join him on the one day in a million when we would have paid to do our job. Our ex-con suspect, Dennis Rivers, had been keeping to himself, work and home. Ron was leaning toward thinking the guy was just trying to go straight. The Palm Beach PD hadn't trailed Rivers. They got pulled in a lot more directions than we did. They'd hate themselves when we told them this story, as we surely would. Ron decided to follow Rivers one last time. The fact that Black Tie Catering was working a lingerie show for the lady members of a local golf club may have been a motivator. Ron showed his membership card from another golf club to gain us guest entry. I'd never seen him play golf, but he seemed to have membership cards from all sorts of clubs.

The bar quite rightly overlooked the eighteenth green. A function room was partitioned off from the bar area by a concertina wall. From the bar we couldn't see the show, but the design of the space was such that the models had to come through the bar to get to a small side room where they were changing outfits. There weren't many people in the bar, but everyone resisted the temptation to say anything. The girls were professional and offered a few winks as they dashed through to their costume changes.

Dennis Rivers was tending bar behind a white-clothed table, pouring lots of chardonnay and vodka tonics. His table was set up against the concertina wall. So he had his back to us, behind the wall. From where we were seated, we were hidden by a row of beer taps but could see the exit out of the function room. We could also see down to the parking lot, where the Black Tie Catering truck sat in the sunshine. I watched a tall model with whippet-thin legs and black garters stride by. She shot me a smile like we were passing on the street. I wondered if I should get something for Danielle. I decided she didn't need the help. Plus, she'd see right through it. She'd figure the gift was more for me than her.

We watched the parade in and out of the function room for an hour. Then the models came out dressed in street clothes and left. We waited another hour as the ladies in the function room enjoyed the catering and traded snide remarks about the shape of the models. Dennis Rivers appeared as the last guests departed. He ran downstairs and I thought we might lose him, but he opened the truck and dashed back up. He grabbed a crate of equipment and dashed down again.

"He seems in a hurry," I said.

"Maybe he's got a date," said Ron as he handed his credit card to the bartender.

He settled up and we took the outside patio stairs down to the Mustang. Rivers spent fifteen minutes shuttling equipment down into the van. When he slammed the rear door closed I fired up the Mustang's engine.

He drove the van back to the Black Tie Catering headquarters. It was a light industrial space with roller doors. It could have housed a mechanic or a distribution warehouse. I guessed they had it fitted out with a full kitchen. Rivers repeated the process in reverse, shuttling the equipment out of the van and into the small warehouse. When he was finished he slammed the rear door closed again.

He almost jogged to his car, a beat-up Camry that I had a sneaking suspicion belonged to a family member. Rivers didn't grab me as a Camry guy. We followed him again. The traffic was starting to build as office workers made early exits. Rivers got onto I-95 and skipped down to Boca Raton. He pulled off and drove to a mall, where he parked outside a large chain pet store. We waited a bit, and then followed him across to the sidewalk. Rivers strode past the pet store and the shoe outlet next door. He turned into a bar and pulled the frosted glass door open and went inside. We wandered up to the door.

The place was called Mango Martini. The outside had tasteful wooden chairs and tables overlooking the beautiful expanse of blacktop that made up the parking lot. Inside was a different story. It looked like Vegas, a mix of dimly lit space, pocked by shots of blue spotlight. The furniture was dark wood and red upholstery. The bar was backlit so all the liquor glowed like a summer sunset. I scoped the room and spotted Rivers.

He was at the bar, chatting with a barmaid who didn't look old enough to drive. He was standing, not sitting, despite the row of empty bar stools. It looked like the kind of place that hit its peak at around 2 a.m. Right now there was more staff than customers. A girl approached, dressed in much the same fashion as the models at the golf club. She wore black trousers that looked painted on, and what I thought to be called a *bustier* on top. A black bra showed several inches above the bustier. As she approached, I had the sense I knew her from somewhere. When she winked at me, I knew I did.

"You following me?" She smiled. It *was* the model from the golf club.

"Just my lucky day. You work here?"

"Can I get you a table?"

We followed her to a counter-height table in the corner of the room, near a dance floor that was lit by UV light. The scuffmarks on the floor made the whole thing look like a crime scene off television. The girl told me her name was Amber. We ordered two beers. I watched her walk back to the bar. She walked differently from the golf club. And it wasn't because she was wearing less clothes at the lingerie show. I'd have called it a tie that way. But at the golf club she had stepped quickly and with purpose, one foot directly in front of the other. Very erect. Now her hips swayed, giving her whole walk an attitude. The word that came to mind was strut. She got to the bar and interrupted the barmaid's chat with Rivers. He nodded and gave the barmaid a casual wave. She pointed haphazardly at a door beside the bar, and Rivers waved again and disappeared through the door. Amber returned with four beers.

"Four?" I asked.

"Happy hour, two for one," she said. She had great teeth and flawless skin. So did every second kid in South Florida. Before the sun got to them.

I wanted to ask her about Rivers. He seemed to be a known commodity here. But if they were both at the golf club job as well they might be friends. The kind of friends that mention when someone is asking questions about them. And I wasn't ready for Rivers to know I was asking after him just yet.

"You do most of your work dressed like this?" It wasn't my intention, but it came out sounding condescending.

"You my dad now?"

It occurred to me that I might be old enough. A group of young guns in summer suits came in. They made a noisy entrance, drawing every eye in the house. They all looked around without looking around. Just to make sure they were being noticed.

"The happy hour crowd," said Amber, rolling her eyes.

"This place always so slow?" I said.

"Those guys are the first of the *double H* crowd. In for the cheap apps and half-price drinks. But later it'll be cheek to cheek."

"Who owns the club?"

"You don't know?" she said.

I took a slug of my beer. "Why should I know?"

"You just strike me as being the kind of guy who would know stuff like that."

"But if I knew then we'd have nothing to talk about."

"I'm sure we could find plenty to talk about."

The guys at the host desk were getting restless. Amber looked at them.

"Gotta go," she said. She smiled at Ron and then moved away. She looked at me over her shoulder as she did. "The club is owned by Mr. Bartalotto."

She swayed over to the group of guys and had earned her tips before she even opened her mouth.

Ron watched her go, and then turned back to me. "Interesting girl," he said.

"Indeed."

"Bartalotto. You think it's *that* Bartalotto?"

I sipped some beer. "Sally will know."

"And if it is?"

I drained the last of my beer and dropped a twenty on the table. I left the extra happy hour beer untouched. "Then I have to ask myself why Dennis *I'm so clean* Rivers is working for the mob."

CHAPTER TWENTY—FIVE

I parked in a space out front of the packing store. A sign hung in the window offered to wrap and pack my Christmas presents. If I wasn't going to think about that two days out from Christmas, then I certainly wasn't interested in October. I locked the Mustang and wandered down the strip mall. The concrete was laced with chewing gum, baked hard by the summer sun. I wore sunglasses despite a light cloud cover. Through them I could see the Chevy Caprice parked further down Okeechobee Boulevard. Two guys inside who just happened to pull over on the side of the road to enjoy a coffee. Apparently they weren't trying to be covert. I hoped they weren't. I hoped they were better than that.

I got to Sally's store and went in. The air was on and made the place smell like the changing rooms at a public swimming pool. The same girl was sitting in the check-cashing booth. I didn't nod. I figured she wouldn't miss it.

Sally stepped out from the rear. He wiped spindles of hair across his scalp. He was wearing a big magnifying monocle on one eye. He was either looking at gemstones or impersonating a one-eyed man with a bad astigmatism. He took the monocle off as he reached the midpoint of the glass cabinet along the wall.

"You find your Heisman yet?" he said.

"Not yet."

"When you do. . ." He winked at me. "So what are you in the market for?"

"Not sure. I'll know when I see it."

"Usually do."

"Heat's off."

"Thank goodness."

"Now's when all the pests come out of hibernation," I said.

Sally nodded. "Exterminators do good business down here. Like waste disposal in Jersey. Always a demand to supply."

"You use someone?"

"I like to take care of such things myself. Every morning and every night."

I nodded. "Thought I saw a pest control truck outside."

"That right?"

I nodded.

"I'm clean."

"You normally get an audience?"

"Every now and then. Nothing to be concerned with."

I leaned on the counter. "You know anything about the Bartalotto family?"

"Sure. Connected to an organization out of Brooklyn. By marriage. Reasonably big potatoes down here but small fry for New York."

"You know a club called Mango Martini?"

"Yeah, I heard of it. Bartalotto owns it. I never been." That didn't surprise me. Mango Martini wasn't Sally's kind of place. A racetrack was more Sally's kind of place.

"I'm thinking there might be some link between my missing Heisman and Bartalotto."

Sally scrunched his face. "Possibly. He could be that kind of guy. Likes to have stuff other people don't got."

"But you mentioned loose lips. Hard to hide a thing like a Heisman."

"And it is. But he's not just a collector. He's the kind of guy who might silence loose lips with a bullet. You see?"

I nodded.

I turned and looked at the rows of shelving. The flotsam and jetsam of other people's lives. "It was brought to my attention that I might not have actually transacted last time I visited."

"Well, we can't have folks thinking the wrong thing of you, can we?"

Sally trudged around the counter and came out and pondered the rows. Then he selected one and walked down the aisle. I heard an *Aha*, and he reappeared, carrying some kind of case. It was for a musical instrument. Could have been a pan flute or sousaphone. He lifted it onto the counter and it squeaked against the glass. The case was blue-gray plastic. Sally flipped two latches and opened it. The inside was plush red felt. In it was some kind of gold instrument, broken down into several pieces.

"What is it?"

Sally looked at me like I'd asked his help with the jumble, three letters, starts with D, ends with G, man's best friend.

"It's a saxophone."

I nodded.

"It's the hottest instrument I ever heard," he said. "Guy like you could do well with a hot instrument like this."

"But I don't play."

Sally closed the case. "And once upon a star you didn't know how to throw a baseball, either."

I nodded. Worst case, it would look great standing in the corner of my living room.

"Everything's there. Mouthpiece, reeds, everything."

"Didn't get claimed?"

"Got it from a guy from Minneapolis. Came to South Florida to play those open-air dance halls, like Fred Astaire played."

"They still have those?"

"Not in decades. Guy used the cash to get a Greyhound back to the Twin Cities. Couldn't take the heat." Sally slapped my back and shuffled around the counter.

"What do I owe you?"

"Excuse me?"

"Sorry, my mistake. Listen, while I've got you. You have any thoughts on a guy using his wife for a spot of heavy bag practice?"

"I do."

"Sort of looking for a performance improvement plan."

"Short of a good kicking?"

"Let's say that's behind the glass. To be broken in case of emergency."

"I have had occasion to deal with similar matters. I find a good talking-to can be effective if the right incentives are in place."

I nodded. "I'll let you know."

"Do."

"Thanks for the sax."

"See Buzz Weeks at the Funky Biscuit in Boca. He'll give you a few pointers."

"Appreciate it. As always."

"I appreciate the heads-up."

I drifted out through the door and slipped my shades on. I stood with the case in my hand until the boys in the Caprice got their shots, and then I walked back to the Mustang and tossed the sax in the rear. I pulled out and headed back toward the coast. I resisted the temptation to wave at the Caprice as I drove by.

CHAPTER TWENTY—SIX

Some days I wished I worked out of a PO box. That way I could avoid walking in on people waiting for me. Lizzy hadn't yet come in. And an early night, no company and a clear head had me on the beach for a run with the sunrise, so I was in the office first. Well second, if you counted Detective Ronzoni, who lay on my sofa in his brown suit. I made a mental note to spend more time at Longboard Kelly's.

"Practicing your B and E technique, Bucatini?"

"It's Ronzoni. And the door was more or less open."

"There are two doors."

"They were both more or less open." He flipped his feet onto the floor and sat up.

"You got yourself some water?" I asked as I moved around my desk.

Ronzoni held up a half-finished bottle from my bar fridge.

I sat down. "What you doing here, Detective?"

"Unlike some, I been working all night. And I got more to do today. So I says to myself, where can I catch a few zees? And then I remember I gotta talk to Miami Jones. So I figure two birds, one stone."

"I'm glad we could oblige. Did you get your pillow mint?"

"Nope. What I got is a complaint."

"I'm not surprised, you breaking into people's offices like this."

"Not against me, lugnut. Against you."

"From whom?"

Ronzoni sipped his water and wiped his lips with the back of his hand. "Newt Bellingham. Ring a bell?"

"Yeah, he's a wife beater."

"I don't know nothing about that."

"That's what makes you such a good cop. Ignorance."

"He's made a complaint against you, smart guy."

"His wife looks like she's gone a round with Ali."

"She's got a beef, she should file a complaint."

"Like her pussy boy husband?"

"Man says he's being harassed."

"If he gets harassed by me, he'll never walk again," I said.

"So I'm trying to decide how formal to make the complaint."

"That so?"

"Yo." He sipped his water. He was a camel. "On the other hand, I'm wondering what you've got on the Baker case."

"Because you've got jack."

"I'm not looking for an information exchange, smart guy. More a download of your data."

"I know what you know. Two burglaries. Not much else."

"I know the guy was trying to sell the wife's Heisman. He told me."

"He told you that, did he? So?"

"So, you're trying to find the buyer."

"Maybe."

"And when you find him, you're gonna call me."

"So you can be BJ's big hero and bring back his treasure."

"Something like that."

"And if I don't?"

"Complaints stack up against a guy. Might end up losing his license."

"The Bellinghams are in West Palm. You're a little out of your jurisdiction, aren't you, Lasagna?"

"Ronzoni. And just because you're screwing the sheriff don't mean squat."

"The sheriff is a fifty-year-old man with a paunch. Not my type."

"I'm talking about the hobby horse deputy."

"Alright, Rigatoni. I'll play your game."

Ronzoni stood, finished the water and tossed the bottle in my blue recycling bin. "Smart move," he said.

I got up and walked him to the door. He opened it and stepped halfway out. I grabbed his shoulder and pressed him hard into the jamb.

"But I ever hear you speak like that about Deputy Castle again, you and I will be taking a visit to the unincorporated county and only one of us will be walking back."

I glared at him and didn't let it go for longer than was necessary. Then I stepped back. Ronzoni straightened his lapels and walked down the corridor, out into the fresh new day.

CHAPTER TWENTY—SEVEN

I was eating a Reuben and drinking an iced tea in the courtyard at Longboard Kelly's with Ron. We were treading water, waiting for something to break. The email provider or the guy from the Heisman Trust, or Dennis Rivers. Anything could set us off. Lizzy was making calls for Mrs. Ferguson and, from the frowns and grunts, not getting too far in finding him. Sometimes people don't want to be found. Sometimes when you do, you wished you hadn't. All in all we were facing a no-hitter of a day, when even an infield error onto first base would've picked things up. But then the day picked itself up and Danielle Castle walked in. She was in uniform and walked with purpose. Marched might be the word.

"Good sandwich?" she asked.

"It's no Katz's deli, but it'll do."

She took the dill pickle off my plate and bit into it. She smiled out of the corner of her mouth. Her *I-know-something-you-don't-know* smile.

"So tell me," I said, biting into my sandwich. The toasted rye bread crunched loudly.

"There's been another burglary."

"A Heisman?" said Ron.

I didn't speak. I had a mouthful of corned beef.

"A Heisman."

Ron and I looked at each other. Just when you can't tread water anymore, the current picks up on you. I chewed furiously. Ron did the talking. We were like a ventriloquist act.

"Where'd it happen?"

"Tampa."

"Tampa?" said Ron.

I swallowed. "Our guy's branching out."

"He is."

"What do you know?"

"Not a lot yet. Tampa PD got the call. Apparently in an aged care facility."

"The guy broke into an old folks' home?"

"It seems. So they did what they do and someone had heard on the vine about BJ Baker, so they looked it up on NCIC and called me."

"Same guy then?"

"Same trophy." She finished my pickle.

"You going over?"

She shook her head. "No, can't justify it. Not for a patrol investigation."

"I thought the sheriff was in Baker's pocket?"

"No. He might be in his debt, but that's not the same thing. He's already put a lot of resources into this and his budget can only stand so much. He says the Tampa PD knows what they're doing."

"I'm sure they do. But they don't know what we know. They're not on the hunt like we are."

She looked at each of us eating our sandwiches. "On the hunt."

I nodded and wiped my mouth with my napkin. "I'm going over there."

"I was hoping you'd say that. I'm coming."

"What about your budgets?"

"Not our budget. I'll clock off now and take tomorrow off. Your car and gas. It's on BJ Baker's budget."

CHAPTER TWENTY—EIGHT

The drive from West Palm Beach to Tampa was one of the most tedious drives in Florida. And there were a lot of tedious drives in Florida. I drove up the turnpike to Fort Pierce, and then west across the flat state. Most of Florida was swamp, so there was not a lot of elevation. I'd discovered that elevation is what makes inland driving interesting. We passed a couple of mounds, landfill covered with turf, and birds in the hundreds, along with a stench that we blew through at eighty miles an hour. I'd grabbed a gym bag and tossed a few things in it. Danielle changed out of her uniform, choosing a white blouse and turquoise skirt. It made it hard to focus on the open expanse of road.

"You not getting too far with the case?" she said as we hit the turnpike.

"What makes you say that?"

"You and Ron didn't look overwhelmed by anything but cholesterol back there."

"We can have lunch, can't we?"

She shrugged. We didn't speak for a couple of miles.

"We were waiting on some things to break," I said.

"Like?"

"Like the emails from the buyer. And the Heisman Trust."

"What about the Heisman Trust?"

"I haven't seen you for a few days, have I? Ron got the idea that if our guy took two Heismans, he might take a third."

"Nostradamus Ron."

"Yeah. So we figured we should try to find out if there were any other Heisman trophies currently in Florida."

"Good thinking. What did you do?"

"We talked to a source. They suggested that they would call the Heisman Trust if they wanted such information."

"A source? That sounds very mysterious."

I shrugged. Danielle turned in her seat and looked at me. She smiled and frowned at the same time.

"So who's your source? Or can't you tell me?"

I breathed in deeply and let it out slow. This was going to go one of two ways. One way was she would see that I was questioning an asset who had inside knowledge of the environment of the case, and could therefore help, regardless of any previous relationships I may have had with the asset. The other way was the other way.

"It was Beccy Williams."

Danielle nodded and turned back to look at the road. "Huh."

I decided not to speak.

After another mile, she did. "This is Beccy Williams, the sideline chick on the football."

"The sports journalist, yes."

"The blond one. Looks like a runway model."

"She could do with a feed, to be honest."

"The one you used to sleep with."

"Used to." Another mile passed. It got hot as we headed inland.

"So you thought she could help. With the case?"

"She's very connected in the football scene."

"I'll bet. So you called her."

"More or less."

"More or less?"

"We met for a drink."

"How nice. Longboard Kelly's?"

"No. She's based in Hollywood."

"Hollywood? Nice beach."

"She has a good view, yes."

"So you had a drink at her place?"

"One or two."

"One or two. How nice." She kicked off her shoes and put her feet up on the dashboard. Wrapped her arms around herself.

"I would have preferred to move things along another way, but it was Ron's idea, and . . ."

"Ron's idea."

"Yeah. Look, she's past history. That's it. She had some information that I hope will prove useful. That's all. It wasn't easy, you know."

"Why, you still have feelings?"

"No. I ended it with her. It just wasn't exactly where I wanted to be."

"I'm sure spending the night with a gorgeous TV bimbo is a real hardship for you."

I was going to defend the bimbo comment but thought better of it. "I didn't spend the night. I got what I needed and I came home."

She shook her head.

"That didn't come out right. I mean, nothing happened."

"You don't need to explain yourself to me." She slumped in the seat and said nothing more.

I couldn't think of anything to say that wasn't going to contribute to the hole I was digging for myself. It was going to go one of two ways. It went the other way. It usually did.

We were passing south of Lake Kissimmee before I thought of anything to say. For once, the silence was uncomfortable.

"Mrs. Ferguson came to see."

"Aha."

"I've taken her on. Lizzy's looking around for me."

"Aha."

"She couldn't afford to pay but that's okay. I'm happy to help."

"Aha."

We drove on in silence. I wished I had saved Mrs. Ferguson's story for another occasion when it might have garnered me some brownie points. We drove the last ninety minutes into Tampa listening to the hum of tires on blacktop.

CHAPTER TWENTY—NINE

The sun was low and into my face as we reached Tampa. The traffic was bad. Lots of people headed for Tampa International or St Pete across the bridge. We got off the freeway and took surface streets the last bit near the airport. The Tampa PD Patrol District 1 offices were in a large complex opposite Raymond James Stadium. I'd been to the stadium before to see the Bucs play the Pats. I didn't know about the police complex. There was a lot of vacant space in the parking lot due to our late arrival.

Danielle had called ahead. That was one thing about cops, even the ones I didn't like, and who didn't think I was as swell as a day out at Coney Island: If they say they'll wait, they'll wait. A civilian receptionist called up and a detective came down to us. He was a large, stern man. Broad in the neck but not in the waist. He had a serious handshake but a generous face. He introduced himself as Frank Templeton. We introduced ourselves and each handed him one of our cards. He looked at mine longer. Detective Templeton led us through a warren of offices and cubicles, not a million miles different from the sheriff's office in West Palm. He offered us coffee. We took water and sat at his desk. It was cleaner than I expected it to be.

"So, Detective, you want me to go first or you?" said Danielle.

"It's Frank. And let me tell you the little I know. Then you can tell me how much of a head start you're gonna give me." He smiled and I noted his desk nameplate said his name was Francis.

"We got a B and E call last night. Assisted-living facility in Westchase. The assailant broke into the townhouse of a resident. Not normally my domain, but the resident is a bit of a celebrity in this neck of the woods. Orlando Washington."

"Wow," I said.

"You know him?" said Frank.

"No. But that's a helluva name."

"That it is. So I get called in because of it being him and because of the nature of the stolen item."

"A Heisman trophy," said Danielle.

"Right on."

"So what happened?" I said.

"Apparently the guy breaks in at night, but old Orlando is not a heavy sleeper. He gets up and disturbs the guy. Guy pulls a gun."

"A gun?" I said. "He's sure?"

"Colt .45. I asked him how he knows this. He says he used to keep that exact one under the counter."

"And you say he's famous?" said Danielle.

"He won the Heisman," I said.

"That would do it, most parts," said Frank. "But after he won it, Orlando, he never played another game. Developed arthritis or something. Career ended before it began. So he opens up a pit barbecue place. Ends up with a bunch of them up and down the Gulf coast."

We absorbed that for a moment before Frank said, "So I heard about the Baker theft. How does that fit with your guy?"

Danielle sat forward. "We've actually got two. A second Heisman was stolen from the Palm Beach area. This time we got a description." Danielle gave Frank the rundown on the Baker burglary and the Bellingham case.

"The cowboy description fits what Mr. Washington told me," said Frank.

"Nothing else stolen by your guy?" said Danielle.

"No. And if it is the same guy, he's now gone from knife to gun."

"My concern is next time he'll use it," said Danielle.

"Oh, he used it," said Frank. "He pistol-whipped Mr. Washington."

"Is he okay?"

"He's a tough old nut."

"I'd like to meet him," I said.

Frank nodded. "You should."

We thanked the detective for his time and he walked us downstairs. Said we'd keep in touch with anything we picked up. I drove out and headed south. The traffic had eased up and a warm breeze drifted in off the Gulf. It was too late to visit an old man in a retirement village, so I headed into the throng of hotels around the south edge of Tampa International. Picked one with Suites in the name. I figured there would be more likelihood of a pullout sofa bed, and I figured there was a good chance I'd be sleeping on whatever sofa the room had. The room was new and spacious. The kitchen had dark cabinets and stainless steel appliances. It was everything my kitchen was not. It lacked any kind of character. But there was a separate bedroom and a pullout sofa bed.

"You hungry?" I said.

Danielle thought about it longer than necessary, and then said yes. We ate pasta and salad at a Carrabba's down the street. We chatted a little, small talk, like we were business colleagues on a road trip. We walked back to the hotel. Jumbo jets flew low over us and landed just beyond the fence. Danielle brushed her teeth and changed into some small white shorts and a t-shirt that said Kale, in the collegiate style of Yale.

"I'll take the sofa," I said.

She looked at me and without a facial expression said, "Don't be silly. Come to bed."

It wasn't a muted endorsement, let alone a striptease, but I brushed my teeth quickly and got into a pair of boxers. I didn't know who had given them to me. Maybe Danielle, but maybe not. Certainly not Beccy Williams. She wasn't the boxers type. When I came out, Danielle was lying on her side facing me. I walked around the bed and got in. I lay on my back with my hands behind my head. Danielle said good night and turned out the light. She stayed on her side, back to me. I stayed on my back, hands behind my head. I stayed like that for what felt like forever.

CHAPTER THIRTY

When I woke the next morning I was alone. I got up and checked the bathroom and living room. Nothing. Danielle's bag was where she had left it the previous night. I shaved and washed my face and wet my hair. I put on a plain blue shirt and chinos, and then walked down the fire stairs to the lobby. I headed for the business center. As I went by the glass door to the hotel gym I saw Danielle inside, pounding the treadmill. She was wearing the same t-shirt and shorts, but her hair was tied back in a ponytail. I used a computer in the business center for about twenty minutes, and then I headed back up the fire stairs. When I got in the room the shower was running. I sat on the sofa and watched a rerun of SportsCenter. Nothing about Orlando Washington and no sign of Beccy Williams. Danielle came out of the bedroom drying her head with a towel. She was wearing a lightweight, black dress. It was longer than a cocktail dress, but she could have pulled it off in any company.

"Hey, you," I said.

"Hey, you. Where'd you get to?"

"Business center."

"Gym."

"I know."

"Had breakfast?"

"Waiting for you."

"Great," she said. "Just let me finish my hair."

Danielle took longer than me but less time than most and came out looking and smelling like roses. We ate breakfast from the complimentary buffet. The scrambled eggs were industrial, but the sausage links were exceptional. We checked out and headed for Westchase. It was just north and west of the airport. The complex where Orlando Washington lived looked more like a new housing subdivision than my idea of an old folks' home. The streets and sidewalks were flat and smooth, the clubhouse looked like a lodge in Aspen, and the gardens and lawns were perfect. I was ready to move in.

We stopped at the reception/sales center. Danielle showed her badge and we got directions to Orlando Washington's home. It was a one-story duplex with a single-car garage. The front was painted in subtle taupe and tan. There was a neat hedge under the front window. All the steps were gone, if they were ever there. A ramp led up to the front porch. I hit the doorbell. The door was answered by a thin, pale woman in a blue pinafore.

Danielle showed her badge again. "Deputy Castle for Mr. Washington."

The woman smiled politely and stepped aside for us to enter. "Yes, the clubhouse manager called."

Decent security.

"You are?" said Danielle.

"Moira. I am one of the home care staff here."

"This is not quite what I thought of as assisted living," I said.

"This is not assisted living. It's independent living."

"Gee, that's what I thought I had." I smiled and she smiled. She was either very tolerant or she got me.

"The community is about keeping people in their own homes, just like any other gated community. Only difference is here there is twenty-four-hour medical and custodial care available on call. For most people in this part of the community, we are hardly ever needed. It's more about them, and their families, knowing we're here. Just in case."

"So you don't have Alzheimer's, that sort of thing?"

"We have many such people. Some here in the duplexes, for those with minimal symptoms or partners to care for them. We also have apartment living for those who need closer attention, and a managed care center for those who need round-the-clock help."

"Three steps to heaven."

"I like to think of it as helping people be as independent as possible for as long as possible." She smiled again. "I'll get Mr. Washington for you."

Danielle looked at me. "Three steps to heaven?"

I shook my head and looked as sheepish as I could. I felt like a cad.

The house was wide and open. Lots of space to get around and lots of engineered wood and forest palette colors. It was in a craftsman reproduction style.

Moira came out pushing a black man in a wheelchair. He looked bent over and frail, like he was slowly curling into a ball. His hands were gnarled, his head hung at an angle. Moira pushed him over. He struggled to look up at us he held his hand inches off his lap, and extended it as far as he could to Danielle.

"Orlando Washington," he said. The voice was hoarse and deep. I could picture a time when it had been deeper.

Danielle took his crooked hand. "Deputy Danielle Castle." She smiled.

The old guy's eyes danced for joy at the touch of her hand. "It's an honor, Deputy."

Danielle turned to me. The old guy didn't have much grip, but he didn't let go of her hand.

"This is Miami Jones."

A broad grin swept across his face. He grudgingly let go of Danielle and I shook his hand. He was skin on bone. He would have struggled to bend a playing card.

"Miami Jones," he said. "Well, that's a hell of a name."

"I was just thinking the same. It's a pleasure, sir."

Moira pushed Orlando to a sofa. It looked like one of those flat, uncomfortable Swedish things. But I figured the last thing a frail old man wanted was a plush sofa he could never get out of. Between Moira and Orlando they got him across from his wheelchair. I moved to help but was waved away by a shake of Moira's head.

"I'm going to wander down and visit with Mrs. Dautry. I'll pop back shortly," said Moira. I'd found from long experience that there were two types of women in nursing. Angels and devils. Nothing in between. Moira was one of the angels.

"Would you like me to put coffee on before I go?"

"I'm happy to do it," said Danielle.

"Great. Y'all have a nice visit." She checked her watch and stepped silently out the door.

"Would you like some coffee, sir?" said Danielle.

"It's not sir. It's Orlando." He grinned again. "And what I'd love is a shot of bourbon. But since the delightful Moira is coming back, we best stick to coffee."

Danielle got up to make it. There was a machine and it looked all ready to go. She just hit the button.

"You get to my age, you start believing you seen it all." He grinned. "But here we are. Orlando and Miami here in Tampa."

I smiled. "Wonder where Jacksonville is today."

He chuckled. Danielle brought us coffee. Orlando had a special cup, break-proof melamine with big handles on both sides. Like a toddler's cup.

"You lived here long?" I asked.

"Three years. My wife and I moved in three years ago."

"Your wife?" said Danielle.

"She passed on last year."

"I'm sorry," she said.

"Me too." He sipped his coffee. "She was a hell of a woman."

"When did you meet her?" I asked.

"You come all the way from the Atlantic to ask about my Delilah?"

"Yes, sir."

"Well then, you lie nice." He sipped again. "We met in college. Long time ago."

"This her?" asked Danielle, looking at a photo on a shelf that looked like a mantel with no fireplace under it.

Orlando nodded.

"She's beautiful."

"Yes, she is. She was all that and more. Funny the things that define us. From the outside. Always so different from that which defines us inside." He looked away to somewhere I couldn't see.

"Like a Heisman?" I said.

He chuckled. "For some, yeah. Some people, a Heisman defines them. Defines the success of their lives, or the failure. It becomes a symbol of who they are as people." He shook his head. "People see what they want to see. Heisman doesn't make you or break you."

We sipped our coffee and watched him. His eyes were clear and bright.

"Let's face it," he said. "Elway didn't win a Heisman. Peyton Manning, either."

"Tom Brady, either," I said.

"Hell, Tom Brady was lucky to even play college ball. Lucky to get drafted. It sure as heck didn't define him."

"Or you?"

"No," he said. He looked serious and when he did, he looked older. "It's a symbol of something you did. Something good, and something important to you at the time. But it's a trophy. It doesn't say you now get to be king of the world, or Super Bowl hero, or a drunk or a loser."

"It's a snapshot, not your life story," I said.

Orlando smiled and nodded. "I like that."

"It's yours to use."

"Thanks, kid. I mean, look at Ernie Davis. Heisman was a record of one great year. Didn't help him one way or the other."

"Who's Ernie Davis?" asked Danielle.

"First black man to win the Heisman. Nineteen sixty-one," I said. "He got drafted by Cleveland but was diagnosed with leukemia. Died never playing a pro game."

"How awful."

"Awful it is," said Orlando. "So he got a Heisman. But the poor guy never got that." He looked at the photo of his wife. "Boy could sure run, though."

"So could you," I said.

"What you know about that?"

"Over two thousand career yards, thirty touchdowns, a national championship with the Crimson Tide, Heisman winner."

"You're like a compendium."

"And you were a battering ram. I've seen footage." The old man smiled and I continued. "But you never played pro football."

He shook his head defiantly. "You know why?"

"No. But I'm guessing it has something to do with the reason you're in that chair."

"Rheumatoid arthritis. Got diagnosed just before the draft. Unlike Ernie Davis, I never got drafted. But I'm still around to tell the tale."

"Has it always been like this?" said Danielle.

"No. When I graduated college I felt like I could run through walls. But after every workout, I couldn't recover as fast. Everything hurt. My hands, knees, ankles. So the pros couldn't touch me. Too risky."

"Detective Templeton said you got into restaurants?" she said.

"Yep. Me and Delilah. Using our grand mama's recipes. Opened a pit barbecue. People knew me around here from the Heisman and all, so we called it Orlando's."

"Detective Templeton said it was good. Like his mother made," I said.

"He wishes his mama made it that good. Falling off the bone, smoky goodness. We even made our own sauces. Ended up with seven locations up the coast."

"You don't have them any longer?" Danielle said.

"No. Got too old. Boys went their own way." He smiled. "Travis is a firefighter in St. Pete. Ernie works at the Hotel Coronado in San Diego. So we sold up and used the proceeds to move into this fabulous abode." He'd finished his coffee and he put the cup down like it was bone china.

"Another coffee, Orlando?" asked Danielle.

"That would be lovely. And maybe just a tiny bit of bourbon this time."

She looked at me like he was suggesting a bank heist.

"I think we can manage that," I said.

Orlando directed me to a small buffet cabinet. Inside, next to some unloved wine glasses, was a bottle of Jack. I took it and dropped three small shots in the coffees. Danielle carried two back to the chairs. I carried my own. I sipped and felt the hint of bourbon.

"So what can you tell us about two nights ago?"

Orlando had closed his eyes and was savoring the flavor and smell of the bourbon. He breathed it in, then opened his eyes and looked at me.

"It's the pain meds. Damnedest thing. They blunt the pain, but they make it hard to sleep. I doze, but I can't sleep more than an hour at a time. My mind fires up and bang, I'm awake." He sipped coffee. "So I wakes up the other night and I hear something. That happens, we supposed to call it in." He flicked at a pendant that hung around his neck. "Panic button, I calls it. Here they call it the *concierge*." He smiled at the word. "Got one by my bed, in the bathroom, most every room. Wear this one. You need help, you call, they come. But I figure, the more I call, the more help they think I need. They force me into one of those apartments. With all the old timers." He chuckled at himself. "So anyways, I get up, come take a look-see."

"And what did you see?"

"There's a man standing right there by that picture of my Delilah. He's got a hold of my Heisman trophy. I'm damned if he ain't polishing the thing. Like he's a pool shark, hustling a game, chalking up his cue." Orlando shook his head. "I mean damn. I don't know how long he'd been at it. It takes me half the damned day to get out of bed. Must have been fifteen, twenty minutes since I heard the noise 'til I got out here."

"What did he look like?" said Danielle.

"Funny looking. Kinda like the country singer. Alan Jackson? He had a cowboy hat and mustache. Big ugly old shades like he was gonna do a spot of welding."

"So what happened?" I asked.

"He sees I'm in my chair, he just looks at me. Tucks the Heisman under his arm, you know, like he's running the ball downfield. I rolled over toward him, just beside where I'm sitting here. He pulls out a gun, points at me." He shook his head.

"You told Detective Templeton you recognized the gun?" said Danielle.

Orlando took some effort to stop his head shaking and get it nodding. "Yes, ma'am. A Colt .45. I used to own one, back in the day. In the restaurant, before everything was credit cards. We saw a lot of cash."

"So what did you do, when he pulled the revolver?" I said.

"Thing is, I know that gun. You want to actually hit someone, you gotta be close, real close. Ain't like the movies. And this guy was all shaky, like he didn't know how to use it. Or maybe he was afraid of it." He sipped his coffee and put his cup down gently. "Plus, I figure at my age, he wants to do me a favor and send me to see my sweet Delilah tonight, I'm okay."

"So?" I said.

"So, I jumped him."

"You jumped him?" said Danielle.

"Aha. I ain't in this chair 'cause I can't walk at all. I'm in here 'cause the pain in my joints is too great to stand for more than a few seconds. But I got some springs. So I jump up and I lunge at the guy."

"What did he do?" I asked.

"I think he expelled himself in his pants, that's what I think." He bent over, cackling. "I tackled him around the waist. I figure I take him to the ground. See what happens."

"And what did happen?" I said.

"He clocked me on the back of the head with his gun." He reached up toward his head but winced with the effort. Orlando turned his head slightly and I could see an adhesive plaster pad had been stuck to his head.

"Were you okay?" said Danielle.

"I was out, I think. Maybe a second or two. I heard footsteps. I looked up and see the front door is open so I think to myself, Orlando, you best push the panic button boy. So I did."

"And then what?" I said.

"Then the security guy came. Couldn't have been more than two minutes. Then the on-call nurse arrived. The security guy called the cops and they arrived maybe twenty minutes later. I told them what I just told you. Security checked all the doors and windows and locked up and I went back to bed."

"And Detective Templeton?"

"Came in the morning. After I got up."

We finished our coffee. Orlando's eyes were flagging, but he was fighting them. The effort of having guests was wearing him out.

"How do you think the guy knew you had a Heisman?"

"Weren't a secret. We used to have it in a case in the original restaurant. Plenty of people would've known about it, seen it. I was in the local papers plenty, over the years."

"So he might have seen it some time ago?"

"At least three years ago, but hell, he might've eaten next to it."

We made motions about leaving and Orlando made no protest. Danielle collected the coffee cups and took them into the kitchen. I motioned to Orlando and he nodded and checked that Danielle wasn't watching.

"Just give me an arm, son." I stuck my arm out and he grabbed the forearm and hoisted himself into the wheelchair.

"You need to get somewhere?" I said. I looked in the direction of his bedroom.

He shook his head. "I'll watch a little TV. Moira will be back directly."

Danielle came out of the kitchen, wiping her hands. We met at the front door and Orlando rolled over.

"Well, it was mighty fine of you folks to visit," he said.

"Thank you, Mr. Washington," said Danielle. "We'll do everything we can to get your Heisman back."

"I appreciate that. It would mean something to my boys."

We both shook his delicate hand and stepped through the door. The sun was high and the sky was so blue it was almost white. Danielle stopped and turned back as if she'd forgotten something, like Colombo.

"Sir, if you don't mind me asking one more thing. Why did you tackle the assailant?"

Orlando smiled. "Because I remember," he said. "I remember good."

"You remember? I'm sorry, I don't understand."

Orlando's grin deepened and he looked at me. He squinted against the bright sky.

"You ask Miami Jones." He pushed the wheels on his chair and rolled back inside. "Miami Jones remembers, too."

He was still smiling as the door closed in front of him.

CHAPTER THIRTY—ONE

I didn't feel like a long and boring drive back to West Palm. I felt like sitting in a bar by the water on one of the Keys off Sarasota. Or zipping down to Sanibel and collecting shells. I felt tired. I headed east through the city and out onto route 60. Strip malls and concrete prefab. I looked at Danielle. She was a million miles away. The Mustang pulled toward home and I pulled against it. The horses won. Then Danielle turned to me.

"You wanna get some lunch?" she said.

"Where you wanna go?"

"Orlando's."

I pulled a U-turn and headed back into Tampa. We found Orlando's. A big banner on the outside proclaimed it as the original location. Inside it was dark and basic. Bench seats, red and white check tablecloths. We sat at a table and a middle-aged woman with a generous smile handed us menus. We both looked around the room. It was generic sports. Nothing of Orlando Washington remained. There were lanterns hanging from the ceiling. A Georgia license plate on the wall next to my head. Pictures of old footballers. None of them were Orlando Washington.

Danielle frowned at the Georgia license plate. "Did he play for Georgia?"

I shook my head. "Alabama."

"Family from Georgia?"

"Some here and Tampa, some in the Florida panhandle. If they follow football, they'd hate Georgia."

We looked at each other. "Let's get out of here."

We thanked the smiling waitress and feigned an emergency. The day was even brighter after the dark restaurant. We wandered back to the car and I started it up. I put my hand on the gear selector and Danielle put her hand on mine.

"I don't want to go home right now," she said.

I nodded and pushed the selector back into drive. Danielle lifted her hand off mine and I pulled into traffic. I didn't know Tampa well, so I did what I always do when I can't think of where to be. I headed for water. We drove out over Old Tampa Bay to Clearwater, and then across the causeway to Clearwater Beach. I drove along Mandalay Avenue until I found a likely spot. We parked the car and took our shoes off and walked along the sand. Small waves, maybe one or two-footers, broke on the shore. The beach was wide and handsome.

We came upon a place on the beach called Frenchy's Rockaway Grill. A thin, bronzed waitress waved and smiled and told us to come on in. We sat at a table overlooking the sand. I ordered a Sierra Nevada Pale Ale. It had been a favorite when I'd played ball in Modesto. Danielle nodded and I told our bronzed waitress to make it two. She delivered them promptly and we clinked bottles and I took a pull, and looked out on the sand and the warm water of the Gulf of Mexico. Danielle's face glistened in the sunlight. Her lips were moist. She looked at me and put her beer down.

"You know a lot about Orlando's career. I can't believe you keep all those stats in your head." she said.

"I don't. I knew he'd won a Heisman, but that was it. He was before my time."

"So how did you know about his yards and touchdowns and all that?"

"I spent some time online at the hotel this morning. Looked up his stats. I figured it couldn't hurt to honor an old man's achievements."

Danielle nodded and sipped her beer. "What did he mean? He said he can remember."

I thought for a moment. "He means exactly what he says. He remembers. The disease and the game might have battered his body, but there's nothing wrong with his memory."

"Remembers what, though?"

"Everything. He remembers being young. Indestructible. He remembers the smell of wet cut grass on his cleats, the feeling of running and having every muscle working in concert. A perfect machine. And he remembers a signal. A call from his quarterback, and the handoff. The leather in his hands. Driving forward, behind his linemen and then, at the last minute, exploding out through the gap. The grasping and clawing at him as he pushes through the line of opponents. He's a gazelle and he flies and he's perfect. And then he breaks out and there's nothing but grass and space and the crowd. And he shuts it all out and runs. Just runs."

I looked out at the water lapping at the sand. Then I turned to Danielle. "He remembers a day when a guy in a cowboy hat and fake mustache would've trembled at the sight of him, not stolen his stuff."

I took a large pull on my beer. The waitress reappeared and I ordered two more and some fish tacos made with Gulf grouper. Danielle waited until the waitress skipped away.

"He remembers all that? Or you do?"

"Maybe we both do."

"So you're saying he was angry? Angry that someone was taking his trophy?"

"He was angry that someone took his youth."

"Pretty brave to attack a guy with a gun, angry or not."

"Maybe. Or maybe he thinks, he's had this great life, his wife is gone, sons are grown and gotten their own lives, and now he's alone with his memories. And this guy is stealing the one important thing left to him."

"His prime," she said.

I smiled and nodded.

Our beers arrived. We drank, watching the gulls playing on the beach. When our tacos came we ate, and then ordered some conch fritters. A sign by our table said there was a two-hour limit on patio tables, but we were in the shoulder season: the summer vacationers were gone and the snowbirds were yet to arrive. Our waitress made no attempt to move us on. She brought us some more beers. The sun started its drop toward the water.

Danielle leaned her elbows on the table and looked at me. She seemed to be examining the lines on my face. "I owe you an apology," she said.

"I can't imagine what for."

"The way I reacted about Beccy."

"No, you don't. I should have just told you."

"I know that's history. We all have history. Hell, I've been married."

"I know," I said. "Your history came to see me a few days back."

She frowned. "Eric?"

"Aha."

"Why?"

"He was concerned about the company I keep."

"Me?"

"More how other company I keep might affect you."

"Huh. I hope you were nice."

"Yes, being nice to your ex is always high on my list."

She shook her head and grinned. "I mean it. He's a state attorney. He's a good person for you to know and a bad one to annoy."

"You're right. I'll invite him round for a game of darts."

She punched my arm. It hurt more than I thought it should. "I'm serious. He's not that bad a guy. I think you'd get along."

I took a long drink from my beer, and put it down. I took her hands in mine across the table. "Eric knows, for absolute certainty, that losing you is the worst mistake he has ever made in his entire life. And I am a reminder of that fact. We are never going to be best buddies."

She looked me straight in the eyes and took the air out of my lungs all over again.

"You wanna dance?" I said. I took her hand and led her to an open area near the bar. I whispered to our bronzed waitress and she skipped away. Jimmy Buffett started up out of the speakers. I took Danielle and held her close. She smelled of jasmine and beer and salt water. She felt like an old glove. We drank a couple more and the bar got crowded and loud. I settled up and we walked barefoot back onto the sand. Danielle put her arm around me and nestled her head into my collarbone. A gull bounced across the sand looking for a bed.

"I wonder what I'd do in Orlando's place," she said.

"Attack a guy? Hope not."

"No. I mean, be on this high, be a winner. Then have it all taken away. Hard to look on the upside all the time."

"We talking about Orlando now?" I said.

"You saying I'm talking about me? I've never won anything."

"You were on the track, had the flashy husband, the house. Things a lot of people would consider wins. You became a cop, dumped the husband and were seen about town with a ne'er-do-well former ballplayer with a Columbo complex."

She laughed. "Sounds pretty good."

"Exactly what Orlando would say. We can all remember something. But we can't live there."

"I just hope I'm not too old to miss out on things."

"Old? Are you kidding? You are young in all the right places, sweetheart."

"Not all the right places," she said quietly.

We came upon a small hotel across from the beach. Blessed be the shoulder season, so they had a room. It was sparsely furnished in cane pieces. It was old and tired, but clean. The kind of place where you don't mind walking sand in on the bottom of your feet. What a seaside motel should be. We showered together and then fell into bed. The bed rattled like a San Francisco trolley car. I lay on my back, hands on my head, as I had the previous night. Danielle was crushed up against me, one leg looped over mine. I could feel her breath on my chest. She was breathing deep and slow.

"I really wanna get this guy now," she said.

"Me too."

"Not for BJ Baker."

"No, not for BJ."

I lay listening to the hum of the air conditioner until Danielle spoke again. "You think we'll get him?"

"I do," I said. "Something tells me he's about to make a mistake. And we'll be there when he does."

CHAPTER THIRTY—TWO

By the time I finished the long and boring drive from Tampa to West Palm Beach my confidence that our Heisman-stealing cowboy would make a mistake had subsided considerably. I dropped Danielle at her house and headed into the office. No one was in. We had left early and without breakfast in order to get Danielle back in time for her shift, so I was hungry. I wandered out to a cafe and got a bagel and black coffee.

I sat on the seawall looking across the Intracoastal. It was bright and sunny, but the humidity was up and interesting clouds were jostling on the horizon. I felt better for the bagel but not for the thinking time. The three Heisman thefts were linked, of that I was sure. And the Cowboy, as Danielle had started referring to him in that typical law enforcement way, had escalated. Maybe not from burglary one to burglary two. We didn't know what he'd had at BJ's as no one saw him. But if the Cowboy was Rivers, it was easy to believe he had access to a knife. And, from the knife at the Bellinghams to the gun at Orlando Washington's, there had been a definitive step up. Knives were often handy and spur of the moment. Guns rarely were. Even if he owned it before, he still had to make the decision to take it, and then actually take it. Getting the gun would have been easy enough for Rivers, especially if he was doing the job for Bartalotto. What I found small relief in was the fact that Orlando described him as holding the gun nervously, like an amateur. And he had not used the gun, or at least not fired it.

I wondered about that as I headed back to the office. The Cowboy not firing the weapon may have been a sign that he was unwilling to do so. That meant it would take another escalation for him to do it. Or it could simply have been because Orlando had tackled him and taken the Colt out of play.

As I arrived at the office I made myself two mental notes. One, if I wanted to regain my confidence about catching the Cowboy, I had to get my skates on and crack the case open fast. And two, I had to stop calling Rivers *the Cowboy*. I took the fire stairs up to the office. Ron and Lizzy had both arrived. I called them into my office for an update.

They both had coffees. I grabbed some water from the cooler and sat behind my desk. Ron and Lizzy took the chairs. I started by giving them a debrief from Tampa.

When I was done Ron chimed in. "Will you tell Ronzoni?"

"Not today."

"So breaking it open? How do we do that exactly?" said Lizzy.

"Danielle is going to rattle the cage of the email provider. I'll do the same with the Heisman Trust. We need to know one of two things: if this is Rivers and where he'll strike next. We get one of those questions answered, and then we grab the lever and pull."

They both nodded.

"So, what's the news here?"

Ron sat up. "While you were in Tampa, I took the opportunity to see what our friend Dennis Rivers had been up to."

"Alibi?"

"Shaky. He hasn't worked for the past couple days. Nothing on."

"So where has he been?"

"That I can't speak to. The Camry he was using after the yacht club job is registered to his mother. It hasn't been parked at the house at all when I've drifted by."

"Could he get from here to Tampa, recon the job, do over Orlando Washington and get back in two days?"

"You did," he said.

I nodded. And I hadn't been in any hurry.

"We need to have a more serious conversation with Mr. Rivers," I said.

"Stake him out?"

"He's not doing any more lingerie shows, is he?"

Lizzy clucked her tongue at me.

Ron shook his head. "They have a charity function at a private residence on Jupiter Island. Thursday afternoon."

"Then we'll catch him right after. What else you got?"

"Got a call yesterday from a hedge fund here in town. They think one of their execs is licking the icing off the cake to fund a mistress or three. I'm on it."

"Have fun. Lizzy?"

"Mrs. Ferguson and her missing husband. I've gone through their bank accounts, credit cards, insurance policies. All the normal stuff."

"And? Foul play or runner?"

"If I had to hazard a guess, and I hate to say it, I think he may have hurt himself."

"Trail?"

"Nothing concrete yet. He upped the life insurance, which goes to Mrs. Ferguson, but is still pretty meager. But here's the thing. He took out five hundred at an ATM in West Palm a week ago. Not a massive amount, but a fair bit more than usual. Then three days ago he filled his tank and got another two hundred dollars at a gas station in Belle Glade."

"Didn't they live there before they moved to West Palm?"

"It's his hometown. He left to go to college and came back after."

"Gone home to mommy and daddy?"

"Both dead. Here's another thing. He lost his job."

"When?"

"Two weeks ago."

"Why?"

"Guy wouldn't say. Not very helpful."

"So he might have found himself at the end of his rope."

"Yes. But I don't get the cash-out. Looks like travel money."

"True." I rubbed my eyes. "Maybe for drugs? Suicide attempt? Ron and I should drop by his workplace, see what's what. You see if anything else floats to the top. Then if there's nothing, I think we've done all we can right now."

"That's what I was thinking. I'll keep digging."

"Thanks, team. Meeting adjourned."

CHAPTER THIRTY—THREE

Ron bought tuna salad sandwiches, and we sat in my office mapping out a plan of attack for his hedge fund executive case. I struggled to keep my mind on things. I was drifting off, thinking about Orlando and the Heisman thief. I had to admit, the Cowboy sounded better. But we needed to focus on keeping the pipeline going. One case does not a business make. And right now, I had one case going nowhere fast, Lizzy was working pro bono and Ron had this job. And he had just finished a well-paying insurance fraud case. Ron was becoming a regular rainmaker.

Ron was eating and laying out the players for me. Who was whom, who was where. Who might look good to hit up for some inside mail. We were interrupted by the intercom on my phone.

"State Attorney Edwards," said Lizzy.

We looked at the door as it opened and Eric Edwards stepped through. He was in a long dark pinstripe, blue shirt, pink tie. That combo shouldn't have worked on him, but it did. He had five o'clock shadow at noon. He was tall and thin, and looked like immaculately dressed bamboo.

"Eric, always a pleasure," I said.

He looked at me, and then Ron. He didn't say hello to Ron, a registered voter, and I knew it must be bad news. "Are you mentally defective, Jones?"

"I'm not the one dressed for a wedding in eighty-five degree heat."

"This is not the time or the place for your stupid humor."

"Actually, given you are standing in my office, I'd say it's exactly the place." I thought calling my humor stupid was a touch harsh.

"I told you to stay away from Sal Mondavi."

"Who?"

"I'm serious, Jones!" he yelled. I'd never seen him yell before. The guy would golf clap at a professional wrestling match.

"Eric, I'm told by sources that you're an okay guy. All evidence is to the contrary, but I'll cut you a break. So listen carefully. Get lost. Get out of my office before you upset me and I decide not to vote for you next time."

He seemed to choke on that last part. "Jones, you are messing in things of which you have no understanding."

"I do that. Here's something else I do. I go where I want, when I want. And if a merchant of a store, say a pawn shop, who has never been found guilty of anything, let alone arrested, has an item that I wish to purchase, then I will visit said merchant to do so. And I don't give a damn what you think about it." I could feel my pulse rising now. I took a slow, quiet breath.

"If you told Sal Mondavi about this investigation you are in all sorts of hurt, Jones. You know that."

"What investigation, Eric? I would think if the Florida state attorney for the Fifteenth Judicial Circuit gave information about a confidential investigation to a known associate of the subject of said investigation, that would be a whole world of hurt."

Edwards stood erect, which made him really tall, especially from my seated position. His jaw was clenching. "You went to see Sal Mondavi directly after I spoke to you," he said, quietly. "Even between us, there is a level of trust and professionalism."

"I went to Sally's pawn shop to pick up an instrument."

He frowned. "What kind of instrument?"

"A saxophone."

"A saxophone?" He frowned more. He looked like a small child who needed the bathroom. "May I see this saxophone?"

"It's sitting against the wall there."

He turned and looked at the case. It was exactly where I had dumped it when I'd gotten back from Sally's. I made a note to take it home and call Buzz Weeks at the Funky Biscuit. Eric stepped over to the case and looked at it like it was kryptonite.

"May I look in the case?"

"You got a warrant?"

He didn't take his eyes off the case. He breathed and his whole body moved. It was like watching air blow through a drinking straw. I figured I'd had my fun.

"Go ahead, look in it."

He bent down and unlatched the case, opened it and looked inside. He took all the instrument pieces out and lay them on the floor. He removed the reeds and a cleaning cloth. He ran his hand around the sides and lifted out the felt lined base. Looked in the empty cavity. Then he carefully replaced everything back in reverse order. He closed the latches and put the case against the wall.

Then he stood and looked at me. "It's a saxophone."

I nodded.

I guess he had nothing left to say because he stepped to the door. Halfway through, he turned to me. "You hurt her, I'll hurt you."

Then he left. I looked at Ron, and he at me.

"You always get the most interesting visitors," he said.

I slapped my palm into my forehead. "Damn," I said. "I forgot to invite him round for darts."

CHAPTER THIRTY—FOUR

I was sitting at my desk signing checks when the phone rang. Lizzy had left me alone in the office to run some unspecified errands, dropping the completed checks on my desk as she went. Bookkeeping was not my strong point. I truly failed to understand people for whom it was a strong point. I heard the phone ring from the front office and I saw the light on my console flash by line one. I hit the button that brought the call onto speakerphone.

"LCI," I said.

"Miami Jones, please." It was a deep voice. Texan maybe.

"This is he."

"Mr. Jones, this is John Carter from the Heisman Trust."

I sat up and grabbed the handset from the console. His voice was the complete opposite of the last guy I'd spoken to at the Trust. This was a football voice. It spoke not only of an understanding of football but of a lifelong love. Of Friday nights in East Texas, sitting in the bleachers, watching high school boys running around on the gridiron.

"Mr. Carter, thank you. I've been waiting on your call."

"I apologize for the delay. I've been on campus in the Midwest."

And they don't have phones in Ohio, I thought. I didn't say anything. It was easy enough for him to drop the phone down and never speak to me again.

"Did your colleague explain my situation?"

"He did." I could practically hear the cowboy hat on his head. "But I'm not sure there's much I can offer you. It is our strict policy to never share details of our alumni mailing list without an official warrant. You can appreciate that the addresses of our Heisman champions are highly sought after. And therefore dearly protected."

"I appreciate your position. But since I spoke to your colleague, another Heisman has been stolen."

"Oh, boy."

"Exactly."

"Unfortunately, that doesn't change the situation. If a burglary has taken place, perhaps the police can get a warrant."

"I'm sure they can. I just hope they can do it before someone gets killed."

"Killed? Why would someone get killed?"

"The last victim, Orlando Washington, had a gun pulled on him. Fortunately this time it didn't get fired."

There was silence on the line for a moment. "How is Mr. Washington?"

"He's a feisty old dog."

Carter chuckled. "Yes, he is."

"You've met him?"

"I had the pleasure shortly before his wife's passing."

I didn't say anything.

"Mr. Jones, I can't help but think you are asking the wrong question."

"How do you figure?"

"It would seem to me that although you are asking about the location of Heisman alumni, what you really want to know is the location of Heisman trophies."

"By and large, wouldn't they be the same?"

"Yes and no. Lots of alumni have passed awards onto family. Others live or spend significant amounts of time in other locations from where they keep their trophies."

"So we can't really know how many Heismans are in Florida."

"Not really. There have been plenty of winners from Florida schools, but no telling how many are there now."

"That's sort of my point, Mr. Carter. I know there are Heisman winners from my alma mater. Finding them is another matter."

"Where did you go to school, Mr. Jones?"

"Miami, Florida."

"And you are now in West Palm Beach?"

"That's right."

"You have a fellow Hurricane Heisman winner in your backyard then."

I thought for a second. It was a short second. "Gino Torretta?"

"If you say so."

"Now that you say it, I've heard him on the radio. In Miami I think. I didn't know he lived in West Palm."

"I'm not saying anything privileged to tell you he splits his time between West Palm Beach and New York City. But I ask myself, if I stole a Heisman in Palm Beach and I wanted another, why go to Tampa when a Heisman winner is in West Palm Beach?"

"Because the thief didn't know where Torretta's trophy would be." I mulled on it some. I wondered if I could hire the Texan on the other end of the line. "No," I said. "Not the trophy. He didn't know about Torretta, period. He doesn't have a list of winners. It's opportunistic. He saw BJ Baker in the paper. Newt Bellingham tried to sell his father-in-law's online. And anyone who'd spent time in Tampa would've known about Orlando Washington."

"Sounds logical."

"So I don't need to find all the Heismans. I need to find the next high-profile one."

"I think they're all high-profile."

"Of course you do. But they're not all in the paper or on television down here every day." I thought on it. Heisman. High-profile. And Rivers would have to know where it is.

"Tebow," I said.

"Excuse me?"

"Tim Tebow. He played at Florida and comes from Jacksonville."

"But right now he's in the NFL. Maybe his award is with him."

I had nothing to say to that. When you really think you're onto something, there's nothing like a pragmatic Texan to bust your balloon.

"Can I make a left field suggestion?" said Carter.

"Please do."

"There may be another player that your perp knows about or maybe not. But if I wanted a guaranteed location I knew had a Heisman, I'd look at a college."

"Sure, but how many winners will have given their trophy to their school?"

"Steve Spurrier '66 gave his trophy to University of Florida so it could be shared with the entire student body. Ever since that date, the Heisman Trust has presented a replica to the college of the winner."

"So UM, Florida and Florida State all have Heismans?"

"Correct."

"So our guy could be headed for Miami, Gainesville or Tallahassee."

"Possible. Could be wrong."

"Could be. But one from three is odds I can play with."

"Glad I could help."

"Mr. Carter, you make me feel like an amateur, but thanks."

"Don't feel sore, son. I spent twenty years as an MP in the United States Army. I didn't always glad-hand college presidents."

"That being the case, let me ask you one more thing. If you had your choice, which of those schools would you hit up for a Heisman heist?"

He was silent for a moment. "If your guy is just taking his opportunities? I'd go for the one where the Heismans were accessible. I know for fact that three are on display permanently at the Heavener Football Complex. University of Florida."

"I was afraid you were going to say that."

CHAPTER THIRTY–FIVE

My conversation with John Carter from the Heisman Trust hadn't given me what I wanted, but it had given me what I needed. *If you try sometimes*, as the wise men said. I now had a path forward. Unfortunately it was a path of thorns.

First I narrowed the field. I called the athletic directors of both Miami and Florida State. Both thanked me for the information. Florida State assured me that their Heisman trophies were not currently on display, but they would add extra security to their storage locations. The Miami athletic director told me they would remove theirs from the Tom Kearns Hall of Fame temporarily, and then offered to host me in the department's recruitment box at Sun Life Stadium for their next home game. That left University of Florida, as I knew it would. The Fates have a funny way of conspiring to ensure such things.

My phone buzzed a third time and Lizzy said "U Florida" and clicked off and I heard the ringing and then someone answered. I asked for the Athletic Department, and then the athletic director. I was told he was out at Jacksonville with the team, preparing for Saturday's big game. I was asked if I wanted the assistant director.

I took a deep breath and said, "Why not?"

"Rollie Spenser."

"Spenser," I said. "Miami Jones."

I heard a snort. "Still using that stupid moniker, Jones?"

"When you're well-gilded the gold sticks."

"Remind me how many starts you had in college?"

"You still got that winning personality, Roll."

"What do you want, Jones? I'm very busy. We've got Georgia this week."

"I know. All eyes on Jacksonville. That's why I called."

"I can't get you any tickets."

"Yeah, that's what I want. Tickets to a Gator game."

"What then?"

I explained to him in broad strokes the Heisman thefts and the likelihood the perp could visit Gainesville next.

"What about Miami or Tallahassee?"

"I called both UM and Florida State. They're taking precautions. Besides, they don't have theirs out in the open like you do."

"I hardly call the Heavener Football Complex out in the open. It's the most state-of-the-art training facility in college sports."

"But not a bank vault."

"Don't worry about us, Jones. We Gators protect our own."

"Gators? What happened to Hurricanes forever?"

"Life moves on, Jones. You should try it."

I could assure him I had moved on, but I didn't feel like saying it. "I see Brady threw for three hundred yards again on Sunday," I said.

"Get lost, Jones. I didn't need you as a backup in college and I don't need you as a backup now."

Nothing clever came to mind, so I didn't say anything. It didn't matter. Rollie had hung up. It was a childish thing to say. But some people brought that out in me. And Rollie Spenser, the guy I played two years as backup quarterback to at University of Miami, was one of those guys.

I dropped the phone in the cradle. I had done my civic duty and warned him. Not that it mattered. I didn't care if someone stole a trophy out of the University of Florida's gleaming collection. But not caring didn't get me closer to solving my case. I figured Rollie Spenser was going to enter my life again soon, whether he or I liked it or not.

CHAPTER THIRTY-SIX

Ron and I had the top down on the Mustang. The air was clear and the breeze offshore, keeping things mild. Ron grinned like he'd won the Lotto. There wasn't much Ron didn't like about South Florida. He never even complained about the heat and humidity in mid-July. But on a perfect fall day with the sky clear and blue, and the wind blowing through his thick gray mane, he was in heaven. I half expected him to lean his head out the window and stick out his tongue.

I drove us down Southern Boulevard and into Palm Beach Gardens. We got to the address Lizzy had given us and pulled in. The big wooden sign said Marv's Quality Autos, and looking around the lot I was reminded that quality was not so much a fact as a value judgment. Compared to a busted wagon and a nobbled old horse there was indeed some fine quality on the lot. Not junkers exactly, not in the old way where duct tape and twine could give a rust bucket another five years. The laws had made most of those go the way of the dodo. The cars were relatively new, not much over fifteen years and nothing younger than five. But they'd all been driven long and fast and hard. The Florida sun had bleached the paintwork and cracked the vinyl interiors, and the long freeways ensured all the odometers had reached well over a hundred thousand miles. It was the kind of place where five C notes could have you driving off the lot paid in full. Almost everything was domestic.

We got out, looked around briefly, and then walked toward a small shed that acted as the sales office. A fat man in gray trousers and a peach-colored shirt came out to meet us. The shirt was opened to the midpoint of the bulge of his gut. Sweat glistened in his chest hair. He wasn't smiling. He was almost squinting, except the sun was behind him. Perhaps he didn't like bright light. Perhaps he knew that someone who pulled into his lot in a current model Mustang wasn't in the market for one of his cars. I had to figure a smile would sell more vehicles, but I've never worked in sales so I could have been wrong.

"You Marv?" I said.

"Nup," said the fat man.

"Marv around?"

"There is no Marv."

I looked at the wooden sign. It was mounted on a ten-foot wooden pole, like something you'd make a patio deck out of. Only this one had been painted white. When I was a boy. The sign itself looked like it had been erected by a post-World War II Boy Scout troop.

"Why you called Marv's Quality Autos?"

He shrugged. "Think there was a Marv once. Before my time."

"How long you worked here?"

"Twenty-seven years."

Ron and I looked around the yard. The pavement had been cracked by decades of heating, cooling and heating again. Little weeds had come through the cracks and turned into fully fledged plants. I wondered how you got yourself out of bed each morning for twenty-seven years to come here. I could tell by Ron's face he was thinking the same thing.

"The owner about?"

"I am the owner." He frowned, which made him look like a sixty-year-old Cabbage Patch doll.

I handed him a card. "Miami Jones. I'm working on a missing persons case. An employee of yours, Sandy Ferguson."

He shrugged and said nothing. He didn't look at the card.

"You know him?"

He shrugged again and blinked slowly, like a massive reptile. He still said nothing. Ron turned from me and walked over to an old car. Then he looked back.

"How much for this Caddie?"

The fat man lost the frown but kept squinting. "You interested in that one?"

"Who isn't interested in a Caddy?" said Ron.

The fat man waddled over to him. He pocketed my card. "That's a beautiful automobile, that is. One of Detroit's finest."

I looked at the Caddy. It had been white, I suspected, when it rolled off the line in Motown. It was the size of an ocean liner, all pure steel and chrome. The hood had been baked so long it looked like a salt flat. The vinyl roof was peeling. It was a testimony to the guys who'd put it together that it was still in one piece.

"Original," said the fat man. "Only one owner."

I could picture the owner buying the thing to impress his neighbors in Queens, driving it for twenty years, and then cruising it down to West Palm where he drove it another ten years in retirement, before he was laid to rest in Shady Palms and the Caddy was laid to rest at Marv's Quality Autos.

"You sell many of these?" said Ron.

"Oh, you don't see too many of these," said the fat man.

"Sandy Ferguson sell many of these?" I said. I looked in the driver's window at the odometer. It seemed the car had spent some time traveling to the moon.

"He didn't sell much of anything."

"You mind if we sit inside?" said Ron.

"Be my guest."

We both got in. The interior smelled like the beach and was stained nicotine yellow.

"He work here long," I said.

"Who?"

"Ferguson."

"About eight years."

"Good salesman?"

"Nope."

"If you want something done right, you gotta do it yourself," I said.

"Damned straight."

"So why keep him so long if he couldn't sell?"

"Staff are hard to come by."

I glanced at the lot again. I could imagine attracting good people would be a challenge.

"So why'd you let him go?"

"Didn't make his monthly quota."

"For how long?"

"Twenty-two months."

Ron was playing with every switch and button. He pushed hard on a preset on the radio and got talkback. It sounded distant and tinny. He turned it off again.

"So why after twenty-two months?" I said. "Why not twenty-one or twenty-three?"

The fat man shrugged. It was a signature move. "Got too sad."

"Sad? How do you mean?"

"Look. Sandy wasn't the most upbeat guy, you know. He was kind of a downer. But I get it, right. This ain't a Starbucks. It's no dream job. But he sold cars before, so I figured he could do it again. But . . ."

"But?"

The fat man looked at Ron. "You wanna make an offer?"

"It is a fine vehicle," said Ron. He turned the radio dial and it came off in his hand.

"But?" I said.

"But nothing. He got sad. He was tolerable as a downer, but sad? He was driving customers away."

I could imagine. "What made him sad?"

"Hell if I know. He just kind of spiraled. Over time, you know. It seemed like every fall when the heat came off, Sandy would just be a little sadder than when the summer started. The rest of us would be happy as pigs in you-know-what for the relief, but not Sandy."

"So what happened when you told him?"

"Nothing. He just nodded and said he understood. Took his last check and left."

"Did he ever give you any indication of where he might go?"

The fat man shook his head. "Not to me."

"Any interests?"

"Nope."

"What did he do all day? You're not exactly beating the crowds off with a stick."

"Guess he read the papers and such. Clipped articles."

"What kind of articles?"

"No idea. Never paid much notice."

I found that hard to believe. I got out of the Cadillac. "You got a water cooler in there?" I said, nodding at the shed.

"This look like a Motel 6?"

"What about a john?"

He shrugged again. I took that to mean yes. I left Ron in the Caddy and walked over to the shed. It was small and dark. Two desks covered in newspapers and invoices and paper coffee cups. A half-naked woman striding a motorcycle on a calendar. The air con was humming despite the mild weather. Perhaps the windows didn't open. The desk at the front had a half-eaten donut on it. I assumed, despite the pigsty, a half-eaten donut would not have been left by a former employee gone several weeks. The rear desk was covered with just as much junk. Not much if it had been made to clean up after Ferguson left. There was a desk lamp and a dirty coffee mug. A loose pile of newspapers and magazines. I flipped through them. Local papers. Some articles had been cut out. Looked like the social pages. On second thought, perhaps pictures had been cut out. A couple of *Sports Illustrated*s. Some pages had been ripped out. Could have been articles, could've been ads for French cologne. At the base were travel magazines, the kind cities or regions send you to help plan a vacation. One for South Georgia. Another for the Gulf coast states sponsored by an oil company. More for Miami Dade and the Everglades. Tampa and St. Petersburg; Charleston, North Carolina; Saint Joseph County, Indiana; Wake County, Indiana; La Porte County, Indiana; Stark County, Ohio. Each had pages torn out.

Behind the magazines was a cardholder full of cheap business cards in the name of Sandy Ferguson. It seemed that Sandy was planning a trip somewhere. Perhaps a surprise for his wife. A real big surprise, given he'd gone and left her behind. I scooped up some of the papers and magazines and stuffed them into a plastic shopping bag I found on the floor. I'd take them to the office and get Lizzy to match the clipped sections and torn out pages to confirm what I knew. Sandy Ferguson had been planning his escape. To where, I couldn't be sure. Perhaps his credit card activity would tell us something in the future. Perhaps he had taken cash out to get away and drop off the map. Perhaps being fired had dashed his hopes, and he'd chosen to end it all.

I didn't know, but I hoped the answer would at least set Mrs. Ferguson free. If she was capable of that. Perhaps their sadness was shared. Perhaps for her to break free, he had to first. That was all above my paygrade. My job was just to break the news. I walked back out into the sunlight. Ron was chatting with the fat man. They had popped the hood and were bent over, examining an engine built before computers existed. I dropped the bag of magazines and papers and walked over to Ron.

"So?" I said.

Ron popped up. He was beaming. "It's a miracle of modern technology," he said.

"You wanna make an offer?" said the fat man, again.

"Absolutely," said Ron.

I was stunned.

Ron continued. "Let me check with the little woman and I'll get back to you."

"I can't guarantee it will still be available. This one is going to move."

"I know it," said Ron. He put out his hand and the fat man took it.

"I didn't get your name," said Ron.

"Barry. Barry Kennett." They shook and Ron smiled and Kennett squinted.

We got back into the Mustang and I pulled out of the lot. "You gonna get yourself a new set of wheels?" I said.

"Goodness, no. It was a miracle of modern manufacturing, though, wasn't it?"

"You think?"

"Absolutely. There was moss growing on the engine block, but the thing still started first turn of the key. What did you find?"

"I think our man was planning a road trip, possibly never to return."

"Why would you leave Florida on a day like this?" Ron smiled. "You hear what I hear?"

"The call of an ice-cold beer?"

Ron settled back in his seat. "That is why *you* are the master detective."

CHAPTER THIRTY—SEVEN

The following morning was mild and wispy shards of cloud threaded across the sky as I ran along the beach and back up to the house. I was throwing together a smoothie with egg white that I'd read about in a magazine and was pretty certain I'd regret, when my phone rang. It was Lizzy. She relayed a message from Jenny Bellingham, asking if I could come to her house urgently. I tossed the smoothie in the garbage disposal and called Danielle. She was on duty but not available. I left her a message and ran through the shower. I hoped the Heisman bandit, as I had decided to call Rivers, had returned. But even as I drove out to Tropicana Palms, I knew I was kidding myself.

I parked behind Jenny Bellingham's Civic. There was no sign of the Ram truck. I knocked on the door. She opened instantly, as if she'd been watching through the curtains. Her face looked like a topographical map. Mountains and valleys, light and dark. Solid skin and flowing blood. The left eye she had bruised in her last fall was refreshed, a lumpy mess of red and black. A perfect right cross. Maybe two. Her right eye was puffy and weeping. The left mandible was swollen like she had eaten golf balls and was hiding them in her cheek. There was dried blood on her chin, where a geyser had opened in her nose and cascaded down onto her shirt. A cartoon turtle on her pajama shirt was covered in dried blood.

She let me in and shrunk back into the dark home. The shelves around the television were empty. Everything that had been there—

the photos, the mementos—had been thrown to another part of the room. A chair lay on its side. She looked at me with a face carved in shame.

"I'm sorry," she said. She was shaking like a petrified canary.

"You have nothing to be sorry for."

I stepped toward her and she recoiled. A reflex action. I gestured for her to sit on the sofa. When she sat I noticed an open wound on the side of her head, above her ear. It had bled over her ear and coagulated. It was a significant split and would require stitches. I went to a cabinet in the kitchen and found a bottle of cheap bourbon. I poured a generous shot and took her the glass.

"Take this."

She sipped it and screwed her face. I stepped through the debris to the bathroom and got a towel and some bandages. I found some gauze and antiseptic cream. I came back. She was still sipping the bourbon. She didn't like it, but she knew how to take her medicine. I sat on the sofa and told her it would sting a bit. She was a nurse, so she didn't believe that one bit. She put the drink on the floor next to a cracked picture of her and Newt in a happier place. It stung a lot. She made no sound. I dressed the wound with antiseptic and gauze and then wrapped her head in a bandage. She picked up the bourbon.

"It'll need sutures," I said.

She nodded. I let her take a couple more sips.

"Tell me."

She stared at the black screen of the television. "He went out last night. Drinking. When he came home he said he'd heard that he could've gotten ten thousand dollars for Daddy's Heisman. He said it was his right and I took it from him. He was so angry." She sipped the bourbon.

"And?" I said.

"And?"

"The wound on your head is fresh. That didn't happen last night."

She stared at the television. Blinked hard. "No. He woke up this morning. Still upset. Before, he was always sorry when he lost his temper. You know, later. Not this morning. He was ranting and raving. I was trying to clean up, put things back on the shelves. He'd wait for me to put something up, then he'd knock it down. Said I was driving him crazy."

She finished the bourbon. In her position I would've had several more. But she needed stitches and might need painkillers, so I didn't offer.

She put the glass down and clasped her hands. "I told him if we could get the Heisman back, he could sell it. If that's what he wanted. He said it was gone for good and it was my fault. He picked up a table lamp and hit me with it, then he stormed out."

I looked on the floor. A shattered lamp with a heavy brass base lay beside the sofa.

"I was going to call Deputy Castle, but I'm scared, Mr. Jones. You hear stories. The police say there's only so much they can do and it happens all over again."

"Actually, there's a lot Deputy Castle can do."

"You said you dealt with this sort of thing before. You think I should just call the police?"

"We'll get Deputy Castle involved soon enough. But tell me, if you had to leave in the next thirty minutes, would you have somewhere to go?"

She nodded. "My friend, Mona. From work. She's been telling me to get out."

"Then that's what you'll do."

"I can't live with Mona, Mr. Jones. This is my home."

"Not anymore, Jenny. Twenty-nine minutes from now you will leave and never come back. We'll go to your friend's place first.

Deputy Castle can help with shelters and such if we need it. Support, too. It's out there."

"Okay, I guess."

"We're going to pack you a bag. Take what you need and what's important to you. Then we're going to the bank. You have an account with your husband?"

"In his name."

"Debit card?"

"Yes."

"How much in the account?"

"I'm not sure. Maybe eight or nine hundred dollars."

"Any investments?"

"Just this house."

"Okay. We'll go to the bank and you are going to withdrawal exactly half of what's in there. Not a penny more."

"Okay."

"Then as soon as you're a little better, you'll go to another bank and open your own account. Deputy Castle is going to arrange for support to help you."

"Half of eight hundred dollars won't last forever. And we have a mortgage on this place."

"You'll be selling this place to pay that off."

"Newt won't like that."

"Newt will learn to deal with it."

She looked around the ruins of her home. "I'm scared, Mr. Jones. Of Newt, of money. Of surviving."

"I'm going to find your dad's Heisman."

"Thank you, I guess."

"Then we'll take it from there."

She nodded.

"Jenny, let's find your bag, collect your things and get out of here."

She shuffled to the bedroom and pulled out a small suitcase. She collected some clothes, her nursing uniforms, some toiletries. She picked a picture up off the floor. It was a young version of her with an older man.

"My daddy," she said.

I nodded. She didn't take a picture with Newt in it. I took that as a good sign. She put her worldly possessions in the back of the Mustang and bid goodbye to Tropicana Palms.

"What about my car?"

"I'll come back for it."

"And what if he comes looking for me?"

"I'll have a word. Suggest that's not a great idea."

I drove her north to Abacoa and left her in the care of Mona, an eagle-nosed woman who didn't completely believe that I hadn't inflicted Jenny's injuries. Mona said they would go directly to an urgent care center she had friends at, so Jenny could get her wounds looked at.

I called Danielle again and told her where Jenny Bellingham was, and asked her to come over to take a report and photograph the injuries. Just in case Newt decided to get clever or greedy. I knew he wasn't capable of the former, and we would have a chat about the latter. I headed back to the office to call Sally and get his wise counsel on the upcoming negotiations.

CHAPTER THIRTY—EIGHT

Sally's wise counsel consisted of telling me not to pick him up at his store. The last thing we wanted, he said, was a posse of federal agents following us. I agreed. The night was still and I could feel the moisture content in the air rising. Somewhere off Grand Bahama a storm was brewing.

I collected Sally from the Cracker Barrel off I-95 in Spencer Lakes. He was crazy for the biscuits. And the store. He loved that the store had thousands of so-called country items, and all except one were completely useless and unnecessary to anyone's life. But they sold by the pallet load. Sally sat outside in Cracker Barrel's one useful product when I pulled up. He was rocking in the wooden chair, in a row of a dozen such chairs. He clutched a paper bag that I bet myself was filled with fresh baked biscuits. He got up and ambled over to the car. We drove out to Tropicana Palms in silence. The plan was simple. It was my show to run. If I wanted Sally's input, I would ask for it.

We parked behind the Dodge Ram, which was parked behind the Civic. Sally grabbed his tool bag and we wandered up the side and banged on the door. The mobile home wobbled on its base as Newt stomped to answer.

"About time a-hole, I'm starving."

Apparently Newt's personal chef had taken the night off and he was stuck with delivery. He opened the door. We were in the dark, he the light. So the first thing he saw was my fist. If he saw anything. He may have just felt it. It was a left shot to the throat. I had thought of giving him my fastball thunderbolt, but I didn't want to put my shoulder out and I didn't want him dead. The left just knocked the wind and the voice out of him. No screaming for help when someone punches you in the voice box.

Newt rocked back but didn't go down, so I gave him a punter's special into the balls. I'd been the recipient of a solidly kicked football into the privates during a high school practice, and I knew that most blows in the groin fostered shock, and if one wore a cup, some bruising on the inner thigh. But actual dead-on contact with a testicle was like shooting an electric current through the soles of someone's feet. Newt gave the standard reaction. He lost all motor function below the waist and fell to the floor. He was clutching his throat as he fell. His hands instinctively moved lower. I stepped inside and dragged Newt into the living room, and propped him against the sofa. Sally closed the door behind us.

Newt was clutching his groin and attempting to yell abuse at me. It came out a breathy whistle. I had to hand it to him. He really was one dumb son of a gun.

I crouched beside him and placed my palm on his chest. "Slow down, breathe. In, out. In, out."

The spasms in his chest and throat steadied and his breathing settled. Sally shuffled to the kitchen and brought back a glass of water. Newt gurgled it down. He tried to talk. It was a whisper halfway between Eartha Kitt and an emphysema sufferer.

"You are so dead," he said. The guy took stupid to a whole new level. "I made a complaint, to the cops." He grinned. "Now you're gone. I'll sue you to kingdom come. I'll be rich."

"You sadly overestimate my net worth and my liability insurance, pal. Besides, this isn't Detective Ronzoni's jurisdiction."

I could see a modicum of concern wash across his face at the mention of Ronzoni.

"Now, let me tell you how this is going to go down. You are going to feel considerable pain. How much pain is up to you. Then we are going to discuss your life moving forward and how that life no longer includes your wife. Then we will discuss strategies for the disposal of this dump, and for your divorce. Okay?"

He wheezed. "You are out of your dumbass mind."

I turned to Sally. "Thoughts at this point?"

Sally reached into his tool bag and handed me a rolled up Yellow Pages, held together by duct tape. It was like a miniature baseball bat. I held it up in front of Newt, and he looked at it like he was looking at a firefly for the first time. Then I swung it hard into his guts. He doubled over and made sounds like he was going to vomit into his lap. I like the guts. They don't bruise. If any real damage is inflicted, it's internal. My next preferences are the groin and the anus. Kicks to either area are debilitating to a guy, and any ensuing damage is in the kind of spot one has to be extremely desperate to show off.

Newt brought his head up, gasping for air. I handed the rolled up phonebook back to Sally. I wondered why they bothered to still print them, and now I knew. Sally passed me a silver shifter wrench. I wasn't at all sure what he expected me to do with it. He saw the look on my face and took it back from me, then leaned over Newt and banged the wrench into Newt's ankle. He let out a howl that I stopped with a chop to the throat.

Sally stepped back. "Never too hard," he said. "You don't wanna break the ankle. Unless you do."

We waited for Newt to recover some.

"Shall we continue?"

He shook his head. "Whatever you want, I'll do it."

"I want you to not treat women like punching bags, for starters."

"What about when they're asking for it?"

I swallowed bile and took a deep breath. My mother—hell everyone's mother—said that two wrongs didn't make a right. I still felt I held the moral high ground. I was instilling a new value system in Newt Bellingham. Kicking the life out of him was what I wanted to do. I closed my eyes. It didn't help. I saw Jenny Bellingham's battered face.

I took another breath. "I'm about to cross a line here," I said to Sally.

He nodded and put his hand on my shoulder. "Get him into a chair," he said.

We lifted Newt into a dining chair and Sally duct taped his arms and legs to the chair. Then Sally directed me to drag him into the bathroom. It was a tight squeeze with Newt in the chair. Sally then told me to lean the chair back onto the side of the bathtub so Newt's head hung back over the tub. Sally started the faucet in the sink and soaked a towel, which he placed loosely over Newt's face. There was a knock at the front door.

"Food's here," said Sally. "Take care of that, will ya? Then wait out there. I'll be out shortly."

I stepped out of the bathroom and closed the door. At the front door I found a young Asian guy in glasses. His hair contained so much gel the spikes in it looked dangerous. I took the food, paid cash and gave him a nice tip. Food delivery is a tough job. I took the bag to the kitchen and opened it. Three large containers of special fried rice and a half dozen egg rolls. I took a roll and sat on the sofa. I strained but couldn't hear a sound from the bathroom.

I didn't feel good. About what I was doing, about involving Sally, about not leaving it to Danielle. I thought back to the call I'd made to Danielle, asking her to attend to Jenny Bellingham. She hadn't asked me why I wouldn't be there. Hadn't asked me where I was going or what I was doing. I ate the egg roll. It wasn't very good and I wished I hadn't.

I waited. Looked around the room. I'd sat in this exact spot with Jenny. It looked the same. I wouldn't have expected Newt to get a maid service in, but he hadn't picked up anything. The shelves around the television were still empty. The cracked picture of the younger Jenny and Newt still lay smashed at my feet. The packet of gauze I used to patch her up had been pressed down in between the cushions where Newt sat.

I stared at the blank television just like Jenny Bellingham had done. Half an hour must have passed when Sally stepped out of the bathroom. He was rolling down his shirtsleeves.

"He's with the program," said Sally. "But he's pretty tired, so he's gonna get some shut-eye."

I nodded.

Sally turned back to the bathroom. "Why don't you warm up the car? I'll be there in a minute." He went back in the bathroom but didn't shut the door.

I got up and tossed the egg roll wrapper into the trash. I looked at the Chinese food and thought about taking it but decided I didn't need the starchy carbs and Newt might. I walked out of the mobile home and sat in the Mustang. I had the windows up to keep the bugs at bay, but left the air con off. Ten minutes later Sally shuffled out to the car. He tossed his tool bag in the back and got in the front.

"How do you know he'll stick to the plan?" I said.

"He'll stick."

"How do you know?"

"You doubt me?"

"Not for a second. I just want to know."

"No, you don't. You want to sleep nights, as long as you can."

"Tell me."

He looked at me. He looked tired. "Learned behavior. Tonight he was introduced to a new way of thinking. He might not pick it up first time. So we reinforce the lesson. A note written on a beer mat when he comes back from the john at his favorite sports bar. A month from now, a chance meeting in a dark parking lot, a swift kick in the groin and a whispered message. Six months from now he'll get a flat tire and go for the spare and find a rolled up phonebook, wrapped in duct tape. Learned behavior."

I started the engine, punched the gear selector into drive, and then looked at Sally. "Sorry I called you," I said.

"I'm not. But I'd appreciate you getting me home before Leno comes on."

CHAPTER THIRTY—NINE

Doing any kind of stakeout in the ritzy part of Jupiter Island was hard. County Road 707 bisected the pencil-thin island surrounded on either side by ten-foot-high hedgerows and security fences. In some places there was only room for one property on either side of the road. One side was beachfront, looking out onto the Atlantic, the other side banked onto the Intracoastal.

The properties were expansive. Many had two driveways. One for residents and guests, the other for the help. It was the latter driveway that Dennis Rivers would have used to enter the estate where Black Tie was catering a charity event. I didn't see him enter because I wasn't on Jupiter Island. The tight road gave no cover, as Ron and I had discovered when we assessed the spot earlier in the day. Best we could do was pull over on the roadside and pretend to have broken down. We tested it. It took six minutes for a very courteous security guard from the adjacent estate to come out and offer his assistance to get us up and running and the hell out of there.

So when Rivers entered, Ron and I were sitting aboard a Boston Whaler on the Intracoastal, motoring up and down just off the rear of the property. Through binoculars I saw the Black Tie van arrive at the side of the massive three-story house. A marquee had been erected in the immaculate garden. The lawn looked like a putting green. Rivers and his cohort set up. A flock of well-dressed, well-heeled women appeared for afternoon tea. The folks on Jupiter

Island made BJ Baker look like the pool boy. BJ may have played NFL football and become a successful media personality, but that only got you waterfront in Palm Beach. The guys who owned the NFL team and the television station had property on Jupiter Island.

We cruised in the boat that Ron had borrowed from a motor boat club he was a member of. We drank soda and ate corn chips and salsa. It was a pleasant way to follow someone. The water sparkled and boats of all sorts and sizes floated around the calm waters. I was surprised there were so many people out. Didn't anyone in America work anymore? We watched the flock eventually dissipate and Rivers pack his kit and get in his van. We sped the Whaler back to Jupiter inlet and left it at the dock. The Mustang sat dockside, and we sped out and got on to A1A and pulled over just before the bridge into downtown Jupiter.

There were two ways Rivers might get back to the Black Tie warehouse. A1A and the curiously named Alternative A1A. The former was faster and more direct. I picked the van up in my mirror a couple minutes later and pulled into traffic four cars behind. Rivers drove directly to the light industrial complex that housed Black Tie. The Camry was parked outside. Rivers and a girl with tied-back hair carried trays from the van into the warehouse. Then the girl appeared. She got into a small Mazda and drove away. Rivers appeared and I started the engine. But he didn't get in the Camry. He carried something back to the van.

"What's he doing," said Ron.

"No idea."

"Make a move?" said Ron.

I hesitated. We'd agreed that confronting him in front of his employers again wouldn't work. We decided to tail him home, and then pay him a visit. But now he was loading the van again.

"Another gig?" I said.

"Nothing on their books."

I turned to Ron. "How do you know that, by the way?"

"I'm dating their office manager."

"Anything for the job, huh?"

"I'd take a bullet." He smiled.

Rivers brought more stainless steel containers out to the van. Then he slammed home the rear doors. The van bounced as he got in. He pulled out and drove toward us. I figured we were made. I reminded myself again that a red Mustang was not the best vehicle for a person in my line of work.

But Rivers didn't see us. As he drove by his left hand was wrestling with the seat belt. His right hand held a phone to his ear. He must have been steering with his knees. He was way too preoccupied to notice where he was going, let alone see me turn around and pull in behind him. Evidently he was calling someone to say he was running late because he drove like a lunatic. We sped through the surface streets of West Palm and onto I-95. We followed him off the exit at Boca Raton and took a familiar route.

"Hello, hello," Ron said in an English accent as we pulled into the mall that housed Mango Martini.

Rivers drove by the club and pulled around the building. Came to a stop at the rear of the club. I pulled into a parking spot to the side of the big pet store.

"You think he nicked something from that house in Jupiter?" said Ron.

"The thought had occurred."

"And he's selling it to Bartalotto?"

"Also occurred." We watched Rivers unload the van into the club.

"What do we know about the Jupiter property? Who owns it?" I said.

"Some European guy. He's into hotels and resorts."

"So unlikely to have won a Heisman."

"Unlikely," he said.

"Think Bartalotto could be using Rivers for other jobs?"

"Why use a guy who went inside for grand theft auto to do break and enters? Bartalotto isn't short of help in that area."

"My thoughts exactly," I said.

I watched Rivers close the van and dash inside. I had no idea what was going on and it was making me itchy. It was the kind of feeling I used to get before I blew off the catcher's call and threw my fastball. At the batter's head.

"We need to know what the hell is going on in there."

We walked around the storefronts and in the main door of the club. It was a different place. There were people everywhere. The music was louder. The volume increase didn't improve it. The girl at the host desk was dressed in the standard lingerie. She looked about fourteen.

"About thirty-minute wait for the club, forty-five for the restaurant." She smiled. Her parents had sunk some serious cash into her impressive dental work.

I looked around but couldn't see Rivers. "The bar," I said.

"Thirty minutes."

I thought about just heading in but figured that plan would work better once I knew where I wanted to go.

"You *are* following me." It was Amber approaching from the bar. She smiled and I decided that great teeth were a job requirement at Mango Martini.

"Whenever possible, Miss Amber," I said.

She faux pouted. "You call me Miss Amber, I'm gonna think of you like my dad. And I really don't want to think of you that way." She raised an eyebrow.

She was good. I was almost ready to cast myself adrift in her life raft. Almost. Another five years she'd have the look down pat and I'd be a goner.

"There a back room here?"

She smiled. "Easy, Tiger."

"Is there?" I said it straight-faced and she dropped the smile a touch. Not all the way.

"Yeah. The function room."

"You do functions?"

"Tons. But not in the function room. We just call it that. It's just a separate room. Functions happen in here." She waved her delicate hands to signal the club in general.

"So you use caterers for functions?"

"Ah, no. We're a restaurant, too. Mainly fried stuff, but that's what people like."

"So what goes on in the function room?"

"Generally nothing. Sometimes Mr. Bartalotto uses it. I think he's in there tonight." Amber looked at the girl at the host desk.

"Yeah, he is," she said. "He's having a private party." She looked at me. "You want me to put you on the wait list?"

I shook my head. She turned her attention to a young couple who came in looking like they had just arrived from a salsa dancing competition.

"Sure you won't stay for a drink?" said Amber. She brushed her straight hair out of her face.

"Maybe later. If you're around."

"I'll be here." She flashed the pearly whites again and skipped away toward the neon bar.

I turned to Ron. "What do you think?"

"Private party?" he said. "And an outside caterer who isn't on official business?"

"In a club that they own and has its own kitchen?"

"It's a puzzle. And Rivers is the piece that doesn't fit."

"I agree, and I'm sick of not knowing how the pieces fit together. Or even how many pieces there are."

I wanted answers. I wanted to find BJ Baker's Heisman. I wanted a result for Jenny Bellingham and Orlando Washington, too. It was time to beat the bush and see what flew out.

I took off across the room, weaving between tables. I didn't know if Ron was following. I assumed he would, but it didn't matter to me either way. I strode past the bar and saw Amber getting a tray of drinks setup. She saw me. She frowned. She didn't know what I was doing. I wasn't completely sure myself.

I headed straight to the door next to the bar. The door I'd seen Dennis Rivers go through when we had followed him to the club before. I didn't stop. Flicked the handle and ignored the sign saying, *Private Employees Only*. I barged through and found myself in a corridor. It was different from the main room. No attempt had been made to make this area look classy. No neon, no spotlighting. The walls were matte black and small halogen cans lit the space. There were two doors to the left, one straight at the end of the corridor, one to the right. The left doors both had glass portholes. One would be a storeroom for liquor. It had a key card lock on it. For inventory control. The second door was the kitchen. I saw stainless steel shelving and bright lighting through the porthole. The end door had a big bar across it. To push in case of emergency. It led outside. I turned right to a plain black door and pushed my way in. Then I stopped. I looked around the room and took it all in. Felt Ron arrive behind me, close enough so I could feel his breath on the back of my neck.

The room was set up with two large round tables. Each seated about sixteen people. That made thirty-two pairs of eyes on me. Plus the two guys standing against the wall. They looked like linebackers in expensive suits. They both pushed off the wall toward me. The tables were filled with people who shared a strong genetic code. Thick black hair and strong noses dominated the room. Everyone was dressed in their Sunday best. There were little girls in frilly dresses and boys in those little suits that make them look both cute and yet a little odd. A generation on, their parents, and a generation beyond that at the next table. Roberto Bartalotto's generation.

The man himself sat with an open mouth and a scowl furthest from the door. He was a heavy man, a solid ring of fat below his jaw. He looked uncomfortable in a tie. Next to him was the oldest generation. A snow-haired woman with large round spectacles and a print dress that looked like an exploded vat of Concord grape jelly. It was a regular minor league mob get-together. Except for one thing. The tables were filled with rounds of sandwiches. Little triangles of sandwiches on three tiered trays. I spotted petite white doilies under the sandwiches. And everyone except the kids had china cups in front of them. Dainty things with roses and such on them. If I didn't know better I'd say the cups held tea. There wasn't a strand of pasta or a drop of red wine in the room. I fleetingly resolved to revisit my stereotypes of mafia families.

The two big guys were a step away. Then from a door on the other side of the room came Dennis Rivers. He was dressed in his white shirt and black trousers. He had his clip-on bow tie in place and carried a tray of sandwiches. His eyes connected with mine and the color washed from his face.

"Dennis?" I said. It was meant to be a thought, but the whole room heard it.

Bartalotto turned to Rivers. "You know these men?"

Rivers looked at Bartalotto and then back at me.

"Dennis?" demanded Bartalotto.

Rivers creased his forehead and looked back at the mobster. "They're with me," he said.

"With you?" Bartalotto turned his scowl on me and looked me up and down. He didn't appear convinced.

"Yes, sir," said Rivers. He looked back at me. "They're my help."

He gave me that same face he'd shown at the yacht club. Devoid of emotion. He could've been holding a royal flush or spit in a bucket. I'd never have been able to tell.

"Get in the kitchen now," he said.

I moved. There didn't appear to be much mileage in staying in the room. Two big guys who would clearly be packing heat, and me none the wiser about what the hell was going on. Bartalotto tracked me as I moved around the room. I got to the door next to Rivers and pushed it open.

"They use the back door in future, Dennis," said Bartalotto.

I didn't hear the response.

Ron and I stepped into a small anteroom. Rivers was using it as a butler's pantry. We pushed through another door into a room that was part storeroom, part kitchen. The tables and counters were topped in stainless steel. Cardboard produce boxes were stacked against two walls. There was a large fridge and a small oven. Trays of food lay on the counters. Most of it looked like finger food, but not anything I'd seen before. I didn't have much time to take it all in.

Rivers flew through the door and drove his palms into my chest, knocking me into the door of the refrigerator. "What the hell are you doing here?" he said.

Emotion had returned to his face. He wanted to kill me. I was pretty good at picking up on that sort of thing.

"I could ask you the same question, Dennis." I smoothed my shirt with my palms.

"Me? I'm working." He was screaming quietly and the effort of keeping the volume down was making the veins in his neck pop out.

"And what sort of work would you be doing for the mob?"

He glanced at the door. "Keep your voice down."

"Why? You think they don't know they're the mob?"

"You guys want me to get canned, don't you?" He glared at me and then Ron.

"It's a fair question," said Ron. "You, an ex-con, working for a bunch of gangsters."

Rivers expelled a rush of air. "You guys are still on about that robbery. The Baker job."

"It was a burglary and yes, we're still on it. We can be dogged like that," I said.

He shook his head and laughed to himself. "Jesus, man. I've told you. I don't got nothing to do with that."

"So says you."

"Yeah, says me."

"Where have you been these past few days, Dennis?" said Ron. "Tampa, maybe?"

"Tampa? What the hell are you talking about?"

"Another Heisman theft. You got an alibi?"

"Alibi? I been at the Black Tie warehouse."

Ron smiled. "You haven't had a job in several days. I checked."

"Yeah, genius. That's why I'd been at the warehouse. After hours no one's there. So I been there prepping all this food." He waved his hands like he was modeling the spread on the Price Is Right.

"And you just happen to be working for an organized crime family," I said.

"Man, you are dumber'n grits. You think it's easy for a guy with time under his belt to get work? They ask me where I trained, what I say? Prison? Mr. Bartalotto knows the score. He don't care about that stuff. He just wants results. And you guys are messing that up."

One of the Gino's in the suits opened the door from the other room. "Problem?" he said. He sounded like he'd just stepped off the plane from Brooklyn. He was pale enough for it to be true.

"No problem." said Rivers. "Just getting my guys set up."

"Well, Mr. Bartalotto wants to know what the hell he's eating."

"Be right there."

The Gino eyeballed me and Ron without moving his head, then slipped back through the door.

Rivers turned to me. "Don't move." He turned and went through the door.

I looked at Ron. He mouthed the words, "What the?" Like we were being listened to.

I shook my head. I had no clue. Rivers came back into the kitchen.

"Tell me, sport, why does a guy who has a whole restaurant at his disposal need an ex-con caterer?"

"It's for his old lady, you moron. She spends winters down here."

"A snowbird?" said Ron.

"Yeah. She lives in Toronto. But can't handle the winters. So she spends them with her son in Boca."

"I thought he was part of a New York family?" I said.

"What am I? Genealogy.com? How the hell should I know? But the old lady is from Canada. That's why I was hired."

"How so?" I said.

"She loves some show on Canadian TV. Called Coronation Street. It's about some losers in England. It's all tea and warm beer and crap like that. But she loves it. So he says what she wants for her birthday celebration, and she says she wants to have a dinner like the morons on this show."

"And his kitchen can't do it?"

"Those guys are all Mexicans, man. They have enough trouble with American food."

"So how do you know anything about this stuff?"

"I didn't. But I have a friend works here at the club. She says to Bartalotto I can do it, so I get the job. That's where I'd been." He looked at Ron. "At the library, man. On the damned Internet. Finding recipes for what these *Coronation Street* types eat. You wouldn't believe what these English put away."

"I thought you said you were at the warehouse?" I said.

"After that I was. I was using their equipment to prep the food. They just have me serve and tend bar. I don't cook nothing. That's what I want to do, man. But I don't got no equipment, so I borrowed theirs. No harm."

"No harm," I said.

"Until you two clowns show up. Now Bartalotto's out there thinking I'm trouble and he's made a mistake. And he don't like mistakes."

"So I hear," I said.

I thought of what Sally had told me. Not big league, but vicious. I looked at Ron. He was the poster boy for sheepish. It looked like we'd got this one as wrong as we would have if we'd run around Palm Beach with clipboards asking people on the street if they'd nicked Baker's Heisman.

"Our mistake," I said. "We'll get out of your hair and let you get on with it."

"Leave? You can't just leave. He thinks you idiots work for me."

"So what do you want from us?"

"Wait there." Rivers dashed out the back.

I heard the slam of van doors and he reappeared. He threw something at me. It was a white coat, like a chef might wear. He tossed one at Ron.

"You want us to cook?" I said.

Rivers laughed. "Hell, no. Serve, man."

"I'm no waiter," I said.

"Then let's go out there and tell Mr. Bartalotto that a couple of private eyes are snooping around his club."

I looked at the food spread. "What is this stuff?"

"What they eat in England, man. That pastry one, that's a Cornish pasty."

"Okay. And what's this? It looks like a bratwurst casserole." A large dish held a row of sausages in a puff pastry.

"That's Toad in the Hole."

"Come on," I said.

"Seriously. It's sausages in Yorkshire pudding."

I picked up a breaded ball the size of a baseball. It was heavy. "And these?"

"Scotch egg. Hardboiled egg covered in sausage meat, breaded and fried."

"And they eat this, you say?"

"Swear to God. You get these out while I warm the entree." He pointed to a tray.

"Meatballs?" I said, picking up a tray of the eggs.

"Sort of. They call them faggots."

I dropped the eggs back onto the counter. "Excuse me?"

"I'm not kidding. They're meatballs made from lamb's liver and kidneys. Covered in beef caul."

"Beef caul?" said Ron. "I don't want to know, do I?"

"It's a thin membrane of fat from a cow's intestine."

Ron appeared to hold back a dry heave.

"It's served with mashed potato and peas. Like meatloaf."

"I'll never eat meatloaf again," Ron said.

"Just get the appetizers out," said Rivers.

Ron looked pale. "Appetizers? I don't know."

"Then help me with this cask ale." Rivers pointed to a small oak barrel on its side.

"They'll need that," said Ron.

"Okay?" Rivers said to me.

"Sure. We'll help you out. You serve this stuff up, you need all the help you can get." I picked up the Scotch eggs and headed out to the waiting mafia family, leaving behind my sick-looking partner, the ex-con cook, and a roomful of Yorkshire pudd, toads and faggots, and I wondered if I had just reached the low point of the Heisman case, or my career.

CHAPTER FORTY

A storm came in the next day. The clouds were massive edifices in the sky, like a hundred atom bombs had gone off. They grew darker and less distinct as the day wore on, until they were one flat mass of blackness. Then the lightning started, and then the thunder. Then it rained. Hard.

I was eating a late lunch at Longboard Kelly's. A turkey sandwich with Greek salad on the side. Mick did a good Greek salad. It was simple, the way Mick liked things. Cucumber, tomato, onion, feta and olives. A vinaigrette of olive oil, vinegar and salt. The rain pelted onto the roof like a drum band. The televisions were all tuned to the weather channel. I had to shout to be heard.

"What do they say about the storm?" I asked Mick.

"This too shall pass," he said, walking away down the bar, rubbing a clean glass with a dirty towel. The philosopher poet.

The sound of the rain was soothing. Like things were being washed away and the earth would begin anew tomorrow. I sipped some iced tea. The weather channel reporter was out in the storm. He was almost being blown away. As if this made their report more credible than the weather guy who had the sense to get in out of the rain.

The front door flung open and Danielle dashed through. She held an umbrella that looked like it had been hit by mortar rounds. Her PBSO-issue rain slicker was cascading water onto the mat on the floor. She stomped her feet a few times and poured off the raincoat and hung it near the door. Then she walked over to my spot at the bar. She sat at the end, next to me. We could see through the bar area out across the patio, where we would sit if the sun were out. The rain was creating a lake around the water feature.

Danielle put her elbow on a crab pot that sat at the end of the bar.

"Some lunch?" I said.

She shook her head. "I ate."

"Okay. So to what do I owe this pleasure?"

She smiled. Her lips stretched and tiny wrinkles formed at the corners of her mouth. "I got some news on the emails to Newt Bellingham."

"How's Jenny?"

"She's doing okay. She was in rough shape."

"I know."

Danielle looked at the crab pot under her arm. An old thing, chicken wire and wood. She fiddled with the wire. She didn't look at me. "How's Newt?"

"I think his wife leaving will cause him to see the error of his ways."

"You think?" She turned her head and looked at me.

"I know."

She turned back to the pot. "What is this thing?"

"It's a crab pot. For catching crabs."

"I know that. I mean, why is it here?"

"It belonged to a guy called Pat McGinnis. Everyone called him Stonecrab Pat. He used to catch crabs and bring the claws in here and Mick would boil them up and put them on the menu. Stonecrab Pat used to carry that pot around like it held the crown jewels. He'd come in here and drink where you're sitting."

"So why is his pot here?"

"One night he left it there. Went home and died in his sleep. No one has ever wanted to move it."

"I'm not going to get weird looks now because I've sat in the guy's seat, am I?"

"You'll get plenty of looks, but it won't be because you sat in Stonecrab Pat's seat."

"Ever the charmer." She did the smile again.

"Tell me about the emails."

Danielle took her arm off the crab pot and turned on her stool to face me. "I heard back from the email provider for the username we were looking at."

"RealPro."

"Right. That was the only user who got the Bellinghams' address. So the provider tracked the IP address, which is sort of like the physical location of every computer in the world."

"Unless the computer was on a network. Then the IP might only get us the location of the network."

"Right. And there are other ways to track a specific computer, but they're not recorded by the email provider. But here's the thing. The location of the IP that sent the email. It's in West Palm."

"Tickety-boo," I said.

"You care to take a drive with me?" she said, smiling.

"Even if you were Thelma and I was Louise."

CHAPTER FORTY-ONE

We waited until the rain abated a touch before heading out. The wipers on Danielle's patrol car still worked overtime to keep the windshield clear. We struggled to see the addresses on buildings. The cable company had told Danielle the account holder was a business. The name gave us no clue what type of business. We got to a strip mall that matched the address on Wellington Terrace. The mall was a Spanish-style, with terracotta roof tiles and whitewashed walls. It was pleasant if uninspiring. Perhaps it looked better in the sunshine.

We drove around looking for the unit that matched our address. I spotted the number and Danielle pulled into a space in front. It appeared to be a cafe and bagel house. We got out of the patrol car and dashed for the cover of the awning. Rain ran off tall palm trees like the proverbial duck's back. I looked in the window of the cafe. It was tinted dark against the sun. All I saw was my own drenched head. I pushed my wet hair back and thought I looked like Kenickie from *Grease*.

We went inside. The cafe was one of those places that doesn't know what it wants to be, tries to be everything and fails to be anything. There was an area near the window with aluminum chairs and tables. Behind that, two lounge chairs and a low table. A bench seat ran along the wall with further tables dispersed along it. At the rear was a condiment station. The counter was glass and displayed premade sandwiches and pastries, all of which looked designed for longevity, not taste. A range of bagels that looked more like Kaiser rolls with small holes in them. A coffee station dispensing house blend by the gallon. The space had the ambience of a railway station concourse at 1 a.m.

Danielle stepped to the cashier and spoke quietly. Demanding to see the owner while dressed in uniform tended to spook the cattle. The cashier moved briskly to a door in the rear. She reappeared with a young woman dressed like a barista. The woman had long blond hair and looked like she did the job to pay for her trips to the cheerleading championships. Danielle and I weaved through the tables.

"Hi, I'm Lisa. Is there a problem?"

"No problem, Lisa. We're just looking for some information," said Danielle. We sat down and Danielle slid a piece of paper over to Lisa. On it she had jotted down the name of the business and the IP address.

"Is this the business that owns the cafe?"

Lisa looked at the paper, and then at Danielle. She wasn't convinced there wasn't a problem. "Yes," she said.

"Is it your business?" I said.

She looked at me. She had aquamarine eyes and porcelain skin. "Yes."

"You're very young to be running a business," I said.

"Am I supposed to just get married and breed?" She didn't say it angrily, but I could tell she had said it before.

"I would've thought you a bit young for that, too."

"Well, I'm not. I'm twenty-three."

"I stand corrected."

"Lisa," said Danielle. "We are searching for someone who may have committed a crime. It's nothing to do with you. But we executed a warrant and discovered that the suspect may have used a computer here. Is there a computer here that someone might be able to access?"

"I have one in the office, but only I and our accounts girl use that."

Danielle looked at Lisa and then at me. She was asking silently if I believed Lisa. I did.

"But we do offer free wifi, obviously," said Lisa.

"Obviously," I said. "And anyone could access that?"

"That's the idea."

Danielle tapped the paper on the table. "Is there any way you can check if that IP address belongs to your network?"

"I can check the settings on the router." She took the paper and went into the back office.

"You don't think young people should run businesses?" said Danielle.

"Young people? What are you, Ma Kettle? I think that girl will be successful beyond her wildest dreams. But she looks too young to vote."

"You think this place will succeed?" Danielle said, looking around the cafe. There were only two customers.

"I wouldn't think mid-afternoon is hardly rush hour for a cafe, but no, I think this place will fail miserably. But I don't think she will."

"Why?"

"She's smart. Had the good instinct to make you come to the back of the shop and not stand in the window like it was a crime scene. She's articulate, she's driven and she's prepared to do the work. She's the owner, but she's wearing an apron. Ready to man, sorry, *staff* the register. But she has an accounts person, which says she understands that cash flow makes or breaks every business."

"And she's pretty."

"That won't hurt, because she'll use it but won't let it get in the way."

Danielle smiled. "So you think she's pretty."

"She's a porcelain doll. Cute as a button."

Lisa stepped out of the back room and looked at us like we had our hands in the cookie jar.

"It's our router," she said. "Does that mean trouble?"

"No," said Danielle. "Is there anyone regular who comes in and uses the Internet?"

"Most all we have are regulars. People who work in this complex, to be honest."

"We're thinking a man. More than thirty but not more than sixty."

She thought and then shook her head. "I don't know. We don't track people like that."

"Really?" I said. I made a point of looking around the mostly empty room.

"It's not always this slow."

"Really."

"Not always."

I smiled. She didn't.

"You think we're doing something wrong?" she said.

"Your cafe is empty."

"What are we doing wrong?"

"In business school they teach you a lot about understanding your weaknesses, overcoming them."

"Yes, I know."

"I didn't go to business school. I played baseball. And in baseball we were taught that the only way to win was to play to your strengths."

She thought about that and nodded. "What are my strengths?"

"Not coffee," I said, standing. Danielle stood with me.

"What do you think my strengths are?"

"Thanks for your time," said Danielle. "If you think of anything, or see anyone suspicious, please call." She handed Lisa a card. Then she turned from the table.

I looked at Lisa and she at me. I put out my hand and she took it. I pumped a quick shake.

"Your biggest strength is you," I said. I felt like Tony Robbins, giving some BS pump-up advice. Except I meant it. She was one of those people. She radiated energy. I let her hand go and followed Danielle out into the rain. It had eased and would no longer knock over a child. It just made us wet as we rushed for the car.

"You want me to drop you at home or the office?"

I looked out the window.

"Or Longboard's?"

"When do you get off?" I asked.

"Not 'til eight."

"Not Longboard's, then. Office, I guess."

She started the car.

"No wait," I said. "Where are we?"

"Wellington. You lost, sweetie? I get you all turned around?"

"Every time I see you. But I gotta make a house call around the corner. Mrs. Ferguson."

"The missing persons case?"

"Yeah."

"What do you know?"

"Nothing. Well, nothing good."

"What?"

"He's gone."

"Why?"

"Don't know. Either midlife crisis or end life crisis."

"And you're giving up?"

I glared at her. That was harsh.

"I'm sorry. I just told her you could help her."

"I did. I spoke with her. They've been sad for so long, she forgets what sunshine looks like. She just wants to move on and I don't think she believes she can do it with him. So she just wants to know."

"So what will you tell her?"

"Not all I'd like. But something. It's okay, I don't have to do this now."

"No. I took the call. I sent her to you. We'll do this together."

CHAPTER FORTY-TWO

It took a couple minutes to get to the Ferguson residence. Where we stopped the pavement was moist but not drenched, like they'd seen a spring shower rather than a tropical downpour. That was South Florida weather. Forty percent chance of rain meant, "Oh, there'll be rain all right, but it's forty percent chance that it lands on you."

The Ferguson home didn't appear to need the rain. The house was a small wood siding job. Maybe two bedrooms, half that number of bathrooms. The front yard was Arizona low maintenance. Red-colored rocks and succulents. I tried not to read too much into it, but it looked like the garden of someone who had given up.

We walked across the paving stones to the front door. I knocked, for no other reason than I wanted to be the one Mrs. Ferguson saw when she opened the door.

"Mr. Jones," she said.

She looked better. Not great, but better. She had done her hair. Not professionally, I suspected, but that wasn't my area of expertise. She wore makeup, not a lot, but it gave her face color and definition. While she might not have been the life of the party, she didn't look quite so sad. She stepped aside and let us in. We waited and she led us through to a small living room.

"Can I offer you coffee? Iced tea?"

"Iced tea," I said.

"Sweetener?"

"No, thank you, ma'am."

Danielle shook her head and smiled politely at the offer. Mrs. Ferguson went to the kitchen. I surveyed the room. The living room bled into the kitchen. Seventies dated with an eat-in table. Three doors off the living room. Four if I counted the front door. The others were two bedrooms and in between a bathroom. That left a door unaccounted for. I looked around again and found it when Mrs. Ferguson closed the fridge after retrieving the iced tea. I saw a door with a window that led out to a laundry room, and I assumed, onto the backyard. It was a modest but decent home. Not large but sufficient for a family of three. Now one.

Mrs. Ferguson returned with the tea.

"I wanted to update you," I said.

Mrs. Ferguson nodded and sat.

"It seems from the activity we've uncovered that your husband went home. To Belle Glade. There's no activity after that. The lack of activity is a concern."

"Why?"

"Because it suggests either he doesn't want to be found, or he has caused himself harm."

She nodded. "If he's left, where would he go?"

"I'm afraid I don't know. As I say, he went to Belle Glade, but a check of motel registers didn't turn anything up. Now he may have moved on, or he may still be there. Our call around was thorough but not conclusive. Some motels don't cooperate."

"Why?"

"Privacy. At this point we have no basis for a warrant."

"But he's missing."

"Unfortunately, the law would suggest he is just gone, rather than missing."

She thought for a moment, looking distantly at the coffee table between us. I sipped my tea.

"Will he come back?"

"I don't know. I wish I could tell you more."

"I can't live like this," she said, tearing up. "Not knowing if I can move on without him. Or if one day he'll just turn up out of the blue."

"There's not much more we can do right now. I suggest you call your bank and put an alert on your account and credit card. If it gets used, they will call you. If it's him, it might tell us where he's gone."

"All right."

"But he may not use the card again."

"Then we'll know nothing."

"Right. So either way you need to think about your circumstances."

"What do you mean?"

"You need to decide how you want to live your life, Mrs. Ferguson. You can choose to assume he's never coming back and take steps accordingly."

"What if he does come back?"

"Pardon me for saying so, ma'am, but you're not happy. I'd go as far as to say you may be suffering from some form of depression. You've been like this for a long time. Maybe your husband was the same and decided his only way out was to run. I don't know. But I know that you have a choice. A choice to get some medical help, some support. And a choice to move on with your life without your husband in it. He can always come back to West Palm, but that doesn't mean you have to accept him back into your life if that will make you sad."

She stared at the coffee table for a long time. Then she looked up toward the front window and blinked. As if she'd just noticed it was daytime.

"We weren't always like this, you know. We used to be happy."

Danielle and I both nodded.

"We had fun. In college. Like everyone else. Our whole lives ahead of us. Then college finished and he didn't win a prize and he pretended it didn't hurt for a while. And then he just gave up. Took a job selling cars. He couldn't have sold gold bars. His heart wasn't in it."

"What prize didn't your husband win?"

"I can't remember now. It was a long time ago. He got moody just thinking about it. He'd go into his den and come back all dark inside. So we learned to never speak of it."

"What was the prize for?"

She looked at me. "Football," she said. "Sandy was a quarterback in college."

I looked at Danielle. Her chin had dropped.

"Your husband got sad after not winning a prize for college football?"

"I know. It sounds insane."

"Ma'am, where is your husband's den?" I looked at the doors leading off the living room. I couldn't account for a den.

"It's outside. In the backyard. It's more shed, really. But he set it up like a den."

"What does he have in there?" said Danielle.

"I don't know. It's locked. I never go in. I always told him to vacuum it himself. I suppose he never did."

"Can we see the den, Mrs. Ferguson?" I said.

She led us out through the kitchen, into a long, thin room that housed a washing machine and a dryer. The country-style door let out into a decent-sized backyard. The grass was well tended but in need of a mow. A lonely rope hung from a tree branch. I suspected that there had once been a tire tied to the bottom of it. A small shed stood at the rear of the yard, under the shade of an old palm. It was the kind of shed you buy as a kit at one of the big box hardware stores, but it had been mounted properly on a concrete slab. The outside had once been a deep green and still was under its small eaves. The rest was the color of key limes. The door had a combination padlock on it.

"You have bolt cutters in the car?" I said to Danielle.

She shook her head.

"Mrs. Ferguson?"

"If we did, they'd be in here." She nodded at the shed.

"Okay." I looked at the lock. It was stainless steel and had a black dial on the front face, where a combination would be entered.

I turned back to Mrs. Ferguson. "You have a soda can?"

She led me back into the kitchen and retrieved a soda can from a bin under the sink. Canada Dry ginger ale.

"Some kitchen shears?"

She pulled a hefty pair of scissors out from a sheaf that was attached to the side of the fridge by magnets. I cut the top off the can, and then cut a section of the aluminum, about the size of a business card.

"What are you doing?" said Danielle.

"You didn't see this," I said.

I cut notches in the aluminum so the piece resembled a fat letter M. Then I folded the top down and the sides up, leaving a pointed section in the middle. It resembled a fist giving the bird. I walked back out to the shed. I held the padlock and wrapped the aluminum around the shackle. Then I worked the finger part down into the hole the shackle was bolted into. I twisted the aluminum shim around the shackle to the inside, back and forth. It took about fifteen seconds and then the lock popped open.

Danielle frowned. "Private detective school?"

"YouTube," I said.

I took the padlock off and looked at Mrs. Ferguson. She nodded, so I opened the door. The windows had been painted so the interior of the shed was as black as tar. I fumbled along the wall for a light switch, found one and flicked it on.

CHAPTER FORTY—THREE

The inside of the shed was a shrine. A shrine to the Heisman trophy. Along one wall hung pictures of every Heisman winner. The first winner, the one-man gang, Jay Berwanger. Tom Harmon of Michigan. Ernie Davis and Roger Staubach were there. Two pictures of Archie Griffin, resplendent in sideburns and Buckeye red, the only man to win the Heisman twice. Reggie Bush was there, despite losing his award in a payments scandal. And newer, digital prints of Palmer and Bradford and Cam Newton and RG3. There was a desk against the sidewall, covered in newspaper clippings and old magazines. Above the desk was a corkboard on which there were clippings. Cut-out articles and photographs of Heisman winners and their post-Heisman lives. As businessmen and restaurateurs and politicians and media personalities. A clipping from the *Palm Beach Post*, BJ Baker smiling his broad grin, chin out, stomach in. Heisman in silhouette in the background, as distinctive as the Statue of Liberty to football fans across the nation. An article on Orlando Washington upon his selling of Orlando's to a national food services company, and moving into a new independent living estate. Their celebrity tenant.

"Look at this," said Danielle.

I turned and stepped to the other sidewall. Danielle was looking at a trophy cabinet. Not dissimilar from one I had seen at BJ Baker's house. There were three tiers. The bottom two were all trophies in the name of Sandy Ferguson. Middle school. High school. College.

Mostly football, but some baseball and one for high school basketball. A very successful career. The top tier of the cabinet was vacant. A small lamp shone down on the space, accentuating its emptiness.

"Room for a Heisman?" said Danielle.

I just raised my eyebrows. I had moved on. Next to the cabinet was a map of the United States. On it were map pins, pushed into cities across the country. A lot in California, the Northeast and the South. Miami, West Palm, Tampa. Gainesville and Tallahassee. Atlanta and Tuscaloosa and Dallas. A thicket around New York. Chicago and Cincinnati. Seattle and San Francisco and Los Angeles. Some of the pins had been circled with a marker. West Palm Beach, Palm Beach, Tampa, Gainesville in Florida. Atlanta, Georgia. Auburn, Alabama. Columbus, Ohio. South Bend, Indiana.

"Why these places?"

"Heisman locations. Those he could find. Some private, some colleges. Gainesville is University of Florida. The pin in Alabama looks like Auburn. Columbus is Ohio State. South Bend, Indiana— take your pick—University of Notre Dame or the College Football Hall of Fame. Heisman nirvana."

"What about the others?"

"Players. Where they live now as opposed to where they played or where they came from."

"I can't believe it," Danielle said. "Ferguson is our guy?"

"What did Sandy do?" said Mrs. Ferguson. I'd forgotten she was even in the shed.

Danielle turned her. "Mr. Ferguson is now a suspect in a series of home invasion burglaries."

"Just because he has some newspaper clippings?" She bit at her fingernails.

"Ma'am, he has newspaper clippings of the victims."

She picked at her fingers. The sadness returned to her face.

"Mrs. Ferguson, this doesn't change anything," I said. "This is simply a symptom of your husband's sadness. You still need to take care of you."

She nodded slowly. "Will he go to jail?"

"If he did this, yes, he might."

"Will they help him in jail? With his illness, I mean?"

"I hope so." It was all I could offer. Prisons didn't tend to do much for one's mental stability.

We stepped out of the shed.

"You'd better call it in," I said.

Danielle strode off through the house. I walked across the garden with Mrs. Ferguson.

"I guess now I know," she said.

I didn't say anything. We walked up the back steps and into the kitchen.

"When you're okay to do it, I want you to come into my office. Lizzy will take you downstairs to meet with a friend of mine. A lawyer."

"You think Sandy will need a lawyer?"

"I do, but this lawyer is not for him. It's for you. You need to get your papers in order. Finances, that sort of thing. If you choose down the road to move on without your husband, this guy will be able to help you."

"You mean divorce."

"Yes," I said.

But this guy's specialty wasn't divorce. I was thinking of a man on the run. I was thinking of depression. I was thinking about life insurance. And a lawyer whose specialty was estate management.

Mrs. Ferguson picked at her fingers again. "It's a lot to take in."

"Yes. Now the sheriff's office will be sending some people to look at the shed. They will also look at things in the house. Do you have someone who can come and sit with you?"

She shook her head. "No." Her eyes were tired but she seemed beyond tears.

"Okay. I'm going to call Lizzy. She'll come and help you through it. I'll also call another friend of mine. She's a doctor. She'll come and talk to you later tonight."

"A psychiatrist?"

"She's a psychologist. But mostly she's just a good listener."

"Okay."

"And when this is done, perhaps you should visit your son. He's at college?"

"Yes. U Dub."

"Washington. Good school."

"I think he chose it because Seattle was as far away as he could get from here."

I put my hand on her shoulder. "I know that feeling. Doesn't mean he doesn't miss his mother."

She smiled. I called Lizzy to come over and Ron to get working on some background. The deputies arrived and Danielle took them out the back. When Lizzy arrived I sat her down with Mrs. Ferguson. Then Danielle and I headed back to our offices.

CHAPTER FORTY—FOUR

Ron was sitting at my desk when I strode into the office. He had my computer up and was working it with the concentration generally reserved for an Apollo launch.

"Our missing car salesman, eh?" he said.

"You just gotta keep pulling threads until the dress falls apart. That's what Lenny used to say."

"Lenny would've used scissors."

"So what do you know?"

Ron stopped and looked at me. "You aren't going to believe this guy."

I sat in one of the visitor's chairs. "Tell me."

"You said he was sad?"

"I'd say he was clinically depressed and untreated for twenty years. Why?"

"He did play college football. Quarterback. Big Ten conference so I don't recall him. But the stats look good. He could play."

"So what happened?"

Ron looked at the screen and then back to me. "He became a finalist for the Heisman, that's what."

"But didn't win."

"Twice."

"Twice?" I said.

"Junior and senior years he came in second. Both years."

"Ouch."

"Senior year by forty votes."

"Double ouch."

"Yeah, and get this. There are six voting regions, right? He won four of the six, but lost the trophy by forty votes."

"Okay. So that bites. But let's face it; it's not the end of the world. Peyton Manning was a two-time finalist. He came second in '97 to Charles Woodson. It didn't seem to hurt him. So what happened to Ferguson?"

"Two things," said Ron. "One, if what you say is true, he was suffering from a depression that was just looking for an excuse to burst out. And two, Peyton Manning got drafted number one and became an instant squillionaire a few months after missing out on the Heisman. It would've cushioned the blow somewhat."

"Did Sandy Ferguson nominate for the draft?"

"Yes and no."

"Go on."

Ron clicked a key and changed screens. "Seems he was due to participate in drills at the NFL scouting combine. He didn't show."

"Didn't show?"

"Two days, no one knew where he was. Says here he claimed to have had bronchitis. Not too many people bought that. But apparently he got a second chance at his college pro day. Six teams turned up to see him work out."

"And?"

"No show again. Everybody put him in the too hard basket. Everybody passed."

"So he goes from there to selling cars in Belle Glade," I said.

"And the knot in his gut just grew every year."

I looked over Ron's shoulder through the window. The clouds looked less threatening but didn't seem interested in leaving.

"So we know who he is. We more or less know why he's doing what he's doing," said Ron. "So what's next?"

"Not what, where," I said. "I think Gainesville. University of Florida looks like the candidate."

"You tell Rollie?"

I laughed. "Yeah. He wasn't interested."

"What is that guy's problem? He was first-choice QB when you were at Miami; you were his backup. If anything, you should hate him."

"Yeah."

"Do you hate him?" Ron smiled.

"I don't care about him. He was, is, a competitive guy. He never understood that it didn't make you less of a competitor to acknowledge when someone was better than you. And he was better than me. At quarterbacking, anyway. He couldn't throw a curveball to save himself."

"He still pissed about the Brady thing?"

"Yeah, but he's assistant AD at a decent program now. And he's going to get in the way. I can feel it."

"So what do you want to do?"

"Wait to hear from Danielle. They've got something to work with now."

CHAPTER FORTY—FIVE

Ron and I waited, got bored and headed to Longboard Kelly's. It was late and the chance of getting anything useful before morning was slim. The clouds were breaking and the patio at Longboard's was resplendent in colored party lights. Muriel threw us each a towel, and we wandered around the patio, wiping the water off the seats while she poured us a couple of beers. We got back to the patio bar, wiped our own seats and threw the towels in the small sink behind the bar. Ron lifted his beer and winked at Muriel.

"On the house, I assume."

"Ha," she laughed. He swept his hand across the view of the patio we had just toweled off.

"We did work for it." He smiled and took a long look at Muriel's large breasts. Her lime green tank top didn't leave much to the imagination.

"Honey, when Mick starts giving out freebies you'll be second in line, right after me." She gave him a great smile and arched her back a little. The effect was to push her cleavage even further out. It would have looked amazing in a 3D movie. She turned and wandered down to the other end of the bar. We both watched her cutoff denims and bronzed legs make the journey. Ron turned to me. He realized he was still holding his beer aloft.

"The view is worth every penny. Here's cheers." We clinked glasses and took a long, cool drink.

"So you still think he's headed for Gainesville?" said Ron.

"That's what my gut is saying."

"Should we be heading there?"

"Tempting," I said. "But it's still a hunch. If it was all I had, I'd go with it. But we know who the guy is now. So Danielle might be able to track him down. There were other places circled on the map. He might be headed to one of them. He didn't leave an itinerary."

We were on our third beer and the patio was filling up with regulars. Ron's golf ladies came in and one of them gave him a little wave of the fingers. We saluted back with our glasses. Danielle walked in from the parking lot, still in full uniform. She looked tired. She let out a sigh.

"Long day?" I said.

She smiled weakly. "We got something."

I slid off my stool and gave it to her. I would have offered her my beer, but she was in uniform and there were rules and she was a stickler for those sorts of rules. I didn't debate it. Impressions count for a lot in her line of work. Mine too, sometimes.

"We asked Ferguson's bank to run any new accounts. He opened a new credit card just after he was fired."

"His wife didn't mention it," I said.

"She didn't know. He signed up for electronic statements only. At the RealPro email address."

"Not too clever."

"I don't think we're dealing with a master criminal here."

"Just a sad, angry man," said Ron.

"So what does the new card tell us?" I said.

Danielle ran her hands through her hair. "A fair bit. The day before the Orlando Washington break-in, Ferguson used the card to get a cash advance at an ATM in the fairgrounds in the city of Orlando."

"Do we know what was on at the fairgrounds."

Danielle nodded. "A gun show."

"Spectacular."

"So we can guess where he got the Colt he used on Orlando," she said.

"Isn't there a waiting period at gun shows, too?"

"Only if you buy from a registered dealer. Sales from one private citizen to another don't require it."

"A lot of private citizens sell guns at the shows?"

"No," said Danielle. "It's mostly dealers, and most follow the rules because it's their livelihood. But some private sellers hang around and sell their own weapons at the entrance to the fairgrounds. For cash. I'm betting that's where Ferguson got his Colt."

I was going to mention that Ferguson was only alleged to have committed the crimes. But she was tired, and it was pedantic until we got to court, and I thought he was as guilty as all hell.

"Doesn't anyone police the show?" asked Ron.

"Sure," said Danielle. "The local sheriff usually. But these guys aren't running around with loaded weapons or making trouble. They're just selling an unwanted shotgun or revolver. No law against it, so the guys on duty don't make trouble where there isn't any." We sipped our beers and Danielle looked into the dark barroom.

"Any other activity?"

"He stayed in Tampa after he hit Orlando Washington. Nothing on the credit card, so he paid cash somewhere that wasn't fussed with ID, or he slept in his car. Either way he rented a car the following morning at Tampa International. Toyota Corolla, Tennessee plates."

"We could've driven right by him," I said.

"Hell, he could've stayed in the same motel. We just wandered up off the beach. I don't recall them asking for ID."

"True. But I've got an honest face."

She smiled. "After that nothing. Yet. We got a subpoena so the bank has an alert on the card. He uses it, someone in card services gets a flag and calls me."

"So we wait and see which shoe drops," I said. She nodded slowly.

"In that case, I think you need a drink," said Ron.

"I'm still in uniform," she said.

"You come in the patrol car or yours?" I said.

"Mine."

"Then what you need is a shower, one of my extra special massages, a glass of wine and a good sleep."

"That sounds like heaven."

"I'll take you. We'll get your car in the morning. I'll just tell Mick." I leaned across the bar. Mick was down the other end, chatting to a regular in a John Deere cap.

"Hey, Mick, we're just leaving a car in the lot overnight, okay?"

"No overnight parking, Miami. This look like the long-term lot at Palm Beach International?"

"Even for Sheriff's Deputy Castle?"

"Five-day maximum, Miami. Then I'll have to have it cleaned." He turned back to John Deere.

Danielle slipped off her bar stool. "Sorry to love you and leave you, Ronnie," she said.

"Don't worry about me. I'm a big boy." He surveyed the patio crowd with a smile. "I can look after myself."

CHAPTER FORTY-SIX

I handed Danielle a glass of Marlborough sauvignon blanc while she was in the shower. When she came out she was wrapped in two towels, one around her body, one around her head. Her glass was empty. Her cheeks were flushed and her eyelids were heavy. I poured her another glass and massaged her shoulders on the patio. She fell asleep mid-massage. I'd felt like that a few times, almost drifting off during a great massage, so I took it as a sign of my prowess as a masseur.

I lifted her up and carried her inside. Muscle might weigh more than fat, but it is infinitely easier to carry to bed. I lay her down, unwrapped the towels, looked at her sleeping beauty for a moment, and then pulled the sheet over her. I did the nightly rounds like a jailer, flicking locks and checking windows and dousing the lights. Then I walked back to the bedroom and stripped and got into bed. I was asleep before I would've hit the letter E in the alphabet song.

I must've slept deep because when I woke I felt good enough to run through a wall. A phone was ringing. Danielle jumped out of bed naked and ran into the living room. I thought about wandering out and watching her chat on the phone in her birthday suit, but I was happy enough with the image it played in my mind so I stayed put. A couple of minutes later Danielle came back in and sat on the bed.

"That was the bank. He used his credit card."

"Where?"

"Last night. At a gas station off I-75."

"Which one's I-75?"

"I-75 outside of Ocala."

"Hit me again."

"Are you awake?"

I was looking at a beautiful woman sitting naked on my bed. It didn't get more awake.

"Getting there," I said.

"I-75 runs from Fort Lauderdale across to the Gulf coast, then up north to the Canadian border."

"Through Tampa."

"Right. And?"

I sat up. "Gainesville."

"Good boy, I knew you could do it." She had her cell phone in her hand. She started dialing a number off a piece of paper. "Here's the thing. He spent twelve hundred at the gas station."

"Lot of gas."

"Yeah. I'm calling the gas station, find out what Ferguson bought." She finished dialing and put the phone to her ear.

"We gotta get moving," she said to me. "You jump in the shower."

"I'm good to go, I don't need a shower."

"Yes, you do."

"You saying I smell?"

"Baby, you're giving off all kinds of manliness, and it makes me hot. But not everyone will agree." She stood and directed her attention to the phone. Her voice dropped an octave.

"Hello. This is Sheriff's Deputy Danielle Castle," she said, walking out of the room.

I sniffed my armpits, got nothing, but showered anyway. When I came out to the living room Danielle was dressed in jeans and a white t-shirt. She handed me a mug of coffee.

"What's the deal," I said, sipping.

"They're not just a gas station."

"Of course not."

"Next door they run a fireworks outlet."

"Fireworks?"

"Aha." She sipped her coffee.

"That seems like a lot of fireworks to me."

"Aha."

"Aren't fireworks illegal in Florida?"

"Only the ones that leave the ground, explode or shoot projectiles."

"That would leave what?"

"Sparklers."

"He bought twelve hundred bucks worth of sparklers?"

She shook her head. "There are exceptions."

"Of course."

"If you own a railroad or fish hatchery and are using the fireworks for safety or to scare away birds."

"Seriously."

"It's in the Florida statutes."

"How would you prove that you own a fish hatchery?"

"Buyer just signs a waiver saying they are buying pursuant to the relevant statutes."

"And Ferguson signed a waiver."

"Aha."

"So he could recreate the 4th of July."

"On a small scale."

"Why?"

"That's the question," she said.

I drained my coffee. "We gotta get to Gainesville."

CHAPTER FORTY—SEVEN

The tires on my Mustang spent more time in the air than on blacktop as we sped north on the Florida turnpike and I-75. I wished we had Danielle's patrol car and its flashing lights, or at least a vanilla Ford Taurus over my red Mustang. But we were untroubled by the highway patrol the whole way. We arrived as the breakfast places were starting to heat up. There was a palpable energy in the streets of Gainesville. It was odd for a Saturday morning in a college town, and odd because the energy resulted from an event that was taking place seventy miles away in Jacksonville.

But it wasn't just any Saturday in Gainesville. It was a Gator football Saturday, and it wasn't just any event. It was *the game*. University of Florida Gators versus University of Georgia Bulldogs. In this part of the world it was bigger than the Super Bowl.

"These people looked dressed for war," said Danielle, as we wove through the streets toward the college campus.

"They're bitter enemies," I said.

"Why?"

"The states are neighbors. What do you expect?" I smiled.

Danielle shrugged.

"The two colleges clash every year and have done so for more or less a century. The rivalry is fierce and at times bitter. The schools can't even agree on when the first game was played, or how many games there've been. It was originally a home and home fixture, but the game is now played annually on so-called neutral turf, at the NFL stadium in Jacksonville."

"That doesn't seem fair to Georgia."

"It's not. But holding the game in Jacksonville rather than at the campus stadia makes the two universities fifty percent more money. So Reggie Bush might have lost his Heisman for taking payments as a student-athlete, but the colleges know where their cookies are baked."

We hit the outskirts of the sprawling University of Florida campus and parked the car. The campus took up a fair chunk of the city of Gainesville's real estate. It took us fifteen minutes to locate and then get to the athletic complex. There were people everywhere. Students, I assumed, but some looked like they had voted for Nixon.

"Now remember, the athletic director isn't here, and the assistant isn't my biggest fan."

"What's his problem exactly? Didn't he beat you out?"

"He did. But it's not about that. He got drafted his senior year by New Orleans. Spent a year with the Saints, but never got a start. His record as backup was 1-4."

"You have that committed to memory?"

I smiled. "I do. But that's not the good bit."

"Oh, there's a good bit?"

"He got traded by the Saints at the end of the year. To New England."

"Your old stomping ground."

"More or less. So he tracks me down. I was in my senior year by then. He calls me up to tell me he's been bought by the Patriots. That he's going to show them how it's done, since I was obviously typical of the quality of quarterback in New England."

"What did you do?"

"What could I do? Nothing. I couldn't believe he'd called me out of the blue to taunt me about the team I supported as a kid."

"Very grown up."

"Very. So I said whatever, enjoy the Boston winters and I hung up."

We arrived at the building we wanted.

"So what happened?"

"Turns out he goes to Foxboro for five days to do medicals, training drills, that sort of thing. Dot the i's before the Pat's commit to him. But the coaching staff have all been in New York for the draft, and they had thrown their sixth round pick at a quarterback. One hundred and ninety-ninth pick overall. And they umm-and-aah, but eventually they tell Rollie that they're going with this other guy as backup."

"Who was the other guy?"

"Tom Brady."

"Him I've heard of."

"Yeah. League MVP, Super Bowl MVP, Super Bowl winner. He's got all the silverware."

"And a hot wife."

"She ain't you, but she's alright."

Danielle smirked. She knew it was a line, but she liked it anyway.

"So what happened to Rollie?"

"Pat's cut him loose. No one else wanted him, so that was that."

"And he came here?"

"Tennessee coaching staff at first, but that didn't work out. People management was never his strong suit. So he went back to New Orleans, got his MBA at Tulane, and applied for a position in the Athletic Department here at Florida."

"Doesn't seem like such a bad deal."

"It's not. You know how many guys would've killed for a snap in the pros? He won a game. But for him, it wasn't enough. He actually thinks the Pat's made the wrong choice. That with him instead of Brady they would have won more titles."

"A touch conceited."

"With a capital C, and a capital all the other letters. But here's the kicker. He blames me."

"You? Why?"

"Because I was a Pat's fan as a kid. Still am, I guess. But he thinks I was like Coach Belichick's right-hand man. Working against him."

She smiled. "But you weren't, were you?"

"I haven't even been to Foxboro Stadium since high school."

"This Rollie sounds a little too much like Sandy Ferguson. Are all ex-jocks like that?"

"You'd be surprised," I said. "There are a lot of guys out there can't get past the glory days. Some just manage it better than others."

She shook her head. "I weep for the species."

"And I thank you for it. You want to take this?" I said, pointing at the building we were in front of. A glowing blue sign read, *Campus Police.*

"I got it."

We walked in to a small waiting area, linoleum floor and low-backed, uncomfortable-looking chairs. A desk topped by glass that went all the way to the ceiling. Like a bank. Except the part of the teller was being played by a hard-looking guy in a police uniform. And he was packing a sidearm, which tellers didn't tend to do.

"Help you?" he said. The safety glass made him sound like he was yelling from the bottom of a well.

Danielle put her badge against the window. "Deputy Castle, Palm Beach Sheriff's Office. Can I speak to whomever is in charge?"

The guy looked long and hard at the badge, and then at Danielle. He was more impressed by the latter but worked hard not to show it. He got off his seat slow, like he had hemorrhoids, and waddled back across the open office area. It was empty. He stepped into an office we couldn't see and disappeared. He was away for about two minutes by my count. Way too long to ask and answer a request from a fellow law enforcement officer. The desk guy came back out and took his sweet time walking back to us. He hauled himself back up onto his perch before he said anything.

"Lieutenant will see you."

He hit a button and the door beside us gave a grinding electronic buzz, so we pushed our way through. The desk guy didn't offer directions, so we walked to the office he had been in. There was an old man sitting inside. He was in uniform and had a thick gray mustache that made him look like a walrus.

Danielle stepped forward. The Walrus blinked. No doubt the desk guy had told the Walrus who she was, but he was going to make her do it again, anyway.

"Lieutenant, my name is Danielle Castle of the Palm Beach Sheriff's Office." She showed him the badge.

He looked at it without really looking. "You're a long way from home, Deputy."

"Yes, sir. We're on a case, a series of home invasion burglaries."

"You don't say."

"Yes, sir. And we have reason to believe the next burglary may take place here."

"In a police station?" The guy was a real card.

"On the university campus."

The Walrus rubbed his mustache. I guess the plus side of having to look so ridiculous all the time was it gave him something to do with his hands.

"Home invasions," he said.

"Yes, sir."

"Don't got too many homes on a college campus."

"No, sir, but we think the suspect might be escalating."

"Escalating? He done anything but houses before?"

"No, sir."

"So I'll put an extra patrol on the dormitories."

"We don't think he's interested in the dorms, sir."

"Well now, missy, you're getting all confused."

"She's not confused, pal, you're just not hearing right," I said.

"I don't recall asking you a question, boy."

"And I don't recall the section in the Constitution that says I have to give a damn."

He shifted in his large seat, but his face didn't change. The walrus mustache hid any emotions he might've had. "You on my campus, boy. You best remember that."

"And your job is to protect the campus. You best remember that."

"You don't tell me what my job is."

"Who does? The Athletic Department?"

"Yes," came a voice from behind me.

I didn't need to turn around. I knew the voice. And I knew why the desk guy had taken so long telling the Walrus we were here.

"That so?" I said to the Walrus.

"No," he said, glancing over my shoulder. "But when the Athletic Department says there's troublemakers on campus on game day, I gotta listen. Like you said, smart boy. Protect the school."

"Troublemakers?" said Danielle. "Sir, I am a law enforcement officer trying to share information."

The body behind Danielle and I pushed between us.

I hadn't seen Rollie Spenser in years. The time had been kind to his face but not his hair. He was lean and long, but I still looked down on him by two inches. He looked about eighteen years old, but his jet-black hair was beating a hasty retreat from the crown of his head. He'd compensated for the hair loss by growing a Burt Reynolds mustache thirty years too late. He stepped into the room and clapped his hands together, like he was ordering attention at a school assembly.

"When we need help from South Florida, we'll call Don Johnson." He smiled like he'd landed a killer gag.

"What?" said Danielle.

"Don Johnson, Miami Vice," he said.

She looked at me. "What is this guy talking about?"

"His fashion god," I said.

Rollie stood tall to me. "We don't need deadbeat private eyes on our campus." He turned to the Walrus. "Lieutenant, please escort this man off the campus."

"What about me?" said Danielle.

Rollie looked her up and down. "You are welcome to stay, Deputy. Unless you feel compelled to leave with this gumshoe."

The Walrus unplugged himself from his chair and stood.

I shrugged. "No good deed goes unpunished," I said. I extended my hand to Rollie. "No hard feelings."

He responded by curling his lip. "Nothing but hard feelings," he said.

"Grow a pair, will you," said Danielle.

Rollie's face flushed. He wiped his hands on his trousers, then took my hand and with a minimum of effort he shook it.

I smiled. "I see you still got those little baby hands."

Rollie snapped his hand back like I'd given him a taser shot. "Get out," he said.

"What did the *Times-Picayune* say when the Saints let you go? Hands better suited to light opera than pro football. That was it, wasn't it?"

"I said get out!" His pencil-thin neck pushed at the seams of his shirt. He was going an unnatural purple color.

I ushered Danielle out of the office. As we walked back through the empty office space, Rollie stormed by and grabbed at the door to the small foyer. He pulled at it with an effort that might have yanked it off its hinges had it opened. But it didn't. It didn't even move in the frame. It was a good door. Instead Rollie ripped his hand off the knob. He growled at the knob and tried again. No dice. Then his brain clicked into gear and he glared at the desk guy.

The desk guy blinked slowly, and then moved his arm even slower until he hit the door release button. The door gave the same electronic buzz it had when we came in. Rollie turned the knob, lurched through the door and stormed out. We waited at the same door for the Walrus to make his way out. He bounced off desks like a dodge 'em car. I held the door open with my foot. The Walrus squeezed by, and then stepped out the glass door to the small forecourt out front. He let the door close behind him. I opened it for Danielle and then stepped out myself.

"Where's your car?" said the Walrus.

"Other side of campus," I said.

"We'll take mine," he said. He wasn't walking across campus for all the sunshine in Florida.

We got in a blue Ford Taurus marked Campus Police. It had a blue and red bar of lights across the roof. The inside looked like a base model Taurus. Lots of gray plastic. The only addition was a radio handset mounted to the dash. He drove about the same speed he walked, like putting his foot down on the pedal could use a few extra calories that he might need later.

"Lot of students about today," I said as we drove around the perimeter of the campus.

"Yep," said the Walrus. The hair from his mustache curled around his lip and went in his mouth. I guessed if you tried hard enough you could get used to anything.

"Busy for a Saturday."

"Georgia game."

"Isn't that in Jacksonville?"

"Yep," he said, watching a group of five young men in Gator colors and no shirts congregated on the sidewalk. "Not everyone goes, but everyone watches."

"Where?"

"Bars, houses, dorms. There's a big screen in the band shell on Flavet Field."

"But you're shorthanded."

"Yep. Lots of guys gone to Jacksonville. Extra hands." We drove around the southern edge of the campus. "How'd you know we was shorthanded?"

"We walked across campus and didn't see a single cop. Then we got to your station and the place was completely empty. So I gotta ask, where is everyone?"

He nodded.

"Plus, they left you in charge. Gotta be pretty short of men to do that."

He didn't look at me, but he sucked his mustache. "You got a smart mouth, you know that."

"Yep," I said. I pointed to a Porsche Carrera that was parked in the same lot as my Mustang. It was one of the old models, classical lines, mustard yellow. It spoke of someone who didn't make a lot of money but carried the pretensions of someone who did.

"That's me," I said.

The Walrus gave a *that figures* grunt, and pulled over. He looked back at me. He couldn't turn far enough to see Danielle.

"Look, you might think we're all hayseeds up here, but I meant what I said. I got a campus to protect. But I also got to look after me. Pissing off the Athletic Department, the boosters? That's a fast track to ending up a rent-a-cop in the local mall."

I looked at the kids walking around us, all dressed like advertisements for The Gap or Abercrombie, and I wondered how he would notice the difference.

"That's your choice," I said.

"You don't know it here. Ain't no choice."

I opened the door. "Thanks for the ride."

"Wait," he said.

I looked back at him.

"This burglary. Where do you think they'll hit?"

I looked at Danielle and then at the Walrus. "Word was Diamond Village Apartments. You know it?"

"I do."

I climbed out onto the street and offered a hand to Danielle. She slammed the door and the Taurus pulled away. I ambled over to the Porsche and looked back to the Taurus and watched it turn left onto Museum Road.

"Diamond Village?" said Danielle. "What was that about?"

"We just drove past a sign for it. I figure it must be on the opposite side of the campus from the football stadium."

"Why do you want him on the opposite side of the campus from the football stadium? What are you up to?"

"Culling the deadwood. I know Ferguson's going to be here. And today, with the game in Jacksonville and every cop and his K-9 looking that way? Today just feels right."

"I agree," she said. "But what about Lieutenant beanbag there? You don't want them looking after the crown jewels?"

"No, I did. I wanted to warn Rollie. And if the director was here, I bet we'd be setting up a perimeter right now around the football complex. But anyone with any brains is in Jacksonville. That leaves Rollie and the Keystone Kops. All they'll do is scare Ferguson off."

"True. But if they're all looking the other way, and we're off campus, who's watching for Ferguson?"

"Who says we're going off campus?"

CHAPTER FORTY—EIGHT

We headed for the Reitz Student Union Building to get some breakfast. The Union was like a mini version of Florida itself. Chain restaurants as far as the eye cared to look. We chose the Orange and Brew cafe and grabbed a panini and coffee. The panini was roasted vegetable and tasted bland, but the coffee was excellent. I took a second cup. There was a lot of foot traffic in the Union. Students were grabbing food and running errands and getting a final bit of study done before the kickoff at three thirty. Everyone was wearing something in the Gator colors of orange and blue. When I noticed that, I finally got the name of the cafe we were in.

"So if Ferguson is going to strike here, when do you think he'll do it?" asked Danielle, sipping her coffee.

"If it were me, two options. During the game today, when every eye on campus is looking at a television screen."

"And option two?"

"Tonight after the game."

"When half the campus is drunk and celebrating."

"Exactly. But that's the negative about that option. What if Georgia wins?"

"They're students. They'll commiserate and get drunk."

"Probably."

"Plus, it'll be dark."

"Yeah, I like dark. That fits with his past MO."

"Of course, it's the only thing that fits with his past MO."

I swished my coffee in its paper cup. It sloshed around in a circle. Everything was a circle.

"If he escalates to doing a big job like this, all bets are off for MOs," I said.

"I agree."

"So we need to be ready for anything."

"Helpful." She smiled.

"Okay, how? How does he get into where the Heismans are?" I said.

"He walks in. They're on display, aren't they?"

"They are." I swallowed the last of my coffee. "We need to see it."

We walked through the campus. There was a large grass area with a band shell at one end. In the band shell a giant video screen had been erected. Banks of black speakers, the height of two men, stood either side. There was video on screen. Anchors for what looked like ESPN. I wondered if I'd see Beccy Williams. There was no sound accompanying the video. Groups of students had staked claims on the grass with picnic blankets and bedsheets. We wandered up toward the stadium. Danielle drew looks from more than a few of the guys we passed. A woman among girls.

We skipped across Stadium Road. There were a surprising number of people around given that the stadium wasn't hosting an event. We got to the plaza in front of the Heavener Football Complex. It was more than a training facility. It was a temple to Gator football. The plaza out front was protected by a life-size statue of a bull alligator. It was an impressive piece of work. The beast looked ready to charge anyone wearing the wrong colors. People gathered around the statue, taking photographs. Granite pavers in the walkway featured the university's All-American players.

A two-story atrium of glass let the Florida sun shine on the trophies in the foyer. The national championship trophies had pride of place. The cathedralesque space was quiet. People spoke in hushed tones as they viewed the history of the University of Florida Gators. High-definition televisions showed highlights of great players and great games. The school's collection of SEC championship trophies stood proudly. I wandered over to the right side of the atrium. I stood back from the line of people passing by the trophies housed there. The distinctive stiff-arm fend of the Heisman. In triplicate.

"That's them?" whispered Danielle.

I nodded.

"They've had three winners?"

I nodded again. "Steve Spurrier, '66. Danny Wuerffel, '96. Tim Tebow, '06."

I waited while Danielle ambled up and looked at the trophies. I could see she was looking at the cases as much as the Heismans themselves. She wandered around like she was a tourist for a while, and then came back to me.

"Angry looking guy, this Heisman." She grinned.

"Actually the trophy itself isn't John Heisman. It was named in his honor after his death, but the model for the statuette was an NYU player called Ed Smith."

"Why do you know that?"

"Why do you know how to crochet?"

"I don't know how to crochet."

I smiled and shrugged.

She jabbed me in the ribs. "You are so going to pay for that later."

We surveyed the space as we walked out, and then we did a slow lap around the football stadium itself. There were only two logical approaches to the football complex, both alongside the Ben Hill Griffin Stadium. Gale Lemerand Drive to the west, Stadium Road to the south. The atrium holding the trophies was on the southwest corner. The Bull Gator stood guard over the intersection.

I wanted to stand by the Gator statue and watch over the
atrium, but I didn't want to do what I figured the Walrus would do,
and spook Ferguson. We wandered away, through Graham Woods,
past a swimming pool. Sound was now coming from the turrets of
speakers on Flavet Field. We skirted some tennis courts and came in
behind the band shell. Flimsy security fencing kept the path
separated from the band shell and the video and audio equipment
inside.

We came out onto the field. The crowd had grown. People
dotted the park on blankets, picnicking and sneaking beers and
harder stuff. Everyone was facing the band shell. The big screen
showed the heaving masses in Jacksonville. The announcers were
screaming over the noise, pumping up an audience that needed no
pumping. We wandered counterclockwise around the field. I was
watching the crowd and the screen, and then bouncing my eyes to
the perimeter. If I were Ferguson I would be loving this crowd. A
big group like this was attracting a lot of attention away from the
stadium and the trophies in the atrium.

Danielle was glancing at her phone. She had a photograph of
Ferguson on the screen. I wasn't looking at it. I'd taken a good look
on the drive to Gainesville, and I figured I was looking for a posture
more than a face. I doubted he'd walk around campus in the cowboy
getup, but I had the costume in the back of my mind.

We did the lap and stood in the corner of the field. The screen
showed the University of Georgia team running onto the field in
Jacksonville. The assembled crowd in front of us booed and jeered
with a passion that surprised me. The boos died away and the screen
cut to the University of Florida team and the crowd erupted into
cheers and screams. It was like a wall of sound that went on and on.
I tapped Danielle's shoulder and we jogged away from the field and
back toward the stadium. I had a bad feeling. Like we'd just seen a
perfect time to break into the atrium.

Once I could see the entrance to the football complex in the distance I slowed to a brisk walk. The plaza was sparsely populated. People were making their way to a television screen to watch the big game. There certainly wasn't any kind of mayhem. I settled onto a small brick wall that surrounded an oak tree outside the Gator corner dining facility. We were kitty-corner from the entrance to the football complex. We sat in the shade and waited.

"I thought something might've happened then," said Danielle.

"Me too."

"We can't sit here all afternoon."

"No."

"Bit obvious."

"Yeah."

On any given day we might have passed for students wasting away the afternoon, or tourists resting our weary feet from viewing all that was Gator athletics. But today we looked out of place. The only people in the whole town who weren't watching the game. If Ferguson were on the lookout for trouble, he'd be looking for us. So I kissed Danielle. Cupped her chin in my hand, turned her head and kissed her. She was hard to faze. She didn't recoil at all. Just leaned into it and gave as good as she got. We stayed like that for longer than was necessary. When we parted, Danielle gave me that half grin.

"Nice diversion," she said.

"Nice wasn't the word I was thinking of."

"Bought us an extra two minutes sitting here."

"That was the plan."

"And then what?"

"I'll do it again."

"Can you keep your mind on the job if you do it again?"

"What job?"

She smiled and stood. We heard a roar from the crowd on the field. Danielle turned in that direction. She was looking at the building that was behind us.

"Florida score?" she said.

"Sounds that way."

The roar was subsiding when I heard a whistle and a bang behind me.

"Fireworks," said Danielle.

I turned and looked. The late afternoon light was fading fast but it wasn't close to dark. But I saw an orange shower of fireworks falling. Two more whistles and two more bangs and starbursts of green and blue. Then a rapid fire of bursts, somewhere between an Uzi and paintball. Then a deep boom and a fireball exploded into the sky over Flavet Field and all hell broke loose.

CHAPTER FORTY-NINE

Danielle reacted fast and got to the field ahead of me. She stopped on a dime and I almost ran into her. The field was in chaos. People were running in all directions. It was like a human pinball. A blond girl in an orange tank top slapped into my shoulder. She spun but caught herself before she fell. Like an ice dancer.

"Are you okay?" I asked.

"Terrorists!" she yelled, and she spun again and ran off.

I turned back to the field. The band shell was indeed a shell. It had been blasted apart. The screen had disappeared and an acrid-smelling bonfire had taken its place. The central fire was still spitting fireworks in all directions at random intervals.

"Fireworks gone wrong," Danielle said.

"Not terrorists."

We looked at each other at the same time, as the same realization hit home in each of our heads. We sprinted back in the direction we'd come from. Emergency services sirens were ringing out across the twilight. Everyone with a uniform and a badge was running to the open field. They were like salmon against the stream of people running away from the blast. We got to the corner where we had been sitting. Where we had kissed. It wasn't so tranquil. People fled down both sides of the stadium. Danielle and I buffeted our way across the intersection to the statue of the Bull Gator. Up the stairs and into the atrium. The space was empty. A security guard was locking doors on the outside, but was on his knees playing with a lock as we dashed by, into the room full of trophies.

Everything was as it should be. The high-definition screens were still showing Gator highlights. The national championship crystal trophies shone in the spotlights. We ran to the Heismans. Three cabinets. Three crude holes in the glass. Three empty spaces. My mouth may have made an audible noise as it hit the floor. Each of the cabinets was missing the front plate of glass. Large chunks of glass lay inside the cabinets.

"Hey, you there." It was the security guy. Finally locked down and completely on top of things.

"Call it in," I said. "There's been a burglary."

"I said don't move." He took out his sidearm. He looked like he'd had some training, but not enough not to do something stupid.

"No, you didn't, genius. You never asked us not to move. Just call it in."

"Don't tell me what to do."

Danielle slowly lifted her badge. "Sheriff's Office," she said. "Call it in."

He hesitated. The training had only gone so far.

"Do it!" she yelled. "Or you'll be the guy that lost the university's Heismans."

He didn't seem to need further prompting. He grabbed a phone from the reception counter and dialed. Then he waited by the front door. He didn't take his eyes off us.

"Were you here when the fireworks went off?" I asked.

"No talking," he said.

"Okay. You're right. You should definitely let the guy get away."

"Yes, I was here. What of it?"

"What did you do?"

"We heard the bang, I rushed out, saw the fireball. Thought it was terrorists. So I followed lockdown procedure."

"Which is?"

"To lock the place down." He looked at me like I was the dumbest hayseed ever to cross his path.

"Were there people here?"

"Not many. Most were off watching the game."

"You don't show it?" said Danielle, gesturing to the array off high-definition televisions.

"No, ma'am. We don't want boisterous fans damaging the exhibits."

"So what did the people do?" I said.

"They all ran out. I told them I was locking 'em in or locking 'em out. They chose out."

"All of them?"

"You see anyone else here?"

"Anyone go out with a big bag or anything? Backpack?"

"Nope."

"There a back way out?"

"Only through the football complex."

After that we waited. The first to arrive was the Walrus. He waddled through the door, took one look at Danielle and me, and shook his head.

"Diamond Village," he said.

I shrugged.

"Doesn't look good for you," he said.

Second to arrive was Rollie Spenser. I figured if Beccy Williams, State Attorney Edwards and Detective Ronzoni arrived, I'd have the full house. Rollie banged at the door, but the security guard didn't let him in. This didn't improve his mood. He banged harder. The Walrus looked up and barked at the security guard to let him in.

"I want that man arrested," he yelled as he stormed in.

"You need to call the police," I said.

"The police are here," Rollie said. He looked at the Walrus. "Arrest him."

"You need to call the real police," I said.

"The University of Florida Police are real police," he spat.

"The Department is a real police department, but this guy is a joke."

"You trying to annoy me?" said the Walrus. "This is my turf."

"And the university's Heisman trophies got stolen off your turf and on your watch."

"You did that."

"And while the perp gets away, you are sitting on your donut-induced backside doing what you do best. Nothing."

"Where are the trophies, Jones?" said Rollie.

I smiled. "And we tried to warn you. A fellow law enforcement officer told you it was going to happen and you blew her off. I'm sure the university president will be thrilled to hear that. Boosters too."

CHAPTER FIFTY

Another bang on the door and another cop came in. This one wore a different badge on his shoulder. He had thick arms and was as black as coal.

"What the hell you doing here?" said the Walrus.

He smiled. "Someone called police?" He had perfect white teeth.

"I am the police," snarled the Walrus.

"Yeah," laughed the cop.

"Who called you? This is a university matter," said Rollie.

"I did," said Danielle. She put her hand out to the officer.

"Deputy Castle, West Palm Beach." The officer took her hand. He enveloped it like a ball in a catcher's mitt.

"Harding. Tell me."

Danielle updated Officer Harding on the highlights. Up to the fireworks.

"And you think it's your guy?"

"He even bought fireworks. We tracked a new credit card."

"One hell of a diversion. Could've killed a lot of people," said Harding.

"I think that was an accident," I said.

"And you are?"

"A criminal," said Rollie.

"Hush," said Harding.

I liked him. He seemed like a pro. And he spoke quietly. But then he had a face that said *do not make me raise my voice*.

"Hush? Excuse me, do you know who I am?" said Rollie. He was going purple again.

"Yes."

"I am the assistant athletic director of this university."

"I said I know."

"So?"

"So that might impress the hell out of him," he said, nodding at the Walrus, "but I don't work for this university. So I don't give a damn who you think you are."

"This is Gator business. You are obviously not one of us."

Harding turned his broad frame to face Rollie. "I am a Gator to my core. I played for this school. So you question my loyalties again, you gonna make me real upset."

He turned back toward me. His face was the wrong side of forty, but his body looked like it could take the field in Jacksonville tonight. He glanced back to Rollie. "And don't think I don't know where you played football, Hurricane."

He said *hurricane* like it was a social disease. I decided to keep the fact that I was also a former Hurricane to myself.

"So you were telling me who you are?"

"Jones. I'm a PI. Helping the PBSO on the case." I glanced at Danielle.

Harding followed my eyes. "I'll bet you are. So where's the perp?"

"The security guy says no one left out front after the bang," I said. "So the back door?"

"That'll be the football complex, but that leads out into the stadium," said Harding. "And from there, anywhere."

"That's why it's been such a joy sitting around chatting with these fine folks."

"Well, if you got some intel sources, drain them," said Harding. "Deputy, please give my colleague here," he looked at the Walrus, "as best a description as you have and he'll put out a BOLO. I'd best check the gym."

"This is still university property," said Rollie. "Any search should be conducted by University Police."

"Since you are not from around here, I'll assume you don't know that the college police and the Gainesville PD have a cooperation agreement. Which means if asked, officers from one department can effectively work as if they are members of the other department."

Rollie didn't back down. He might have small hands, but being hog stupid made him a tough QB. And a dumb person.

Harding looked at the Walrus. "And we are cooperating right now, aren't we?"

"Yep," said the Walrus. The man knew which side his pastries were buttered on.

Harding took the security kid to search the football complex. Danielle called the PBSO to see if there had been any more credit card purchases. I didn't really know what to do.

So I typed in a text message.

3 Heisman stolen at Florida U. Perp escaped. Got Intel? Fess up now!

I went through my contacts and fired off text messages across the board. I wasn't much of a texter. I hoped Lizzy had gotten some kind of rate that meant I wasn't buying a beer for each message I sent.

Harding reappeared from the gym. "Nothing. Guy's a ghost. You got anything?"

Danielle shook her head. So did I.

Then my phone rang.

CHAPTER FIFTY—ONE

It was Detective Ronzoni.

"You really are the worst private eye in the history of the world."

"So you better not go into private practice, and steal my mantle," I said, walking away from our little congregation.

"You seriously tracked the guy to Gainesville and let him slip through your fingers?"

"What can I do for you, Fusilli?"

"Ronzoni. And it's what I can do for you."

"I already own a paperweight."

"I got your text." I could hear him smiling down the line.

"I figured this call wasn't just 'cause you were missing me."

"You wanna know where your man is?"

I felt a frown coming on. It wasn't a joke. Ronzoni had no kind of sense of humor. I heard him suck some water from a bottle.

"You there, Miami?"

"What do you know?"

"I know where your guy is holed up. But I can't imagine he'll be there all night."

"What do you want, Ronzoni?"

"I want you to catch this bad, bad man."

I was revising the humor thing. "What else do you want?"

"I want the credit."

"The credit?"

"Yeah. I can't get up to Gainesville now. But I figure I don't need to. I got you there. I tell you where he is, you get him and you make sure I get the credit. You like my plan?"

"Ronzoni, you find the guy, I'll get you a goddamned parade."

"Don't need a parade, Jones."

"Okay. You got it. What do you know?"

"Do we have a deal?"

"I swear on a naked picture of your mother."

"He's in a hotel near the interstate."

He gave me the details, down to the room number.

"How you know this, Ronzoni?"

"I called the motel. He checked in under his real name."

"You know what I mean. The guy didn't use his credit card. We're watching it."

"He called home earlier today."

"Home? You mean his wife?"

"Yo."

"How do you know that he called?"

"I got a wiretap on it."

"You got a warrant for that?"

"I will do, if need be."

"Their house is in Wellington. Little outside your jurisdiction, isn't it?"

"So sue me."

I smiled. "There might be hope for you yet, Vermicelli."

"Ronzoni. And don't go getting all misty-eyed. Just don't let the guy get away again."

"Yes, boss."

"And remember who gets the credit."

"You'll get a commendation for this, Batman."

"Good. And Jones. You armed?"

"Yeah."

"Castle with you?"

"Yes."

"She armed?"

"Yes. What's your point?"

"When the guy called his missus, earlier. He called to say goodbye. Know what I mean?"

"Yeah. Now get off my phone so I can get this guy." I clicked off and turned back to a little group. They were all looking at me.

"What the hell was that?" said Harding.

I looked at Danielle. "Palm Beach PD."

She raised an eyebrow.

"We know where the perp is staying."

"Where?" said Harding.

"Motel near I-75."

"Right. You're coming with me," he said. He turned to Danielle. "You too, Deputy."

He told the security guy to hold the fort. Then he looked at the Walrus. "You get back over to your campus and see if you can be of some use for a change."

Then he looked at Rollie. "And you. I don't know what the hell you can do."

Rollie stood there with his big mouth open. He looked like a Venus flytrap.

"There's a lot of glass on the floor," I said. "Find a broom and sweep it up. Thatta boy."

CHAPTER FIFTY—TWO

I sat in the back of Harding's Dodge Charger. There was the standard steel mesh screen that made it hard to see out the front. I preferred the Crown Vic. There was more room in the back. I figured the cops couldn't care less about the relative legroom in the back. Danielle was up front with Harding. He used the radio as he drove and called for backup.

"You carrying?" he asked Danielle.

"Yes."

"What about you, hotshot?" he asked, glancing in the rearview.

"Yes," I said.

"Legal?"

"One hundred percent."

"What about the perp?"

"He has a Colt .45, we know of," Danielle said.

"Six-shooter? I'll take my Glock 40 over a six-shooter," he said.

"Only takes one," I said.

"Right enough. But you say he hit Orlando Washington with it?"

"That's right," said Danielle.

"So it may not even fire."

"Oh, it fires," I said.

"That's always my assumption," he said, "but how do you know?"

"It's how he got into the trophy cases. One bullet into the safety glass of each case. You'll find the slugs in the base of each one."

"You're an observant fellow."

"That's why they pay me the big bucks."

"That right?" he said, looking at Danielle.

She rolled her eyes.

We sped past a mall and a strip of chain restaurants. I could see the freeway cloverleafs approaching through the side window. The interstate was guarded by a phalanx of tall, brightly lit signs for a variety of hotels and motels. It looked like a thousand other freeway interchanges across the country. Only this one was home to more Heisman trophies than Manhattan.

"This is how it goes down. We wait for backup. Then we go in, that's Gainesville PD. Deputy, you follow." He looked in the rear view mirror. "You, hotshot, bring up the rear. You are here out of courtesy, nothing more. Clear?"

"Crystal."

"And you don't draw your weapon unless you absolutely have to. Clear?"

"And preferably not even then," I said.

I saw him nod in the mirror.

He pulled off onto a side road just before the interstate. The street was home to the line of motel signs. Harding drove past the motel we wanted and pulled into the one next door.

From the outside they looked identical. Old, poorly kept and cheap. Two floors in a U shape around a central parking lot or maybe a pool. The kinds of places that took cash and weren't too fussed about ID. The motel we wanted was decked out in green trim and matching sign. The one we waited in was blue. Within two minutes another GPD cruiser bounced into the lot. This one was a Crown Vic Interceptor. We got out. Harding gave the two other cops the lay of the land. We moved off like a little train. The two motels were separated by a small hedge. Harding led the train over it. I walked eight extra paces onto the sidewalk and went around. Danielle followed Harding. Perhaps it was a professional thing.

We got to the motel reception and waited outside while Harding went inside to get a key. I liked the way he thought. Breaking a motel door down took a battering ram and a whole lot of unnecessary effort. He came back out with the keycard in his hand.

"Second floor," he said. He looked a little disappointed. With good reason. Second floor was harder than ground floor. Less chance to do recon. Harding pulled his Glock. His two colleagues followed suit. Danielle unclipped her weapon and took it out. I left mine in its holster. Harding looked at me and nodded.

We passed by the rental car with the Tennessee plates. Wormed our way up the stairs and along the balcony. All the rooms looked across an open patch of cracked pavement. We shuffled past an alcove that housed a red vending machine and an ice dispenser. The ice groaned. When we got to the room, Harding and one cop crossed past the window and the door. The drapes were pulled. The other cop and Danielle pressed against the piece of wall between the window and the door. The only place for me to stand was right in front of the window, which I didn't fancy at all. I hung back. Harding checked all the faces and then slipped the key card in and out of the lock swiftly. It was a well-practiced move. Maybe he'd sold software after college and spent a lot of time in business hotels. I always had to try two or three times with the card before I got the green light.

Harding pulled up the latch hard and pushed the door open. He put his weight right into it. He had assumed the lock would be on it, the little chain in a round notch. But it wasn't. He drove the door back into the wall. The first cop charged in yelling *Police!* The second followed from the other side of the door. He was yelling *Police*, too. Harding came back off the wall and followed the other two. He wasn't shouting. Danielle pointed her gun down and flipped around and into the room. I waited for the shouting to stop. There were no gunshots. Two calls of clear. I realized that Ferguson had gone.

I stepped past the window and around the door and into the room. Two twin beds and four people didn't leave a lot of space in the room. Harding, Danielle and the two cops were looking at each other. Then they looked at me and parted and I realized I was wrong about Ferguson leaving.

CHAPTER FIFTY—THREE

Harding stepped aside and I saw the table. It was a low built-in, positioned between an old wardrobe and a small sink. It had a battered white chair beneath it. It wasn't the kind of desk where one wrote a book. It was more a flat space to throw your keys and wallet and receipts, and all the other crap you collect in your pockets when you are traveling the interstate. Sandy Ferguson hadn't used it for writing a book or tossing his travel debris. He had created a shrine. It was like a miniature version of his shed. But much more impressive.

Six Heisman trophies were lined up on the desk. Together they looked less like statues of a football player and more like large versions of plastic toy soldiers. A battalion of men, nothing more than their hands to defend themselves. Thrusting their arms out, not so much in anger as defiance. Above the line of Heisman trophies, Ferguson had stuck an enlarged photograph to the wall. I didn't need to analyze it to know it was Ferguson as the college hero. It was a posed shot, in full uniform, cocked on his right foot. His arm was extended back, ball in hand. Ready to nail a pass. But he wore no helmet and his hair was freshly combed. He looked young and alive. Everything his wife said he had been, and nothing she was anymore. Nor him, I suspected. One of the beds had a cowboy hat sitting on it. The cops went through the drawers and the wardrobe. Looked under the bed and in the bathroom. It was a fast search. Not too many places to hide anything in an industrial-strength interstate motel. I watched them work from the doorway.

"No weapon?" said Harding.

Three no's.

"He's still got the Colt," he said.

"And he hasn't gone anywhere," I said. I stepped out onto the balcony and looked along the row of rooms. The green motel sign glowed like a beacon. From behind the motel the interstate roared by like a constant, crashing ocean. The halogen lights on the motel lit the parking lot halfheartedly. Ferguson's rental car was directly below me. I heard Harding order his men and Danielle out of the room. He was concerned Ferguson might return at any time. I leaned on the wobbly balustrade and looked into the failing light. Gainesville glowed a couple miles away. Then I looked back down to the parking lot and saw Sandy Ferguson.

He was walking slowly, hunched over. He carried a takeout bag from the Waffle House down the street. He was shorter than I expected him to be. Five eight, maybe five nine, given the poor light. Not a modern-day quarterback. He was nuggety. Squat and broad in a way his college photo didn't show. He was one of those QBs who rushed as much as they threw. His golden hair had darkened a shade or two and had thinned on top. He wore a forehead like furrowed ground. Despite the mild evening he wore a leather jacket. I assumed to hide a gun. Same reason I was wearing a jacket. He trod heavily through the light of the halogen lamps.

Then as he stepped into a dark patch he looked up instinctively. He glanced up at his room. And saw me. Nothing registered immediately. I could be a guy in an adjacent room, hanging on the balcony, having a smoke. But he did some kind of arithmetic and figured I was right in front of his room. He stopped moving. He stood in the dim light looking up at me. Then Danielle came out of his room, slipping her gun into her holster. Ferguson had seen enough. He dropped his dinner on the black pavement and ran.

CHAPTER FIFTY-FOUR

I didn't need to do any arithmetic. I'd already done it. In retrospect I wished I hadn't. It would have given me more thinking time. But I knew that to my left the balcony passed three more rooms before turning around the side of the building and running down as a fire escape to the area backing onto the freeway. To my right it was eight rooms back to the stairs we had come up in single file. So I jumped off the balcony. Not the smartest move, but definitely the fastest. I only fell five feet before I landed on the roof of Ferguson's rental car. I made two neat dents in the roof. They'd take some explaining. But I wouldn't be the one doing the explaining, so I didn't care. My feet slipped down the face of the windshield and my knees slammed into the glass. It was hardy stuff. It didn't give an inch. My knees screamed. As I slid off the hood I heard Danielle yell for Harding and take off along the balcony. She either wasn't as stupid or she'd had more time to think, but either way she didn't follow me over the edge. She would have done it much more gracefully.

I took off across the parking lot. I saw Ferguson across the street, running through a vacant lot toward some trees. I ran across and was nearly taken out by a minivan. The driver slammed on his horn to make sure I was okay. I charged across the vacant lot. It was a rectangle of dead grass surrounded by asphalt. Like another motel or restaurant was supposed to go there but had never been built. I ran across the lot until I got to the trees. There were more of them than I had first thought. Now they looked more like woods. It was dark in there. Ferguson could have been five feet in, pointing his gun at me and I wouldn't have known. So I stopped and listened. I heard the angry snap of branches to my right. I tore off into the woods.

Branches thwacked at my face and arms. Underfoot was a minefield of roots and fallen limbs. I pushed hard for less than a minute and then burst out into a small housing subdivision. A neat cul-de-sac of freshly painted townhouses. I looked around the street. Held my head still and froze my eyes as best I could. I detected movement in a break between two blocks of townhouses and saw Ferguson charge into more woods. I followed. I was closer now. He hadn't gotten through the woods as quickly. He needed to come for a run on City Beach. Or lose a bet with Danielle and spend a week drinking tonic and lime. I chased the noise he made as he bulldozed his way through the foliage. For a minute or two we ran, surrounded by darkness, determined limbs holding us back. Then I burst out into the open again. I was next to some kind of warehouse. Ferguson was stumbling across a lightly used parking lot. I followed him toward a much longer warehouse. It was well lit. Ferguson ran up a ramp and in through a door. I lurched up the ramp and hit the door. A sign on it read: *Employees Only—AMF Bowling.*

I flung the door open. I was in a corridor that led into a kitchen. The smell of frying food hit me like a punch in the guts. I ran through the kitchen and out into a room that looked like a bar. I ducked under a space in the bar where it folded over itself. Following the stares of people sitting at high tables enjoying Buds and fries, I ran out of the bar. Into a bowling alley. The thunk of balls on polished wood and the crash of pins echoed around the room. Rows and rows of light polished wood lanes. Machines whirring and spitting out heavy bowling balls. Screens above each lane telling the players just how bad it was. Ferguson had run down onto the lane level and was stumbling across the floor, right where the players were trying to let their balls go. He was heading toward a wall and dead end. His shoes were slipping hopelessly and he was huffing and sweating from his run. His hair was matted with leaves and twigs. I was Clark Gable in comparison. I stepped down onto the smooth lane run-up. I didn't apologize for walking across people's lanes. It was pretty clear to all why I was doing it. Besides, for people who spent their Saturday nights bowling, this was sure to be a month's worth of excitement.

Ferguson glanced to the right down the lanes and saw a utility door that led behind the pins. He redoubled his efforts. It made him slip and slide more. I wasn't exactly Katrina Witt myself. So I grabbed a sparkly green ball that barely fit my fingers and I wound up. I don't bowl. And least not often and never on a Saturday night. But I do know sending the ball down perpendicular to the lanes is poor form. I heard someone say that I couldn't do that, but I begged to differ. I sent it down across the run-up and watched all the people dance about getting out of the way. I didn't know if it was a strike or a split, but whatever it was, it hit Ferguson in the heels and sent him tail over teakettle. He landed with an ugly thud. I followed the ball and stood with a lane's width between us.

"It's over, Sandy."

He looked at me. His eyes were dark and sunken. His mouth had the same permanent downward turn that his wife's had. He blinked several times. Then he burst into tears. He sobbed so his whole body shook. He didn't breathe for the longest time, and then when he did it was in spasmodic gulps. I didn't want to watch, but I wasn't taking my eyes off him.

"Leave him alone," said a woman in a pink bowling shirt.

"Lady, this doesn't concern you," I said.

A big guy with no hair on his head and a very poorly executed goatee stood up behind the woman. "You don't talk to her like that."

"Sir, please back away."

He didn't say anything. He just kept moving toward me.

"Sir, back away."

"Bite me," he said.

Ferguson let out the high-pitched yell. "He said back away!"

The big man put his hands out and backed away. Not so much at Ferguson's demand as at the Colt .45 he was pointing at the guy. Talk about clearing a room. The balls and pins and beer bottles fell silent. The whole alley emptied out. We were left alone with the whirring of the ball return machines. They rattled and sang. Ferguson was still on the floor. He dropped his hand holding the Colt back into his lap.

"Are you okay?" I said.

Ferguson laughed without mirth. "Not for a long time," he said. He was grinning.

"Why?" I said.

"Why what?"

"Why take the Heismans? What did you hope to achieve?"

"They were mine. I deserved them."

"I'm pretty sure BJ Baker's has his name on it."

He laughed again. "BJ Baker. He didn't need it. He came from money. He had everything. What did I have?"

"You think he was successful because he won a Heisman?"

"You think he wasn't?"

"You had choices; you could've done anything after college. There's more to life than football."

"Ha! What do you know?"

"I know."

"What do you know? You're just one of BJ's stooges."

"Hardly."

"So why are you here? Why you after me?"

"Orlando Washington."

Ferguson's face shrunk some. "Is he okay?" he said.

"No thanks to you."

"I didn't want to hurt him. But he charged me. Jumped out of a wheelchair and charged me."

"What about Jenny Bellingham?"

"Her husband's a moron."

"I agree."

"He didn't even know what he had."

We fell silent for a while. I felt a breeze at my back as if someone had come in through the front door.

"How did you get into BJ Baker's house?"

"He had a party."

"You were invited?"

"Ha, no. It was a charity event. I paid to get in. Cost me five hundred bucks."

"And you just walked in and grabbed it?"

"I saw it in the paper. I knew where it was. I walked out by the pool. The room was open so I went in and took it. I had it in a satchel under my suit coat for half an hour before I left."

I smiled. Not a guest, indeed. "You should have left it at one," I said.

"Why? My whole life I've got nothing. These guys got everything. It was my time. I'm not hurting anyone, just taking what's mine."

"People were hurt today."

"Where?"

"The fireworks."

"How did fireworks hurt anyone?"

"You set them off behind a video screen, as a diversion."

"So?"

"So they shot into the screen and the screen exploded. The whole band shell went up."

"I didn't mean that."

"The law of unintended consequences."

"I'm sorry if anyone was hurt. But I'm not sorry I took my trophies."

"Well, you're done now."

"Says who?" he said, looking at his gun.

"Says me." It was Harding. He had his feet splayed and his Glock pointed at Ferguson.

The other two cops came down from the concourse level, guns drawn. Danielle drifted in across the lanes, stepping deftly over the gutters. They formed a perimeter around Ferguson. I felt my gun under my left wing, but I left it where it was.

"Put the weapon down and stand up slow," said Harding.

"I can't," said Ferguson.

"What's that?" Harding spoke loud and clear.

"I can't!" Ferguson yelled.

"Sir, you need to drop your gun."

Ferguson looked at me. He was sad and tired. Just like his wife. I couldn't imagine what it had been like for their son growing up.

"Time to go," I said.

He nodded his head. He leaned forward and pressed the gun into the floor and pushed himself up. He got on his knees and then slowly stood. On his feet he looked delicate. Like he was a cardboard cutout of himself. He held the gun limply by his side.

"Drop the gun," said Harding.

Ferguson looked at me.

"Your son would like to see you," I said.

He shook his head. "He thinks I'm a failure. He's right."

"I'm sure he doesn't think that."

"He deserved a better chance."

"Sir, I will not ask you again. Drop the weapon," called Harding.

"Your wife is worried about you."

A tear ran down his cheek. "She was something. She really was." He looked off into the distance, twenty-five years into the past. "She deserves to be happy."

He looked me in the eye. "Will you tell her I love her?"

"You tell her," I said.

"Tell her I'm sorry."

Ferguson lifted the Colt and pointed it at my head.

Gunshots exploded on either side of me. Ferguson's torso burst in a cloud of red. Four well-trained law enforcement officers with hours on the range hitting the largest visible target as per regulations. Ferguson collapsed. Gunpowder and bloody mist hung in the air. Harding stepped forward and removed the Colt from Ferguson's hand with his foot. He checked the pulse at the neck, as per regulations. The ragged mess that was Ferguson's chest told me everything I needed to know. Harding pronounced him unofficially dead. Official pronouncement could only come from the medical examiner. But it was enough for everyone to holster their weapons. Harding stood and moved to me. He held open my jacket and looked at the piece sitting snugly in its holster. He dropped my jacket, nodded at me, and then turned to one of his men.

"Call it in," he said.

I turned and strode out of the bowling alley. People were still milling about in the parking lot. Rubbernecking. I ignored them and walked around the side of the building and back into the woods. I went about ten paces in. Then I stopped, put my hands on my knees and threw up.

CHAPTER FIFTY-FIVE

The Gainesville PD conducted interviews in the bar of the bowling alley. It was supposed to be a sports bar. It was more like a hospital cafeteria with televisions. I got interviewed. Then Danielle. Then the cops. The alley was closed down for the night so I couldn't even get a drink. The beer taps behind the bar mocked me. I was thirsty and hungry and tired. But I wasn't sleeping or eating anytime soon. My throat and eyes burned dry.

The medical examiner arrived and made his pronouncement. Sandy Ferguson was dead. Crime scene guys in white coveralls arrived to take photographs. I promised some cop from Gainesville PD that I would visit the station house before I left. The shooting was righteous, he said, but they wanted to make sure all the T's were crossed. It wasn't the first time I'd seen someone get shot dead. I'd even done it myself. At no time did I feel like describing the event as righteous. I didn't bother mentioning that to the cop.

Harding was talking to the crime scene guys when we left. A patrol officer gave us a ride back to the motel in his Interceptor. Definitely more legroom. He dropped us in the parking lot of the motel and turned right around. I wasn't sure why he'd taken us there. Perhaps he thought we'd come to the motel in our own car. But we'd come in Harding's Charger. I didn't think to mention it.

Danielle and I stood in the dark parking lot looking at each other. She looked tired. I must've looked like hell warmed up in a microwave. There was a fleet of patrol cars all parked nose in around Ferguson's rental. The door to his room was open. Cops were milling about like cops do at crime scenes. One was unspooling some yellow and black tape. Crime scene, do not cross. We wandered up the steps to the second floor. Walked along the balcony. All the drapes were closed in each room. We got to the door and a young guy in uniform turned full on to block our way. He had smooth skin, like he'd never yet had to shave. He gave us an easy smile. He was there to stop rubberneckers.

Danielle flipped open her badge. "We're with Harding," she said.

He looked at both of us. He'd been listening to the radio chatter. Probably watched us just get out of the cruiser in the parking lot below. He nodded and turned, allowing us through.

The room was dimly lit by cheap table lamps. Another cop was wandering around the room. It was a short trip. The two beds took up most of the real estate. The neat bedspreads were polyester green. A color that no one would steal. The cop was looking at the bathroom. There was nothing to see. He looked at us as we stepped into the room, glancing at his partner by the door, and then back at us.

"Waiting on crime scene guys," he said.

"We just wanted to have a look," Danielle said.

The cop nodded and scooted around us.

He nodded at Danielle. "Don't touch anything," he said as he leaned against the doorjamb.

There wasn't a lot to touch. The cowboy hat was still on the bed. The six Heismans were lined up. I looked at Danielle. I had a sudden urge to not be in the room. To not be in Gainesville. To get a drink. Danielle was looking at the Heismans. She put her fingertip on one of the statues. Touched the statue's face. Lightly ran her fingertip down the Heisman's face. Ed Smith's face. Sandy Ferguson's face.

She turned to me. "Let's get out of here," she said.

She dropped her finger from the trophy and edged between me and the bed. She got to the door and the two cops parted for her. She asked them if one of them could give us a ride back to the university campus. I thought they were going to arm wrestle for the privilege. I took one last look around the vanilla motel room. Then I picked up one of the Heisman trophies and slipped it under my jacket, below my holster.

The young cop drove us the few miles back to the campus. The lot was mostly empty. We thanked the cop and got in the Mustang and followed him back to the interstate. I edged left up onto I-75 and hit the gas hard. We did forty miles in twenty minutes and pulled off the freeway near Ocala. I parked in a Best Western, got a room at reception and asked about a bar. It was loud and busy. A band was in the back, playing country music. I ordered four beers. We each slammed one at the bar, and carried the other to the dance floor. We danced. We drank. The music was loud and the vibe was lively. Danielle danced with a few guys in cowboy hats. It was too loud to talk. She was sweating so much she looked like she'd run a marathon.

When it got late we stumbled back to the room. We each took a shower in the dark. The air conditioning rattled over the sound of the interstate traffic. I lay on my back under cool cotton sheets and watched the lights play on the ceiling. Danielle climbed in and crushed up against me. She sobbed for half an hour against my chest. I lay still until she fell asleep.

CHAPTER FIFTY—SIX

The sunshine streamed in my office. Anyone who sat in the visitor's chair would be like an ant under a magnifying glass. There wasn't a single cloud in the sky. Ron had been up on the roof to confirm that fact. Now he sat on the sofa, waiting.

I was waiting with him, reading the paper. The mayor's photo was on the front page, with BJ Baker and the sweatless visage of Detective Ronzoni. Credit where it wasn't due.

Ron and I were happy to wait. It was the quiet before the storm. The window was open a crack and a soft breeze was drifting in off the Atlantic. I heard the deep rumble of the car as it pulled into the lot next to our building. The thunk of expensive doors as they were slammed home. Ron raised his eyebrows and waited.

The front office door flew open. I heard the marbled window in the door rattle in its frame. Lizzy was out front but she didn't speak or get spoken to. The door to my office burst open. BJ Baker took up the entire space. The shoulders of his blazer touched both jambs. He was dressed in what I would call yachtie formal. Blue blazer, white cotton shirt and tan trousers. He looked at me and his nostrils opened and closed like an angry bull.

"Who the hell do you think you are?" he said.

"Miami Jones," I said. "Says so right on the door there."

I leaned back in my chair. I was enjoying myself. BJ Baker stepped into my office. I noticed his lackey, Murphy, was behind him.

"Excuse me?" roared Baker.

"In due course, possibly. But we've got a bit of ground to cover first."

Baker frowned. "Look, Jones, I don't know who you think you are."

"Didn't we just cover that? It's on the door. Just had it done."

"Jones!" he bellowed.

I thought he might come across the desk at me. I half-wanted him to. No doubt he could do some damage. He was past his prime but still in fine shape.

"Where the hell is my Heisman? The police say they don't have it."

"You didn't pay them to find it."

"No, I paid you, damn it."

"Yeah, let's talk about that."

"Is that what this is? Blackmail?"

"Not all. It's called fee for hire."

A sheet of paper sat on my desk in front of me. I pushed it across the desk with my forefinger. BJ Baker gave me a stern look, the sort of withering stare that probably sent his house staff into a mad flap. I just raised an eyebrow and smiled. I was having a little too much fun.

Baker stomped forward and ripped the paper off the desk. "What the hell is this?" he said, before he'd even looked at it.

I didn't say anything. He was a smart guy. He'd figure it out. He frowned at the paper, and then looked at me.

"An invoice?" he said.

I nodded. "For services rendered."

"I'm not paying this. And you try to blackmail me by withholding my Heisman, I'll sue you so fast your eyeballs will spin."

"Your Heisman has been found and delivered, as agreed. Now we require payment."

"Delivered? Where?"

"All will be revealed in the debrief that occurs after settlement of invoices. Corporate policy."

"I won't pay."

"Ron?" I looked at him in his magnolia print shirt and linen trousers. "What happened to the last guy who didn't pay his invoice?"

"All unpaid bills are referred to collections."

"Who does collections?" I said.

"Catfish Tony out of Brooklyn. I got his business card here." Ron pulled a business card out of God knows where and looked at it. "Yeah. Catfish Tony. His motto is 'they pay or they float.' Catchy."

Baker looked at Ron, and then me. "You think I'm scared by that?"

"No. It's just a slogan. But I don't think a heavy trophy would float, do you?"

"You wouldn't."

"No, I certainly wouldn't. But I am not responsible for the actions of third-party collection agencies."

"You don't want me as an enemy," he said.

"You're right, I don't. But I sure as hell don't want you as a friend. So pay your bill, before I have to spread it all over South Florida that BJ Baker welches on his commitments."

"I never."

"You'll find everything in the invoice properly accounted for."

"I don't have my checkbook."

"That's okay. We take Visa or MasterCard. With an extra 10% processing fee."

He glared at me. I really was having too much fun. I'd pushed my luck for no real reason other than Baker was a blowhard. And that wasn't a crime. But then I wasn't the police. And I just didn't appreciate being treated like a doormat.

Baker grimaced and put his hand out, toward his manservant, Murphy. Murphy reached into his breast pocket and pulled out a leather-clad checkbook that he appeared to have after all. Why bother with a man-bag when you can have a man. Baker opened the checkbook, and put out his hand again. Murphy slapped down a gold pen. It was like watching surgery. Baker looked at the invoice, then leaned over onto the desk and wrote out a check, ripped the check from the book in one swift move and handed it to me. Murphy took the checkbook and pen back. I thought about suggesting that the check better be good, but thought the wiser of it. Baker was a jackass, but he was the kind of guy who would take a bounced check as a character flaw.

"Thank you," I said.

"Now where's my Heisman?"

"Just one more little thing." I pushed the intercom button on my phone.

"Lizzy? If you have a moment, could you join us?"

"What the hell now, Jones? All I asked for was you to get me my Heisman and the guy who took it. So far you have failed on all counts."

"The guy who took it was shot to death."

"Not by me," he snarled.

Lizzy stepped through the open door. I hadn't really needed to use the intercom. She could hear everything that was being said. But I was making a point. She walked around BJ Baker and stood at the end of my desk, between Baker and me.

"Mr. Baker. From the very day you hired my firm to find your trophy you have seen fit to abuse, belittle and degrade the very people who were working hard to find it for you."

"Excuse me?"

"This time, I cannot. On no less than thirteen occasions you have called this office and yelled at and abused my office manager, Miss Staniforth here. I believe you owe her an apology."

"Now see here."

"Mr. Baker," I said firmly. "Apologize. Now."

The big man gritted his teeth. He would have been a sight on a football field. His eyes drifted to Lizzy and his face softened, if only a touch.

"Miss Staniforth. I am deeply sorry for my conduct. If I have caused you any offense, I apologize wholeheartedly and ask only for your forgiveness."

It was better than I thought it was going to be. He sure was a smooth piece of work. I thought for a second that Lizzy might tear up.

"Apology accepted," she said. Considering the circumstances, this was pretty magnanimous of her.

Baker kept her eye for a moment, nodded, and then shifted his gaze to me. "Now. For once and for all. Where the hell is my Heisman?"

I leaned back in my chair. "Mr. Baker. Go home. Your Heisman is waiting for you."

He looked puzzled for a moment, and then he turned and directed Murphy out the door. As Baker reached the door, he turned back to us.

"Good day," he said. Then he left.

I looked at Lizzy and then Ron.

Ron smiled. "Say what you will about him, but he does have good manners."

"When he remembers to use them," said Lizzy.

I nodded. "So what was all that about Catfish Tony?"

"You don't like Catfish Tony?"

"You sit at home and think these things up?"

"I sit at Longboard Kelly's and think these things up. Catfish. You know, as in, if you mess with him, you'll end up with the catfish. On the bottom."

"Sterling work. Really."

"So where is his Heisman?"

"A friend of Sally's is installing it back into its cabinet at BJ's house, as we speak."

"That's going to freak him out."

"I know."

We grinned like Cheshire idiots at each other.

"So when did I become office manager?" said Lizzy.

"You prefer secretary?"

"No."

"So office manager."

"Does that come with a pay raise?"

"Why don't you go home and pray on it?"

"That means no."

"Who knows? Perhaps I'll get some divine inspiration."

"Perhaps you'll get struck by lightning," she said, and she strode out to her desk.

"Equally possible," I said to no one in particular.

CHAPTER FIFTY—SEVEN

I left Ron lying on the sofa, mapping out a plan of attack for his investment banker case, and Lizzy to do the banking. I drove up to the hospital. I asked around and finally located Jenny Bellingham. She was checking the chart for an old guy who was complaining about the television reception. She saw me and her face registered a mix of happy and sad. Sad because I was a bridge back to a past she wanted to forget. Happy because I was a bridge to a better future. I hoped I was made of sturdy enough stuff to get the job done.

She told me she had a break in thirty minutes. I waited in the cafeteria. It looked like a cafeteria. A little antiseptic and bland, easily maintained and difficult to break. It could have been in a school or a museum. Only there was none of the life of those sorts of institutions. No noise or hubbub. People crouched close and spoke in hushed tones. I drank a stale coffee and ate a Caesar wrap that was so cold it made my teeth ache.

Jenny Bellingham arrived after forty-five minutes. She did the nurse shuffle that made nurses walk light on their feet. Nurses were only second to ninjas when it came to sneaking up on people.

She grabbed an iced tea and sat down opposite me.

"How's it going?" I said.

"All right." The bruising had faded a little. She looked like she'd been in a car accident and the airbag had hit her in the face. Maybe that was what she was telling people.

"Things okay at Mona's?"

"Sure. She's a saint."

"But?"

"Well, I can't stay with her forever."

"Just take it one day at a time. Forever will take care of itself."

"I'm going to have to find somewhere to live. I'm starting from less than scratch."

"We can fix that."

"How?"

"I have a real estate agent friend who has taken on the listing of your home. She's having it cleaned today."

"Newt won't agree to that."

"He already did."

She frowned at me like I'd spoken in Chinese, but she said nothing.

"Plus, I found your dad's Heisman."

"Thank you, I guess."

"It's with the Gainesville Police Department. And it's gonna stay with them as evidence until you get a divorce. As soon as the divorce is final you'll get it back, and you're going to sell it."

"I couldn't, Mr. Jones. It was Daddy's. It's worth more to me than a few thousand dollars."

"Jenny, I have a friend who has a lot of experience selling things like that. And he tells me the trophy is worth at least one hundred thousand. Maybe double to the right buyer."

She looked at me but didn't register any shock. Maybe she couldn't be shocked anymore.

"That's a lot of money."

"Yes. It is."

"But it still feels wrong."

"It's not. Trust me, Jenny. If your dad were here, he'd agree. He'd want his little girl to be free of this." I waved my hand around the room. "He'd want you to be happy. More than any trophy. I bet you are the greatest prize he ever got and he'd be happy to know his Heisman got you a new life."

She nodded. "Maybe."

"We don't have to decide that yet."

"Thank you."

We sipped our drinks in silence for a while. A man pushing a saline drip on a pole sat at a table nearby.

"Did Deputy Castle speak with you?"

Jenny Bellingham nodded. "She put me in touch with a support group."

"And?"

She looked me in the eye. "It doesn't make it feel any better. But it helps to know other women have made it through."

"As will you, Jenny. As will you."

CHAPTER FIFTY—EIGHT

A brilliant pink sunset exploded across the horizon. I watched the colors play across the huge marshmallow clouds. Danielle stepped onto the patio with a bottle of wine. Beads of condensation dripped down its side. She poured me a refill, then sat down on the lounger beside me and topped up her own glass.

"How was the review board?" I asked.

"Fine. As expected. Ferguson had a loaded weapon and he pointed at you with the intention to harm. Gainesville PD will find the same way."

"How do you feel?"

"I'm okay. I'm not sorry I did it," she said, sipping her wine. "I'm just sorry I had to."

"Thanks for that."

She smiled, almost begrudgingly. "Someone tries to hurt you, I have to stop them."

I nodded.

She looked into her wine glass and then at me. "Can I ask you something?"

I nodded.

"Why didn't you draw your weapon? He could have killed you, and your gun was still in your holster."

"I guess I felt like I was the negotiator. Trying to be on his side. Once you guys arrived I figured you had me covered."

Danielle nodded. "I guessed it was something like that."

We looked at the last of the sun as it dipped below the flat Floridian horizon. We both knew it was a lie. But I didn't see an upside in verbalizing it. The PBSO would make her see a shrink and maybe in doing so it would come out, and she'd want to talk about it. And if she did, I would. But until then I figured it was of no benefit to tell her I didn't draw my weapon because I knew Sandy Ferguson wasn't going to shoot me. I knew at that point his delusion had exploded around him and he was left with plan B. And he'd put the pieces on the board for plan B before he even disappeared. We assumed he had left to take his own life. He'd topped up his life insurance before he was fired from the used car lot. He was, in the deepest part of his sad mind, looking after his family. If he took his own life, Arlene Ferguson would get nothing. So he chose suicide by cop.

I knew he wouldn't shoot me. But he would force the cops' hands. They would have to take him down. And they did.

I was sorry Danielle had been there. I was sorry I hadn't seen Ferguson's plan B earlier than I did. But as he picked himself off the floor of the bowling alley, I knew.

"They didn't let me go see her," said Danielle. "Arlene Ferguson. I thought I should be the one to tell her."

"Understandable on both sides. But the PBSO isn't going to send you in after being involved in the incident."

"Yeah. I'm sorry about your husband. PS, I shot him."

"You and three other cops."

"Did you see her?"

"I did." I sipped my wine. It was rapidly going warm.

"What did she say?"

"If anything, I think she was just glad it's over. She'll probably wonder if she could have done more for him, but she's not there yet. She needs help herself, before she can worry about anything else."

"What will she do?"

"She doesn't know. Too soon. Her son is flying down from Seattle for the funeral. She's going to go back with him, for a visit. Turns out he's a psych major."

"Figures."

"Yeah. Then she'll see. She's from Ohio. Think she might head back that way."

"Will she be okay?"

"I really don't know. She's been sad for twenty years, she says. Forgets what happy feels like. She needs help with her depression. She does that, maybe she'll be okay."

Danielle sighed, deep and long.

"Hungry?" I asked and she nodded.

We stepped in out of the warm air. Danielle sat on a barstool at the orange counter while I put a plate of antipasto together. I took some salami and Parma ham and lay them out on a platter. Put some cornichon in a small ramekin. Laid out some pickled veggies and some cheese, fresh buffalo mozzarella and Parmigiano-Reggiano that I sliced into slivers with a vegetable peeler. I popped a bowl of olives on the platter and we carried our food and drinks out to the patio.

The lights of Riviera Beach twinkled across the Intracoastal. I tossed the warm wine in our glasses onto the lawn and refreshed our drinks from the cold bottle. As I sat down Danielle spoke. "You ever feel like Ferguson?"

"Depressed, you mean? Not like that."

"No. I mean, he became sad because he didn't make it, win the Heisman. Become a pro footballer. And you played in the minors for what, six years? But you never made it to the majors. You ever think about that?"

I ate a cornichon and screwed my face at how sour it was. I ate another. Then I sipped my wine.

I took a breath. "I did get to the majors."

Danielle turned in her seat. "You did? You never told me that."

"I don't really talk about it."

"Why?"

"Because it sounds like a sad story. And people just don't get that it wasn't."

"When? How?"

"End of my fourth season at Modesto. I'd had a good year. Probably my best ever. I got bumped up to Triple A with the Sacramento River Cats. The A's organization had a few injuries, it was late in the season. We were in the race for a playoff spot against the Angels. I got called up. Me and Joe Blanton. For twenty-nine days I was in the Oakland A's bullpen."

"That's incredible."

"It was. Moving from A to Triple A was two levels up, but it was like changing from an older bus to a new one. Not that different. But the one step from Triple A to the majors, that was like going from a Greyhound bus to British Airlines first class. Everything was bigger, better, faster, brighter."

I smiled at the memory. I could still see the floodlit grass at the Coliseum. It was not one of the prettier stadia in the MLB, but the fans were passionate. I was wide-eyed for the whole twenty-nine days.

"So that doesn't sound sad."

I smiled. "The A's had one hell of a roster. Zito, Harden, Hudson, Mulder. Duchscherer in relief. Great pitchers. Blanton was lucky, he got a couple games. I never did. Twenty-nine days and I never threw one pitch in anger."

Danielle had gone quiet. That's what people did at this part of the story.

"So the A's finish one game short of Anaheim and miss the postseason. Then the organization make changes. Mulder and Hudson get traded. Blanton did enough to keep his spot. I get traded to the Mets, and they send me to Port St. Lucie. That was it. That was the majors for me."

"I'm sorry," she said.

"See, that's what everyone says. And at the time, I would have agreed with you. I thought I could match Blanton. With Mulder and Hudson gone, and Zito ended up having a terrible year the next year, I might have had a shot. But other people didn't agree. Billy Beane didn't agree. And he had a great method for finding talent. But I didn't cut it. Even in the Mets' organization. I still had chances. I was mostly fit, had a good arm, nice curve. But in The Show, everyone has that. You need more. Mostly, it's between the ears. Doing the things you can do when it really matters, not just in training. When the pressure is really on. Other guys took those moments better."

I took a long slug of my wine. "So people think that's so sad. But here's the thing. I spent twenty-nine days in The Show. Twenty-nine incredible days. Sure I would have loved to have pitched an inning. To have thrown my stuff on some of those great players. Tossed my heat, or weaved a curve. I'd have loved that. But I still got to spend twenty-nine days in the majors."

Danielle nodded and looked at the rippling water. "I wish Sandy Ferguson could have looked at it that way. He missed his life because he couldn't get over missing the Heisman."

"I don't think the Heisman caused his problems. That was just how it manifested itself. His demons were always going to catch up with him. Sooner or later."

She nodded again. "Well, I for one am glad you didn't make it in the majors."

"Gee, thanks." I smiled.

"I don't mean it like that. I mean I'd have never met you."

"Exactly. If you live in the past, you miss out on the now. And the now is when great things happen."

"My poet warrior."

"Something like that."

"Is there another bottle of wine going?"

"Always. But you want to be careful," I said.

"No, I think you better be careful."

I smiled. "That a promise?"

"It is. Tomorrow morning. First thing. You and I are going to be doing push-ups."

"What's the prize?"

"If I win, we both go vegetarian for two weeks."

"You trying to kill me?"

"I'm trying to help you live forever."

"And if I win?" I said, standing to retrieve another bottle of wine.

"Name your prize."

I looked down at Danielle reclined in her lounger, moonlight bouncing off her face. And I smiled.

GET YOUR NEXT BOOK FREE

Hearing from you, my readers, is one of the the best things about being a writer. If you want to join my Readers' Group, we'll not only be able to keep in touch, but you can also get an exclusive Miami Jones ebook novel, as well as occasional pre-release reads, and other goodies that are only available to my Readers' Group friends.

Join Now:
http://www.ajstewartbooks.com/reader

ACKNOWLEDGEMENTS

Thanks to all my readers who send me feedback. A big shout out to Beth for the edits, Marianne Fox and Donna Rich for the proofreads, all the betas, especially Heather and Andrew, and the folks at the Tiki Hut in Fort Pierce, FL, where this book was conceived and partially written over plates of peel'n'eats and cold bottles of Kalik. You all make my life and my work better. Any and all errors are mine, especially but not limited to the one for the road. That's never a good idea.

AUTHOR'S NOTE

Depression is a serious illness that affects millions of people worldwide. If you or someone you care about exhibits any of the signs of depression, including but not limited to ongoing sadness, feelings of emptiness or hopelessness, fatigue, difficulty concentrating, insomnia or thoughts of suicide, seek assistance. For a list of helplines in various countries, visit AJStewartBooks.com/helplines

ABOUT THE AUTHOR

A.J. Stewart wrote marketing copy for Fortune 500 companies and tech start-ups for 20 years, until his head nearly exploded from all the stories bursting to get out. Stiff Arm Steal was his fifth novel, but the first to make it into print.

He has lived and worked in Australia, Japan, UK, Norway, and South Africa, as well as San Francisco, Connecticut and of course Florida. He currently resides in Los Angeles with his two favorite people, his wife and son.

AJ is working on a screenplay that he never plans to produce, but it gives him something to talk about at parties in LA.

You can find AJ online at www.ajstewartbooks.com, connect on Twitter @The_AJStewart or Facebook facebook.com/TheAJStewart.

Made in United States
Orlando, FL
22 April 2022

17087065R00164